RAVEN

DEFIER OF ROME

ADAM LOFTHOUSE

B

Boldwood

First published in Great Britain in 2025 by Boldwood Books Ltd.

Cover Design by Colin Thomas

Cover Images: Colin Thomas

Map Design by Simon Walpole

A CIP catalogue record for this book is available from the British Library.

Paperback ISBN 978-1-83678-502-6

Large Print ISBN 978-1-83678-501-9

Hardback ISBN 978-1-83678-500-2

Ebook ISBN 978-1-83678-503-3

Kindle ISBN 978-1-83678-504-0

Audio CD ISBN 978-1-83678-495-1

MP3 CD ISBN 978-1-83678-496-8

Digital audio download ISBN 978-1-83678-498-2

This book is printed on certified sustainable paper. Boldwood Books is dedicated to putting sustainability at the heart of our business. For more information please visit https://www.boldwoodbooks.com/about-us/sustainability/

Boldwood Books Ltd, 23 Bowerdean Street, London, SW6 3TN

www.boldwoodbooks.com

For Michael, Wayne, Harry, Joe, and Tom.
Shield brothers.

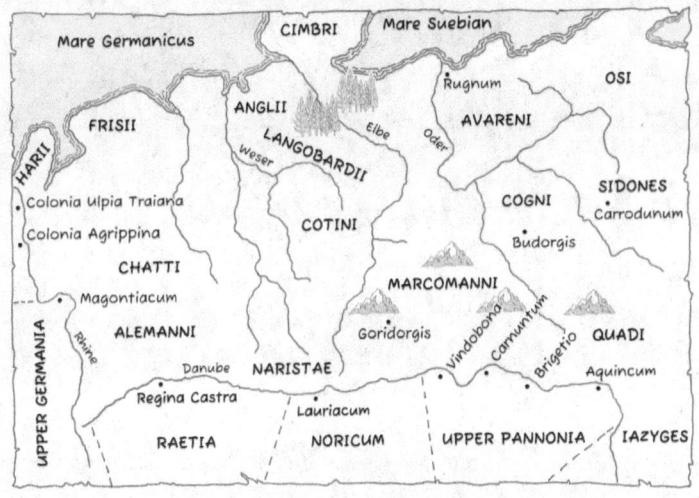

PART I

1

It takes years to build a legend. To turn fear into reputation, and reputation into immortality.

It takes mere heartbeats to shatter it to dust.

Back when I was young, when my beard was more black than grey, my muscles still firm, my face unlined and void of old scars, I was building my legend faster than Rome was conquering cities of fine-cut stone.

From east to west my men would ride, the endless expanse of grass and forests our home. We slept where we wanted, ate what we wanted, and fucked who we wanted. No man would stand in our way, even if he possessed the finest mail, the sharpest blade and a war host at his back; all men knelt in the mud when Alaric and his Ravensworn rode past.

And what did they see, these lords and chiefs who knelt in the dirt and prayed to the Allfather that the dreaded Ravensworn would ride past their hovels and leave their sour ale, stale bread and ugly daughters untouched? They saw a lord of war. A cold-faced killer at the head of a horde of men and metal. They saw a blood-red banner, streaming in the wind with a black raven swooping through the claret. They saw a man in his prime, flowing locks of dark hair, Loki-cunning eyes framed by a scowl, above a long, thick beard. Gleaming mail, beneath a deep blue cloak, pinned with a brooch of silver. Boots of the finest leather, pillaged from the cold and lifeless feet of a slaughtered Roman officer. A black pommelled sword, well-oiled and freshly sharpened, in a scabbard of wood lined with the wool of a newborn lamb. When the blade was freed from its sheath, the length of glimmering iron ran from hip to foot, four fingers wide, there was no sword to match it in all of Germania.

When that weapon was bared, men died.

Chieftain-killer, battle-turner, mercenary, pirate, Wotan-wise, Loki-cunning, Oathbreaker. I have been called them all. I revel in the names whispered in the hearth flames; timid tribal leaders and their retainers, speaking half in fear and half in reverence. For all men knew, it wasn't Rome and her emperors who settled land disputes and wars of honour in the far reaches of the wild lands, however much they thought they controlled us with their frumentarii agents creeping through our forests, the senate installing client kings whenever and wherever they saw fit. It was Alaric and the Ravensworn that turned the tide when German met German in the storm of blood and iron.

For the right price, of course.

And so it was on that glorious midsummer's day, as I sat atop my horse with my war host at my back, a grovelling chieftain at my feet; I felt the breeze tickle my beard, the sun caress my face, and I knew I was destined to carve my legend in blood. Men would speak of my deeds for generations.

'And what is in it for me?' I asked the quivering chief, whose mouth moved like that of a fish, his whole body trembling under the weight of his rust-pitted mail.

'We will pay, Lord, and pay well.' I liked it when men called me Lord. I had no right to be called it, not really, but men did anyway. Even chiefs, like that wet trout who grovelled at my feet.

'What will you pay in?' I asked sceptically, looking at a collection of scrawny mud huts with patchy thatched roofs and half-naked children ducking in and out the canvas flaps that passed for doors in this part of the world.

'We got no coin, Lord, but we can pay you in cattle, even offer a few horses,' he said in more hope than expectation. It was evident in the quivering of his voice, plain as porridge in his wide, hopeful eyes.

'The fuck do I need cattle for?' I scoffed. 'If me and my men need food, we'll just eat yours!' This was greeted with a roar of approval from those of my men within earshot, just as I had intended. 'And as for horses, well, look around. Does it look like we need them?' I swept my arm in a grand gesture, indicating the five hundred sworn men behind me, each on horseback and with a remount in tow. 'Now, what are you going to offer me?'

He knew what I wanted, had known all along. He'd known as soon as he'd sent a runner east to beg for me and my men to visit his village. Did I say village? I meant shithole.

I watched as his heart sunk, his shoulders slumped, and he stood leaning forwards, his head drooping as he studied the holes in his boots. 'Wait here, Lord,' he said with a sigh. 'I might have something more to your liking.'

He went off into the collection of huts. A woman approached him and the two spoke in low tones. Their conversation took a turn for the worse, it seemed, as she began to shout and scream whilst slapping the chief repeatedly over the head. She was his wife, I guessed. I also guessed he was reluctantly going to grab some chest of silver or precious jewellery he had either hidden in his hut or buried underneath. Clearly, she didn't think us worthy recipients of such a gift.

But we got it anyway. He scurried back with an object wrapped in cloth. I felt my men move closer, drawn in by the potential of gleaming silver or precious jewels. Each man in the Ravensworn knew they were to get a cut of whatever we were paid, and whatever they pillaged on the job would be thrown into a pile at the end for each man to take their equal share, depending on his rank and importance. Of course, some men thought to hide certain wealth from their fellow Ravensworn. Well, all of them did. In spite of the fact all knew that any man caught would be flogged then sent packing without so much as a coin. But men are greedy, heartless and selfish. When there are gold or silver coins on offer, or intricate links of gleaming metal hanging from a woman's neck, no man thinks of sharing it with his brothers in arms. I am no different, just not afraid to admit it.

The chief staggered as he rambled towards me. I still sat atop my horse, a fine brown and white mare. I'd named her Hilde after an old lover. She tossed her head and snorted as the man edged closer. I'd had a retired Roman auxiliary cavalryman ride with my warriors for a while. He'd taught a few of the lads the basics of training a horse for war; it had been by far his most useful contribution to the Ravensworn. He only lasted a few months before taking a spear in the belly on a raid against the Cimbri in the north. I was reaching into the depths of my mind to remember the man's name when I noticed the chief on his knees to my left, hands extended and offering the cloth-wrapped package. I looked down at him and smiled. 'Aristides,' I said, and the chief looked up at me and frowned.

'Lord?'

'Aelius Hadrianus Aristides,' I muttered in guttural Latin. I had a basic understanding of the language; it came in useful when trading amber for silver. 'The gods only know why these Germans and Gauls give themselves such stupid names when they scurry over the river to take Rome's money for murdering their own people.' Again, the chief looked at me then my men in confusion, for I still spoke Latin. The Aelius Hadrianus part of the name symbolises that Aristides entered Rome's service during the reign of Emperor Hadrian. Aristides would just be some shit Greek name his officers threw at him when he had made his mark and agreed to sixteen years' service in an auxiliary unit. That's how Rome treated people. They couldn't give a fuck who you were or where you were from; just as long as you could make a mark on a wax tablet and shove a spear into a barbarian's neck, you were in.

But I digress. I sprung down from the mare with all the vigour and swagger of youth. The chief fell on his arse when my boots hit the ground next to where he knelt. Snatching up the cloth-wrapped package, I opened it quickly to reveal a glimmering torc of silver lined in gold. It was, I thought, quite beautiful. There was a picture engraved in the centre, but the lines were old and the engraving filled with dust and dirt. I squinted, holding it up to the sun to try and get a better look.

'It is the Allfather, Lord,' the chief said, rising slowly to his feet. 'See, his face his hidden under a large beard, but one eye is covered in a patch. The triangle at the top is his great hat, and the two marks either side are the ravens.'

The ravens. Thought and memory. Huginn and Muninn. My hands shook as the realisation of what I was seeing, holding, hit me like Donar's hammer. Me, Alaric, Lord of the Ravensworn, had been given a torc depicting the Allfather and his two ravens. It was perfect; better than that. I coughed, rubbed the sweat from my palms on my cloak. 'This is some gift, Chief Wulfric,' I said with newfound respect.

Wulfric was the chief of the Fenni, a small and inconsequential tribe buried in the middle of some marshland in central

Germania. They had very few warriors, no armour and less swords. In this country, if you've got no swords, you have no chance of keeping hold of your cattle. No cattle, no food. Simple. Wulfric was young, not long since risen to the rank of chief after the passing of his father. He had many lessons to learn, did Wulfric; he was about to be taught one now.

'Tell me again, Chief Wulfric, exactly what happened.' I always do this, get men to explain a story to me twice. You would be amazed at how much the same man can change his version of events.

'They came in the night, Lord. Twenty men, maybe thirty.' See, there already. The first time the whoreson spun his tale it was fifteen men, maybe twenty. And that was not an hour ago. 'They wore all black, Lord. Faces darkened with soot, black tunics and cloaks, black shields and boots. They were silent as the grave. We didn't even know they were here till the cows kicked up a fuss.'

Again, this version differed from his last. The first time he regaled me with this woeful story of treachery and loss, he said he hadn't seen the raiders, but one of his men had told him they were all in black. Now, here he is, explaining to me in detail what they looked like. I don't mind a fool, a simpleton with a small mind, unable to string together a coherent sentence. But a tribal chief, openly lying to me? Now that I can't have, won't have.

'Some of us rallied, Lord. Grabbed what weapons we could and chased them off, but they'd already taken the cattle away into the night. That's when the killing began...'

He trailed off then, did Wulfric, eyes downcast, that quiver back in his voice. Pathetic.

'How many men did you lose?' I asked. It was five the first time he told me.

'Seven, Lord. Good men too, hard workers, honest people.'

I smiled. Smirked, more like. Wulfric had the sense to not look upset or angry. He just stared at me with those pathetic fishy eyes.

'Where are the bodies?' I asked, as innocently as I could.

'Lord?' Wulfric replied, eyebrows rising to hide behind his straggly straw-coloured fringe.

'The bodies, man! You say seven men were killed, so there must be seven bodies, no?'

I struggled to hide my laugh as Wulfric looked round in exasperation, searching for an answer that wasn't forthcoming.

'We buried them, Lord,' he said eventually.

'Where?' I asked. 'Show me the graves.'

I followed the hapless Wulfric through the ramshackle of huts his people called home. The ground was soft under the soles of my boots, and twice I nearly lost my footing. Cursing at the mud splashes that blotted the black leather, I reached the back of the huts to find a freshly filled-in grave.

In Rome, I know, it is common for the deceased to be sent to their gods on great pyres of flame. A coin will be placed on their tongues for the ferryman, who will row them over the River Styx to their final resting place in Hades. Their ashes will then be sealed in an urn, and either placed in the family's mausoleum or buried in a grave beneath a tomb stone. In Germania, we are less dramatic about death. The elders say we come from the earth, we are as much a part of it as it is of us. When we die, we simply return to it. In other words, our dead, rotting corpses are chucked unceremoniously into unmarked graves, and then quickly filled in with the same mud that was dug out. Job done.

I looked upon this unmarked grave, a brown patch amidst the endless green, and knew it was not big enough to be the final resting place of seven newborn babes, let alone seven full-grown men.

'If there's seven men in there, Wulfric, then I'm old One Eye himself,' I said, turning to Ruric, my second in command. Ruric scoffed a laugh, hefting the shaft of his axe, aiming the head at Wulfric.

'It is a deep grave, Lord. Took us a whole day to dig it deep enough.'

'Hmm,' I muttered to myself. 'And how do your womenfolk feel about seeing their men dumped one atop the other, lain to rest till the end of days?' I asked, my Loki-cunning eyes fixed on Ruric, a knowing smile on both our faces.

'They... they didn't say they were offended, Lord.' His voice shook with fear now. I imagined I would see the piss stain growing on the front of his woollen trousers at any moment.

'I'm going to ask you one more time, Wulfric, Chief of the Fenni. How many bodies are in this grave?' I clutched the gold and silver torc in my palm, fingers running across the engravings that shaped the outline of Wotan's face. I hadn't yet decided if I was going to take on the work Wulfric was paying me to do, but I was damn sure I was leaving that wasteland with that torc.

'Two, Lord,' he said with a sigh. I looked at him then, my dark eyes boring into his. I've always considered myself to be a strong judge of character, and to me, everything about Wulfric seemed off.

'Your men, or theirs?' I asked in a quiet voice.

'Ours, Lord, honest.'

I paused then, letting the silence stretch out. 'And how did your men die?'

'They fought the raiders, Lord, with nothing more than their wood axes.'

'No one else fought with them?' I asked. Wulfric opened his

mouth to speak, but I held up a palm in warning. 'No more lies, Wulfric. I swear to the Allfather if you lie to me again I will kill you here and now.'

Again, Wulfric's mouth opened and closed like a blubbering fish caught in a net. 'No one else fought, Lord. We all stayed in our homes.'

And there was the truth. Men had raided their village in the night. Only two men had possessed the courage to leave their beds and fight them. Wulfric clearly wasn't one of them. 'You have been raided by a tribe, a common occurrence in these lands. And yet, with your women and children unprotected and vulnerable in their huts, only two of your men had the balls to step into the night air and face them. A sad day, Wulfric,' I said, shaking my head.

'Yes, Lord,' he mumbled, eyes downcast. Let's face it, there wasn't much else he could say.

'So, you want me to attack this tribe, wipe them from the pages of history. That right?'

'Yes, Lord. Too long we have lived in fear of the Harii. We're not the only ones to have suffered this; I know of three other tribes that have lost men to their raids.'

'So why not band together? Surely four tribes of men can handle the Harii?' The Harii were ferocious, a warlike tribe based in the northwest of our land, near the Rhine border with the Romans. They were infamous for their night raids; men dressed all in black, charcoal blackening their faces; they stuck to the old ways, worshipped the old gods in secret groves deep in forests of pine. They were not to be trifled with, even by me.

'No one fights the Harii, Lord.'

'But you expect me to?' I asked with all the savageness I could muster. I had five hundred men at my back, certainly more than enough to take on the Harii. But I would lose men, for no man storms the home of the Harii without being bloodied.

'You are Alaric,' was all he said. I guess he hoped I would take it as a compliment.

'And you are a *nithing*,' I spat. A *nithing* is a coward, a man without the courage to fight for his loved ones. There is no shame in shitting in your breeches before a fight. I've seen men vomit, piss dribbling down their trousers, a foul-smelling brown patch spreading on their arse. Yet still they stood when the iron clashed and the blood flew. 'I have no time for *nithings*. But I will go to the Harii, and fight them if need be. Not for you,' I said to Wulfric before he could blubber his thanks. 'For the other tribes who have suffered at their hand. And I will accept this as payment,' I said, showing him the torc I still held. 'The Ravensworn will leave immediately. You will hear from me when it is done.'

I walked off without another word, mounting my horse and cantering away before Wulfric could feed me any more bullshit.

2

'You don't believe him, Chief?' Ruric asked as we cantered through the marshland. We were an hour or so gone from the village Wulfric and his tribe called the capital of their lands.

'Of course I don't,' I said. 'You?'

Ruric weighed up an answer in his mind; I could see the cogs working behind his huge forehead. 'He was telling the truth for the most part. I just think he exaggerated a bit is all.'

'A bit?' I scoffed. 'He's a coward, and a liar. Plain as day,' I said, with absolute confidence. 'Get me Birgir.'

Ruric returned shortly with the young lad. He was a runt, an urchin we picked up in Goridorgis, capital of the Marcomanni. A proper capital, that one, walled and garrisoned, not a place you'd want to assault. I stopped my horse and dismounted, gestured for Birgir to do the same. 'Keep the men moving north,' I said to Ruric. 'We get out of this marshland and turn west, understand?' Ruric nodded and moved off, heading the vast column of mailed men that cantered past.

'I have a task for you, young Birgir.' I placed my hands on his shoulders and steered him away from the prying ears of the men. 'I want you to ride back to the Fenni. Find a secluded spot on the road south from their village, and wait.'

'Wait for what, Lord?' Birgir asked, his pale face set in a frown.

'If I am right, and I usually am' – I couldn't stop the smile from spreading, even if I'd wanted to – 'a man will come up the road, a Roman. He will have with him a bag of gold, and may even have a couple of soldiers as an escort.'

'Roman soldiers, Lord? This far north?' Birgir shook his head and spat, held his thumb against his head, the universal sign to ward off evil.

'Yes, Birgir. Romans, right on our doorstep. Now, listen. Don't get too close, I don't need to hear what is spoken between them, just if coin changes hands, understand?'

He nodded. There was a gust of wind and the wispy blond strands of Birgir's first beard rippled. He rubbed them, clearly proud of the straggly thing. I remembered the first dark hairs that had sprouted from my chin, and my father's mocking voice when he caught me combing them with a bone-carved brush.

'That's a Hel of a beard you're growing there, lad. How old are you now, eighteen?' I knew he wasn't, but I also knew he would revel in being called older than he was.

'Fifteen, Lord, sixteen this winter,' he said with pride.

'Bet you get all the girls after you, eh! Anyway, all I need to know is which road the Romans take out of the village. When they're gone, come find us. We'll be camped at the conflux, where the River Elbe meets the Saale. Got it?'

The conflux was one of my favourite places to make camp. In fact, we had partially rebuilt an old Roman outpost from back in the dark days when the curs ruled half our land. The water seemed sweeter, the rivers shallower, the current swirling in lazy circles. There was also always an abundance of fish, and I liked nothing more than fresh fish.

'Why, Lord? Why are the Romans doing this?' Birgir asked, awakening me from my fish-themed dream.

'They are trying to trap us, lad. Get us to believe something that isn't true. Goad us into making a rash decision. These are dangerous times, Birgir, and I'm counting on you.' With one last clasp of his shoulder, I left him to find his horse. I made my way back to the head of my men.

* * *

Two days later, Birgir returned to us. I was sitting outside my tent, which, like most of our possessions, had been pillaged from dead Roman soldiers. I sat on the grass, watching the morning dew reflect the first shimmering gold rays of the sun. Birgir galloped into the camp, followed by three angry sentries, who he had clearly not stopped for. I watched with a half-smile as he stumbled from his horse and slumped to his knees in front of me.

He was covered in dust from the road, his horse lathered in sweat, and both were sucking in great heaving gasps of air. 'Good morning, Birgir,' I said, the half-smile still on my face.

'You were right, Lord!' he blurted out. 'Just as I got back to the village, a man with an escort of eight soldiers came from the south. They were Roman for sure, and he handed Wulfric a large pouch of coin.'

I nodded slowly, considering what Birgir had said. 'How do you know it was coin?'

'Wulfric tipped some onto his palm. I'd recognise the glimmer of gold anywhere, Lord,' Birgir said through a grin.

'Did you hear what was said?' I asked.

'No, Lord. But they were speaking Latin, I think, but I was too far away to hear properly. You did say to not get too close.' He looked suddenly worried, as if I would lose my temper for him not gaining any further knowledge.

'Good, you did well, Birgir.' He smiled at that, relief plain on his face. 'That man, the Roman, what did he look like? Were his clothes of high quality, did he look like he might be rich, important?'

'No, Lord. He wore a stained tunic under an old cloak. His men the same, none had armour but all were armed. But they rode and walked in formation, the way the legions do.'

I nodded again. So, the man wasn't a high-ranking officer then, but a frumentarius – a grain man. Even so, a play against me of this magnitude wouldn't be of his own initiative. I had no doubt some Roman senator was planning this, scheming in the steam room of his marble baths in a luxurious villa. Gods, I hate the Romans.

'Eight men in the escort, you say? And they came from the south?' Birgir nodded. The men could only have come from two places: the Tenth legion at Vindobona, or the Fourteenth at Carnuntum. I sent a swift prayer to the gods for it to be the Tenth.

'Which way did they leave? Back south?' I asked optimistically. Though I thought I already knew the answer.

'No, Lord, west. The same road you took. They must be a day behind me.'

I nodded slowly. 'Any chance they saw you? You must have needed to cut across their path at some point?'

'No, Lord. I gave them a head start, then took the road north, cutting west across the land before re-joining the road. They're definitely behind me, didn't seem in a rush.'

'You have done well, Birgir, as I knew you would. Wait here.'

I walked into my tent and stood inside, waiting for the flaps to swing shut. A man in my position can never be too trusting. I commanded five hundred men, cutthroats and thieves all. I had chests filled with silver and other precious materials, and on more than one occasion had found myself scratching my head in confusion as I counted the chests and found one missing. When the leather flaps had swung shut I walked to the far left corner and lifted my cot and dragged it as quietly as I could out the way. In an unremarkable leather pouch, hidden in an old tunic, were the keys for the chests. I quickly unlocked one, chose a silver arm ring from among the mound of silver and gold. Locking the chest, returning the key and sliding back the cot, I walked outside and presented the waiting Birgir with the arm ring. His eyes lit up at the glimmering metal and he swaggered off into the crowd of warriors that had gathered to hear his news, his new arm ring secured on his scrawny bicep.

I called Ruric to me and impolitely told the rest of the men to be about their business. Ruric sat on the grass next to me, a conspiratorial grin on his face. 'What news, Chief?' he asked.

'The Romans have shown their hand. Now let's call their bluff, shall we?' I ordered him to get the men ready to ride, but wouldn't tell him where to. I walked to the river and gazed at the swirling waters. It amazed me, that the two rivers were such different colours, each with their own mesmerising patterns where the different currents swept the water in separate directions. The River Elbe was the cleaner of the two, the water the colour of dull iron. It also had a faster, more direct current that ran inexorably south, as the water came directly from the northern sea. Where the River Saale drifted off from its bigger brother, the water was brown, the current less strong. I thought it must be due to the lack of fresh water that entered its domain. The river was the shorter of the two, and therefore needed less new water. It also flooded less, and at low tide was so shallow you could ride your horse across at certain points and not get a speck of wet on your boots. I was lost in these thoughts when Ruric came back to me.

'Everything is ready, Lord. Are we going to the Harii?' I could sense the nerves in his voice. We easily had the numbers to pick a fight with the Harii, and on an open plain the battle would be over in less time than it takes a Roman sand clock to count an hour. But the Harii didn't fight in sunlight on open plains, they ambushed you whilst you slept, rolled up in your cloak in the dim interior of a harrowing forest. As I said, no one picks a fight with the Harii lightly.

'No,' I said. 'I will go there alone. We'll split the men up when we get further north. When we reach the River Weser, each file leader will take his men separate ways. But let's keep that between us for now.' I grinned as I spoke and knew it to be a thing of pure evil. I had a plan, and it involved my favourite pastime: killing Romans.

3

The Harii lived in the very northwest of our land, right on the Rhine border with the Romans. They had previously lived more centrally, but even they had needed to give in to the pressure caused by the great migrations of other tribes to the north and east. The Suebi, as they were most commonly known as now, were a vast tribe, led by a king. Very few of our tribes had kings. Many chiefs would of course call themselves king, but they only ruled small tracts of marshland and could put no more than fifty poorly armed warriors in the field. A true king had an army, and his tribe would be given tribute by the smaller tribes that bordered his land. The Suebi were such a tribe.

So, as they swallowed up more people, those people imposed themselves further west. The Harii had uprooted and settled in the swamps that bordered the sea and the Rhine. It suited them, I thought as I rode down an old Roman road, surrounded by half-sunken carts and carriages in the stodgy land either side. It was impossible to assault the home of the Harii. There was one road through the marsh into their land, and the same road took you back out again. They could fight off an army of thousands with just their small number. They might have to if I didn't get there before the frumentarii agent.

The road itself was a work of art. Long, flat wooden beams sunk into the soft ground, connecting beams running through the middle, giving support for the cobbles laid on top. It must have been over a hundred years since that road was built, and still it was smooth and comfortable to ride on. I hated the Romans, I hated them even more when I had to admit they were good at something. Unfortunately, they were good at quite a lot.

I was alone now, whistling softly to myself as I left the open marsh and entered a dark patch of wood. Each of my file leaders had taken their men in a different direction. It was a risk I was taking, but a considered one. I had five such leaders, and each commanded one hundred men. I had taken the idea from the Romans, who were, as much as I hate to admit it, brilliant when it came to warfare. Their armies were drilled to within an inch of their lives. It left no room to think when they met with the enemy – each man knew his role, each knew what every trumpet blast signalled. More importantly, each officer had the freedom to make decisions on the field that could affect the outcome of a battle, and that is what I wanted to install in my men. Five cavalry wings each numbering one hundred men can cause carnage in a battle if given the right leadership, and I had chosen my file leaders well.

Now I had released them into the wild. I was as cunning as Loki, or so I believed. The trickster lived within me, and I was going to lead Rome on a merry dance. I spied two ravens circling above the trees; I thought it a good sign. The Allfather watched over me, guiding me through the choppy waters that was the politics between the tribal chiefs.

I heard the slightest rustle in the trees to my right, a noise so faint it could have been made by a creeping squirrel. I snapped my head round and there must have been fifty black-clad warriors, all with spears with leaf-shaped blades, pointing at me. By the gods, they were good. 'Morning, boys,' I said as cheerfully as I could. 'The chief at home?'

'Alaric of the Ravensworn, been a while since I have seen you in our lands. Why are you here? We have no quarrel with any of the tribes, nor do we wish to start one.' The man that spoke was Emmerich Fridumarson, and I knew him to be the leader of the Harii's warriors. Not a man you'd want to cross blades with.

'Emmerich Fridumarson, good to see you, old friend.' The men of the tribes had long since taken to using their father's name with 'son' at the end as their second name. It always annoyed the Romans, which is, I think, as good a reason as any to do it. 'I need to see the chief. It's urgent,' I said, not wanting to waste any time. For all I knew, the frumentarii agent was hot on my heels.

'As I just said, Alaric, we've got no quarrel with our cousins, and we don't want one either. What do you want with the chief?'

I sighed. Emmerich was a big man, tall and broad-shouldered with light brown hair and a beard that dropped almost to his belt. His face was blackened with charcoal; he wore a black tunic with no armour and carried a huge double-headed axe in one hand. I doubted I could heft the thing with two. 'We share a problem, your people and I,' I said, not wanting to talk details in front of fifty men. I wasn't sure who I could trust.

Emmerich met my eye for a heartbeat, then another one. 'Rome?' he asked, arcing a great bushy eyebrow. I nodded.

I was soon shown to the chief of the Harii, through a maze of small paths through the dense undergrowth of the forest that I doubted even my most skilled tracker would have been able to find let alone follow. Deeper into the woods we went, the canopy of the thick trees blocking out more and more of

the sunlight. The silence was eerie, just the steady trudge of
my boots the only sound. I had been asked, none too kindly, to
dismount Hilde and she was now being led by a warrior at the
rear of our column. Emmerich stalked the ground as silently
as a cat. I wondered at the level of training the warriors must
go through, for the man must have weighed twice as much
as me.

Eventually we came to a small clearing, a patch of yellow
sunlight amidst the endless darkness. There were warriors
everywhere. Some sitting outside the small round huts that
must have housed up to ten, others chopping wood or rolling
dice. Others were drinking vast quantities of dark ale, and
laughing at some poor bastard who had not only reached his
limit, but seemingly passed it some time ago. He was retching
and coughing on all fours, huge amounts of ale cascading from
his gagging mouth. I smiled. Such things were to be seen
commonly around my own camp of an evening. I had once had
a man, Gerlach, his name, who had drunk a whole barrel,
although he hadn't lived long enough to brag of his efforts.

The warriors stopped their horseplay when they saw me, the
whole camp falling into a muttered silence. Alaric of the
Ravensworn was here. Battle turner, Loki-cunning, chief killer,
oathbreaker. I heard it all whispered on the breeze as I swaggered by, saw each man reach instinctively for his sword. *Alaric is
here*, they were all thinking. *Only blood will come of this.*

* * *

'Well if that ain't old Alaric, then I'm old One Eye himself!'
exclaimed Ketill Lambertson, chief of the Harii and an old
comrade of mine. He was a bear of a man, as you would expect
of someone who led the most feared tribe in all of Germania.

His hair was chestnut brown, his eyes pale grey, and his mouth was rarely found unsmiling.

'Ketill, old friend, good to see you.' I showed him my teeth, one of those smiles that starts with your lips but doesn't spread to your eyes. He noticed the expression and nodded sombrely. With a motion of his head, he beckoned me into the round-house he had emerged from. He didn't invite Emmerich to follow.

'Am I to assume you haven't just dropped in to see an old friend?' he asked as we both took a seat on the old rug that covered the floor. I scanned my surroundings before replying. Most chiefs had long halls these days, huge great buildings of solid timber, warmed by large heath fires running down their centre. There would be a raised dais at the far end where the chief would sit at the high table, surrounded by his family and guests of honour. Running parallel to the hearth would be long benches and tables, where warriors would feast and drink the winter away, waiting for spring and the start of the raiding season. It seemed that this trend hadn't reached the far north-west and the Harii. Ketill's hall was a small roundhouse, identical in every way to the other roundhouses that encircled it. There was a small fire in the centre with smoke billowing out from a crudely constructed chimney. Sparsely decorated, it didn't even have proper flooring, just the rug that must have been older than our parents, covering packed earth. The walls were bare wood and there was a small cot, with only a couple of pans and a few cooking utensils suspended from pegs and hooks near the hearth.

'Afraid not, Ketill, I bring dark tidings.' I told him all I knew, which was little enough. He listened intently, his pale eyes glistening silver in the light of the flames. There was a silence when I finished as he considered my words.

'How do you know this to be true?' he asked after a time.

'I don't *know* as such. But, as I said, Birgir saw the Roman hand the coin over to Wulfric, and the Roman left the lands of the Fenni on the westerly road.'

'So? That does not mean the whoreson is coming to my door.' A knife appeared in his hand; I have no idea where from, as he was wearing only an unbelted tunic. He toyed with the blade, flipping it in the air and catching it repeatedly.

'I was told that the men that attacked the Fenni wore all black, their faces covered with soot. They howled the wolf cry as they slaughtered the men of the village. Someone is trying to frame you, Ketill, a Roman. And that Roman is on his way here. I would be extremely interested to hear what he has to say.'

'You think he will threaten me?' Ketill asked. He always was quick of mind. 'I join his conspiracy or Rome attacks me and wipes my people from history?' I nodded. 'All this, to get to you?'

I nodded again, aware it sounded ridiculous spoken out loud. 'I have been declared an enemy of Rome, I am a danger to their Pax Romana, as they like to call it.'

Ketill laughed, a joyous belly laugh that left him gasping for breath. 'The mighty Alaric! Slayer of Romans, feared throughout the lands, a warlord sent from the gods!' He laughed again, tears streaming down his face. 'I think, my friend, that you overestimate your own importance in the eyes of the Romans. They've not long since invaded Dacia, they have trouble in Britannia, from what I hear, and there is always some war going on in the east. Why would they go to all this trouble for little old you?'

I shrugged, trying to hide my embarrassment. I had doubts now, for Ketill spoke a lot of sense. I liked to consider myself a big fish in a small pond. Sure, I was feared and respected, and all of the smaller tribes paid me due respect when my men and I rode through their lands. But I only had five hundred men; they were good men, but only five hundred. Rome had more than forty thousand on the Danube and Rhine borders alone. What possible threat could I pose to them?

'I know how it sounds, but I've got a feeling in my bones. The same feeling a man gets when he knows he's being watched, or just before a battle. They *are* coming for me, and I need your help.' I didn't have many men in this world I could confidently call a friend, but Ketill, I thought, was one. If he refused to help me, then the best I could probably hope for was to die with my blade in my hand and spend eternity feasting and fighting in the Allfather's hall.

There was a disturbance on the other side of the curtain that passed as a door, and Emmerich poked his head through. 'Sorry, Lord, but there is a man here, a Roman. He says he needs to speak with you urgently, Lord, and in private.' He said the last bit whilst looking at me. An icy shiver ran up my back. I stared at Ketill then, trying to gauge his reaction from his turn of expression. He smiled and when he looked at me, he had the look of a trickster about him.

I gulped down my fear.

4

I don't know if you've ever tried hiding yourself away in a tiny, barely furnished roundhouse, but it isn't easy. Ketill giggled like a small girl as he stuffed me under his small straw cot, then piled blankets on top to disguise the bulge of my body. The air was close and muggy beneath the straw, the stench horrific. I thought of the roasting meat staked above the cooking fires I had seen on my way through the camp; the barrels of dark ale. I fought the urge to vomit at the rank smells that leaked from the cot. I resolved to burn the thing as soon as the Roman was gone.

The silence that ensued when Ketill left the roundhouse was overpowering. Just the sound of my breathing, the thumping of my heart. Ketill hadn't said what he was going to do, and I half thought he would listen to what the Roman had to say and then decide whether to give me up on the spot.

I didn't have to wait long. I heard Ketill's feet thump on the mud, the sound of the fabric door being ripped back. 'Come in, sit,' he said, presumably to the Roman agent. There was a muffled reply before what sounded like two people entering the cramped space, although I couldn't say for certain how many people were in the hut. My pulse quickened, for my chances of being spotted increased with every additional set of eyes in the room.

'Thank you for seeing me,' the Roman said in halting German. Ketill, I knew, spoke no Latin, so the whole conversation would have to take place in our native tongue. It would drag it out whilst the Roman tried to wrap his tongue round our words. I had to stifle a groan just at the thought of it. I sensed, rather than heard, two men sit down by the fire. I assumed them to be the agent and Ketill. That left the other man, the Roman's companion. I was certain I had heard three sets of booted feet enter the roundhouse, but I could hear no sign of the second foreigner, just the muttered small talk between the agent and Ketill.

Suddenly, I got my answer. A great weight set itself down on top of my legs, crushing them below the knee. I hadn't seen the Roman soldier – for I assumed that was who he was – as he entered, but he must have been bigger than the horse he had rode into the Harii lands. I winced, scrunching up my face and mouthing a curse. 'You comfortable over there?' Ketill asked the man. I could hear the smile in his voice. Silently, I cursed again.

The soldier clearly had no grasp of our language, for I heard the agent repeat the question to his man in Latin. The soldier shuffled slightly and asked the agent if he should move. The agent didn't consult with Ketill, just told him to stay where he was.

'Time is of the essence, Ketill Lambertson, chieftain of the Harii, so I will get straight to the point,' the agent said in broken German. His voice was high-pitched, and in my mind, I pictured a short man, slight of stature with black hair and a face like a weasel. I had no idea if I was right of course. 'My name is Ambrosius Trajianus Valerius, and I am an imperial agent of

Rome. I have come here today to ask for your support on a matter in which you could have a considerable impact.' He spoke slowly, his girlish voice struggling with the tongue-twisting words of our language.

'What's that then?' Ketill replied, blunt as an old blade.

'Alaric of the Ravensworn. He has become a problem, an itch that Rome has been unable to scratch. Are you familiar with the man?' Again, he spoke softly, almost patronisingly.

'I know Alaric. He's an old comrade of mine. We did a bit of raiding together back when we were young men. He even helped me to become chief of the Harii, after a particularly bloody battle with the tribe. I would go so far as to call him a friend.' The threat in Ketill's voice was clear. There was an edge there, gruff, solid and unmoving, like the marble that covered the emperor's palace in Rome.

'Ahh,' Trajianus said. 'I was afraid of that.' I could picture him wincing slightly, smacking his lips together and settling his face in an apologetic frown. 'So, you are saying you will not help us in this matter?'

'As Hercules as my witness, I swear I will do nothing to aid Rome in her hunt for Alaric and the Ravensworn. What's he done, anyhow?' Ketill asked with genuine curiosity. I was also curious, for I have done many things over the years to displease the mighty empire. I wondered which one had finally tipped them over the edge.

'We put a new king on the throne of the Quadi, a few years ago. Areogaesus, as I am sure you are aware.' I heard Ketill grunt in acknowledgement. 'Well, there was an agreement between us and the king...'

I heard no more of what was said, although by then I knew the gist of it. Areogaesus was king of the largest tribe in the south, on Rome's northern border. When they set him on the throne, it had been agreed he would not raid into Roman lands, nor would he trouble the Marcomanni, his neighbours to the west. With some *slight* encouragement from myself, he and I did both, gaining much wealth and losing few men. Rome was not happy, and four cohorts of the Fourteenth legion spent an entire year camped in his lands, ensuring he didn't get up to no good. I had, it seemed, crossed the line.

But I didn't get the opportunity to revel in the memory of my glory and deceit, for the Roman soldier atop my legs shifted, ever so slightly, from his right arse cheek to his left, and a whole world of pain shot up my left leg quicker than an arrow. First my foot cramped, then my calf, and before I knew it my whole leg was alight in burning pain. I nearly screamed out, but bit down on my tongue till I could taste the iron tang of my own blood. My leg was tense, taut like a bow, and it took all my self-restraint to not move it. I swear to all the gods if Donar himself had strolled into that roundhouse, hefted his great hammer and swung it at my head, I would have considered it a mercy.

For what felt an age I lay there, body tense, blood welling in my mouth. Eventually the soldier got up, and I was faintly aware of him pacing the room. The pain in my leg calmed, and ever so gently I rolled it first right then left, the shooting pain becoming momentarily worse before mercifully receding.

'Do you have a plan?' I heard Ketill ask as I slowed my breathing and wriggled my head against the irritants of cold sweat that streamed down my forehead.

'I do,' Trajianus replied, his high-pitched voice filled with arrogance. 'We have two alae of cavalry, joined with a vexillation of auxiliary currently patrolling the eastern banks of the Rhine. We know Alaric has come this way and that his Ravensworn will be holed up nearby. I intend to tempt him into the open and then have the men massacre him and this wolfpack of his that have caused Rome so much grief.' I grinned at the term wolf-pack. I suppose I must have felt a certain degree of fear, given the amount of effort Rome seemed to be putting into the extermination of the little band of merry men I had put together. I was also flattered.

'Which units?' Ketill asked. I knew what he was doing. Getting me as much information as he could. Also, I assumed, still in two minds as to whether or not he should hand me over to this Roman dog.

'The First Ala Noricorum and the Second Ala Asturum cavalry wings, who have been borrowed from Britannia especially for this. For the infantry we're calling in the First Batavian. Not quite the force they once were, but still a formidable opponent.' I really was flattered. Two whole wings of cavalry, one of them shipped across the narrow sea, just for me. Not only that, but Rome had also employed the Batavians to face me in the field.

The Batavians had once been the cream of Rome's army. Used as shock troops during the invasion of Britannia, they had won great fame for their heroics at the battle of the River Medui, in the southeast of that miserable island. But, during that infamous year where four men battled for the purple, they had revolted against Rome, and inevitably lost. They fought on both horseback and foot, and had the incredible skill of being able to swim rivers in full armour, using their mounts to propel them across the water. Despite not being the force they once were, the thought of facing them in the field was not exactly a prospect I relished.

'What makes you think Alaric has come west? My people are based a stone's throw from the Rhine and your lands, yet you came from the east. You're not telling me everything, Trajianus, and I don't like it.' I heard Ketill rise to his feet as he spoke. Heard the gravel in his throat, the menace in his voice.

'You may not like what I am about to say, Chief Ketill, but I want you to listen to the end.' Trajianus spoke as if he was about to explain something simple to a small child. 'We set an ambush back east, in the lands of the Fenni. The Semnones, led by their chief Euric, raided the Fenni. Twenty warriors he brought with him. They covered themselves in charcoal and wore just black tunics. Wulfric, the Fenni chief, had some problems with a couple of his men. He thought one might even challenge him for leadership of the tribe. So he didn't tell them of the plan, and when they rose to fight off the invaders, they were killed by Euric and his men.'

I grinned ruefully beneath the straw cot. Rome really had pulled out all the stops to see me buried. And it also proved that I was right, not simply suffering delusions of grandeur, as I'm sure Ketill must have thought.

'Let me guess,' Ketill interjected before Trajianus could speak again. 'These men lived just long enough to say they were attacked by the Harii in front of witnesses. And now I have two options: help you get Alaric and his men to a battlefield of your choice, or do nothing and have Rome come after my men for revenge. Revenge on an attack we had nothing to do with in the first place.' Trajianus made a dismissive noise, but confirmed the accusation in his shrill voice. I could almost see Ketill's cheeks flushing red. I sensed the soldier near me tense, imagined his hand hovering round the hilt of his blade. The tension in the room was palpable. An unnatural silence stretched for what felt an age. 'Get out,' Ketill said eventually. 'I need to think.'

5

Ketill seethed. He paced in the small confines of his roundhouse as I sat atop the rank cot I had been hiding under, picking straw from my long dark hair, and knocking back ale to try and eradicate the aroma of old farts.

'These Roman dogs,' Ketill sniffed. 'They think they can come into our lands and manipulate us, play us off against each other. It makes me sick.' He hawked and spat into the small fire.

'That's how they work, Ketill, they've been doing it successfully for centuries. The question is, brother, what are we going to do about it?' I let it hang in the air. Ketill was angry; his blood was up and I could see his fingers itching for the hilt of a blade. The Roman's words had angered him, brought to the surface everything he hated about Rome. I was prepared to milk that cow for all it was worth.

'There's no way I'm giving you up. Not a chance. But we need to know exactly where these bastard troops are so we can plan properly. And then this cur and his lapdog need to die' – he motioned outside the canvas door to where Trajianus and his companion were no doubt waiting nearby – 'so they can't run back to their masters and warn them.'

I nodded my head in agreement, a wicked grin fixed to my face. 'I took the precaution of splitting my men up before I came here. I told each file leader to ride in a different direction. Each one has my banner. With luck, the Romans will spot the columns and think it my main force.'

'But that could bring them all together?' Ketill asked. I knew what he was thinking. He wanted the three units kept separate, so they would be easier to pick off. Me? I wanted them all in one place, on an open battlefield where I could enhance my legend and give the Allfather another reason to invite me into his hall when my time on middle-earth was done.

'Exactly, brother,' I said, grabbing hold of his shoulders. 'Get them on ground of our choosing, with them all to our front. Leave no chance for their little tricks or deceptions. With the Harii and the Ravensworn, we can crush them like the lice they are.'

'I can put one hundred and fifty warriors in the field, you?' Ketill asked, his voice mocking and full of sarcasm.

'Five hundred. That's a lot of men, Ketill.'

'Against how many? Assuming the Roman forces are full strength, that's two hundred and forty cavalry, at least! Plus five hundred Batavians. Not good odds.' He shook his head and slumped down by the hearth, prodding at the flames with a stick.

'But you are Ketill Lambertson! And you command the Harii! Those Romans will shit their breeches the moment they see your men in the field. And not to mention the small reputation my men have. We can win this, my friend, but I need you with me.'

Ketill grunted and then fell silent for a time, his silver eyes lost in the flames. 'To Hel with them!' he said suddenly, launching the stick into the fire. 'The whoresons have left me no choice anyway. Let's kill the bastards!' We locked forearms in the warriors' embrace, before Ketill enveloped me in a crushing bear hug.

The relief I felt was overwhelming. Ketill, as I said before, was a good friend. But I wouldn't have been surprised if he had of chosen to sell me out. He had a responsibility to his people after all, and despite his tribe's fearsome reputation, I knew he didn't throw them into battle without careful consideration. 'Now then, what are we going to do about our friends out there?' I hooked my thumb towards the canvas door. Ketill grinned, and it was a thing of pure evil.

* * *

There was a small opening in the back of the roundhouse. A loose plank of timber that when removed left just enough room for a man to squeeze through. I asked Ketill why he hadn't shown me this earlier, and in his typical way he just laughed and pointed to the stinking pallet. We joked about how he hadn't considered his ever-growing belly when he'd had the thing installed, but it was just wide enough for me to scramble through. The sunlight hurt my eyes. I had been under that straw cot so long I had forgotten the sun still shone in the world outside. I squatted with my back against the roundhouse and wondered how I could have possibly thought it dark beneath the canopy of pine when I arrived earlier that day.

Voices woke me from my daydream as Ketill welcomed the Romans back into his home. His apology for sending them outside almost sounded genuine. Smiling to myself, I nearly missed the Roman soldier that trudged not ten paces from me, lowered his breeches and began urinating up a tree. Loki must have been watching over me then, for if the Roman had turned his head slightly to the left he would have seen me there, hunched in the shade, a short sword ready to plunge into his heart. But I have always considered myself a descendant of the trickster; always found an edge against any opponent foolish enough to cross my path.

I stayed rooted to the spot, as unmoving as stone, my heart thudding in my chest. Birgir had told me he had seen the Roman with Wulfric, and that he'd had two soldiers with him. Was this the one that had crushed me earlier as I lay under the straw cot? Or was this the other soldier, and was Ketill inside with two men? Our plan had been for me to rush inside at Ketill's signal, I deal with the soldier whilst Ketill took out Trajianus. Indecision grew within me; stay with this one or wait for Ketill?

My heartbeat reached a frantic tempo, so fast and hard I thought my ears would bleed. The soldier whistled a tune as he pissed. I recognised an old marching song from the legions, something about a whore and cheap ale. I found myself humming along in my head as I crept forward; my palms itched with sweat and I had to adjust my grip on the sword as I moved. I inched closer, carefully treading on the endless carpet of broken twigs and dried leaves. Ten paces, five. Surely he would turn now? Surely he could hear me? But he kept whistling, and just as he did a little jig to shake the last drops from the end of his cock, I plunged the sword through his back and into his heart. He dropped to the dirt without a sound.

I stood over him, scanning the immediate area, but everyone

was the other side of Ketill's roundhouse and my only observers were the birds. I cleaned the blade on the hem of the corpse's tunic and studied the man more closely. He was short, I realised. Slight of build and had not yet grown his first beard. Nor would he. With a start I turned on the balls of my feet and rushed to the small crack in the back of the roundhouse. The dead man was not the one who had nearly suffocated me with his great bulk, couldn't have been; there simply wasn't enough of him.

I returned to the back of the hut, and peering through a crack in the wall, I saw Ketill engaged in a desperate battle with two Romans. He was armed with just a short sword, same as me. The two Romans had been relieved of their weapons before being admitted to Ketill, but both had knives. I ripped the loose plank from the wall and hurtled inside. Such was the cacophony of the fight, no one noticed until I bellowed a war cry and slammed into a huge man.

He really was huge. Arms bigger than my thighs, legs rooted to the dirt deeper than the forest that surrounded us.

Maybe I exaggerate.

But I threw my whole weight into that charge, and when I slammed into him he barely moved. I rebounded off him with thunder in my head and blood seeping from my nose. He recovered first and jabbed his knife at my chest. If I wasn't still staggering backwards, he would have probably punctured my lung. As it was, the knife whistled under my armpit and snagged my tunic. It caught in the folds for just a moment, and I used that time to grab his arm and propel myself to him. His knife hand was trapped on my left, so I gave him a savage headbutt following up with a swing of my sword that buried itself high in his shoulder.

The Roman sank to his knees, cursing me in Latin. I wasted no time and drove the point of my blade into his neck. Black blood spat all over me. The Roman gurgled and writhed, hands reaching to his neck in vain as he tried to stop the inexorable tide of his lifeblood from spilling to the dirt. Eventually he breathed his last. I looked up, panting like a dog to see Ketill doing the same, standing over the body of Trajianus. 'I think that went well,' I said through bloodstained teeth.

6

Dawn the following day found me back on my own. Atop my mare, I scanned the open valley around me, half convinced I would see a column of Roman cavalry galloping straight for me. But all was quiet, just the chirping of the birds and the odd gust of wind. I remember thinking how beautiful the land was; flowers everywhere in full bloom, a patchwork of colour against the never-ending tide of green. The grass each side of the track was long, covered in morning dew that glistened in the sun's first rays. When I inhaled deeply, all I could smell was the scent of summer. Life's simple pleasures; you just can't beat them.

My tranquillity did not last long, however, as soon I heard the thunder of hooves on the road ahead. I panicked for a moment. I was riding up a short but steep rise, a small ridge directly to my front. The hoofbeats grew louder, and my heartbeat matched them. I scanned to the left and right, but there was just grass, swaying in the breeze. I pulled hard on the reins and turned the mare to the right, then the left, frantic in my indecision. If they were Roman – or any of the many chieftains in this part of the land that wanted me dead – I would have been finished.

Pleasingly, a blood-red banner with a black raven appeared over the small ridge. Baldo, one of my file leaders, and his column of one hundred cantered over the rise. Baldo the Brave, he was known as. Or Baldo the Reckless, as Ruric called him. He was short and generously built, with large ox-like shoulders atop a rounded frame. The men of his file would laugh as he cursed and wriggled his way into his mail in the mornings, but the laughter soon stopped when he brandished his axe.

'Mornin', Chief,' Baldo said through a mouth sparse of teeth. 'Still alive then?'

What a stupid question, I thought. *Clearly I'm still fucking alive.* I bit back the retort though, knowing my irritation was aimed more at myself and the fear I had felt until seeing my banner. 'How was your fishing trip?' I asked with an arched eyebrow, still trying to slow my raging heart.

'Oh, we got ourselves a big 'un all right. If you come up here, you might just see its head on the horizon.' It pays dividends to be concerned when Baldo showed you as many of his missing teeth as he did me then. It normally means he has done something incoherently stupid.

I walked Hilde to the top of the rise, shielding my eyes from the rising sun as I cast my gaze east. Sure enough, Baldo had snared himself a mighty fish on the end of his hook. A fish the size of five hundred Batavians, in fact. They were immediately recognisable. They wore long-sleeved shirts of chain mail and dyed red trousers. Each man had a circular shield decorated with a black centre with a red ring around the rim slung from the saddle on the right side of his horse. Their longswords hung on their left and kept one hand on the reins whilst the other held a long ash spear.

They were led by an officer with a white plumed helmet, and I could just make out pale milky skin under the polished steel, and assumed the man wasn't from the tribes.

'Donar's beard, Baldo! You really did catch one!' I didn't know whether to laugh or cry. I had intended for my men to be spotted by Roman forces patrolling their western border. I hadn't banked on the fact my captains would let them get *quite* so close.

'What d'ya reckon, Chief? Run like the wind or stand and fight 'em?'

There haven't been many times in my life I have been speechless. Once, when I was eleven or twelve, Frida, a peasant girl who helped her elderly father on the farm my father owned, had dropped her tunic and shown me her breasts. To this day, I don't think I have lain eyes on a finer pair. How *do* breasts that large and soft stay so perk?

Anyway, I digress.

I gaped at Baldo, giving him a dumbfounded look as I switched my gaze from his gap-toothed grin back to the five hundred hardened warriors cantering merrily down the road to bury their spearheads in our guts. 'Would you like to stand and fight them, Baldo?' I asked in the most sarcastic tone I could muster.

'Yeah. Well, can do. Up to you, ain't it.' Baldo shrugged as he spoke, as if we were discussing nothing more significant than dinner plans.

'Right, okay. Let's stand and fight, shall we? I'm sure we'll be fine.' Bizarrely, even as I snorted in ironic laughter at what I thought was my own cheap joke, the men around me readied for battle. Helmets were fastened, palms spat on as men loosened swords from sheaths. Spears were produced and handed from man to man. I thought to myself that these men really would do anything for me, and they really are stupid.

'Stop! Stop, you idiots!' I commanded in my best battlefield voice. The tumult died away; the smell of leather remained. 'Would you really stand and fight those whoresons?' I asked, pointing to the approaching Batavians, who had begun to get too close for comfort.

'We'd fight for you, Chief,' Baldo said with a casual shrug. 'Not much we wouldn't do for Lord Alaric, ain't that right, lads?' A chorus of 'aye's greeted this. I admit I felt a swell of pride, the hint of a tear in my eye. These warriors, outlaws and cutthroats to a man, were completely loyal to me and each other. Whoever said there was no honour amongst thieves?

'Well, that is touching,' I said. 'You know, you men mean a lot to me too. And that is why I don't want you to throw away your lives fighting those bastards!' I jabbed a finger in the direction of the Batavians. I could hear them now, feel the low rumble of the ground shaking under the impact of their hooves.

'So, leg it then?' Baldo asked.

'After you, Captain Baldo.' I bowed low in my saddle, motioning to the open road with my outstretched hand. That got a laugh from the men, and quick as the wind we turned and fled back west. Baldo, I had to admit, had done his job remarkably well. As we galloped off away from the rising sun, the Batavians were unable to follow, their horses apparently too tired to form another charge. I reconsidered my opinion of 'Baldo the Reckless' that day. The man Ruric considered to be headstrong and rash had in fact planned his retreat from the Roman auxiliaries perfectly. Knowing he had the better mounts, he had led them on inexorably, just staying out of reach, all the time knowing his men had an extra reserve, an edge over his foe. I remembered also the loyalty his hundred had shown to me, and I never forgot it.

* * *

It was late afternoon when we caught up with Ruric and his Hundred. The Raven banners met in the centre of a wide-open plain. I scanned the ground and nodded in approval at the patches of grass that were a lighter shade of green than the others. At the base of a small rise there was a whole line, maybe even half a Roman mile long and at least a spear's length wide. 'How goes it?' I asked, eyes still scouring the land.

'All you asked is done, Chief,' he said in a tired voice. I suppose I must have been in my mid-thirties back then, though I still considered myself a young man. I looked at Ruric and for the first time I noticed the age lines around his pale green eyes, the grey tinge his once yellow hair now held. He was old, I realised – he must have been fifty if he was a day. Ruric had been with me since I had first set out on my own, banished from my tribe for committing a grievous crime, though that is a story for another day. What would I do without him? Perhaps one day soon he would decide he was too old for the life of an outlaw and want to buy some land and settle down to see out his years in peace. My father had done the same thing when he had passed his peak, and the old bugger was still going strong. Who would replace the man that had been my sounding board for more years than I cared to remember? True, I had Baldo and three other solid captains, but they weren't Ruric. They lacked his calmness and his ability to offset my fiery temper. It was something I would have to consider.

'You look tired, old friend,' I said, clasping a hand on his shoulder.

'I'm fine, Chief. Don't you worry about me. Though it's true I ain't as young as I used to be!' he said, arching his back and wincing. 'Carrying a bit more timber than I used to an' all. Killed me, doing all this.' He motioned to the different shade grass. 'You sure this is going to work?'

I shook my head. 'No, but it's the best plan I have.' I shrugged, trying to appear calmer than I felt. 'There's five hundred Batavians hot on our heels and two wings of cavalry around here somewhere. Over seven hundred men coming our way, Ruric. It's going to be one hell of a fight.' Ruric nodded, rubbing his short beard. 'You heard from any of the others?' I asked.

Ruric shook his head and I frowned. I had been expecting my whole force to be waiting for me when I arrived at the open fields I had chosen before I had journeyed to meet Ketill. To find just Ruric and his Hundred here was concerning. I looked at the sun, judging the time to be a little past midday; there was a lot of daylight left for the Batavians to catch us and force battle. I made a quick decision.

'Get me Birgir. Then get your own Hundred with Baldo's in a battle line on the top of the ridge.' Ruric nodded and strolled off, leaving me to ponder in silence.

7

The Batavians found us just before sundown. They cantered into the open field, their commander halting and riding slowly across the front of our line. I had the men form up, fifty men wide and four deep. The men in the front rank were the biggest of us. They were coated in mail and had solid, round shields. Each man had a single-headed axe that he would use to hook atop his opponent's shield and tear it down. The men in the second rank were lightly armoured, most with just a leather cuirass, and each held a long ash spear, which they would thrust two-handed into chests and groins when their comrade to the front had forged an opening with his axe. The rear two ranks were a repeat of the first, so I could rotate the ranks as they tired.

We trained at this regularly. I knew I had at my disposal the best fighting force in all of Germania. There were tribes like the Marcomanni, or the Quadi, who could put vast amounts of warriors into the field, but none who could match my men's skill and discipline in battle. This was something else I had stolen from the Romans. The success of their armies was not due to the numbers they put in the field – for when they fought they were nearly always outnumbered – but because of their training and discipline.

Taking on a Roman legion in open battle was of course well beyond us, but I thought we could handle a force of seven hundred auxiliari, as long as we got the timing right. I stood in the centre of my line, willing the sun to hurry its descent. We were just two hundred. I had no idea where the rest of my force were, and I had arranged with Ketill for the Harii to arrive early the next day. If the Batavian commander decided to attack, we were on our own.

I stepped from the line and shielded the sun from my eyes to scan the horizon for Birgir. I had sent him out earlier in the day to track my three missing columns. There was no sign of him, or my men. A trumpet sounded from the Batavian formation; to my dismay I recognised the three short blasts as the order to form up. They were going to attack.

Sure enough, the Batavians were soon dropping their packs to the mud and forming into a giant boar's snout, still atop their horses. I gulped. They were perhaps half a mile off and had already begun a slow advance towards us. I scanned the horizon one last time; the sun had not yet begun to submerge beneath the endless green sea. I knew we would have to fight.

'Ruric, Baldo, to me!' I bellowed, tightening the chin straps of my helmet. Some chieftains had fancy helmets, with gold inlay or wolves' heads on top. I like mine to be plain, undistinguishable. It made no sense to me why some men would want to put a target like that on their heads. Men would be drawn to it, like a moth to a flame's glow. It was a status thing, I thought. Insecure leaders needing their men to see them in their battle glory. I had no need for such trivial things. My armour was plain, my sword undecorated and my fingers free of jewelled rings. I had a different kind of status, forged in the blood of lesser men. I needed no decoration to remind men of who I was, or why they should fear me.

Ruric and Baldo forced their way to my side, each man hefting a shield in one hand and spear in the other. 'Right, my friends,' I said, licking my dry lips. 'Looks like we're on our own. Keep it tight, no one leaves the shield wall. We let them attack us, and hope Ruric's little "surprises" slow them down. We just need to hold out till sundown. Questions?' Both men shook their heads, determined expressions on their faces.

I sent them away to tend to their men and stood in resolute silence. The familiar sounds of men preparing for battle were all around me, as well as last-minute pisses and the stench of rotten bowels where some men's nerves had gotten the better of them.

I counted the passage of time through my own heartbeats. The Roman commander – a tribune, judging from his armour and white-crested helmet – rode along the front of his men, whirling his sword through the air. The auxiliaries all had lances ready – a dangerous weapon; longer and heavier than a spear, weighted at the business end, and the tipped iron point would easily tear through armour and flesh.

They were roughly a hundred paces from our position on the crest of the ridge, and forty or so paces from the first of the traps Ruric and his men had sown in the ground. Almost too close to the first trap, I thought, for they would still be walking the horses and the rear ranks would have plenty of time to stop when the front faltered. I held my breath as the Batavians advanced, willing their tribune to spur them into a premature canter or for an over-eager centurion to lose his discipline and lead a charge.

Neither happened.

They walked their horses into the first of the pits my men had dug. The front rank of the Batavian force – including their tribune – were lurched unceremoniously from their mounts as their horses plunged onto the stakes buried in the pits. I nodded, silently congratulating Ruric on his fine work. The pits weren't just deep, they were long. I thought when I'd looked earlier in the day that it was just the lighter patches of grass that concealed the 'lilies', as the Romans called them. The lighter grass would mark where it had died when it was cut from the earth and been left in the summer sun all afternoon. But whether through sheer luck or design, I did not know, Ruric had further concealed the length of his work.

The ditches were perhaps the length of two spears, too far for the rear horses to jump with no run up, and since their stricken comrades were blocking their path, they would not get that. The rest of the force merely stood and watched as their comrades clambered from either horse or ground. Remounts were called up from the rear and soon the tribune was dressing his lines for another advance whilst a party of men killed the wounded horses and dragged their corpses clear of the ditch.

'They gonna jump it, Chief?' Baldo asked at my shoulder. I had been so transfixed by the carnage to my front I hadn't seen him approach. The ditches were wide, but the tribune would be able to ride around the flanks with ease. They would, however, then need to approach at a different angle. Ruric had dug the ditches along the shallower incline to the ridge we stood on, which was clever. Now the tribune knew the land was booby trapped, he would have to reconsider his plan of attack, and maybe attack up the steeper side of the slope.

'I think they might try,' I said, hoping I was wrong. Without even striking a blow, we had cost the Batavians a few men, many horses, and a lot of time. The sun was kissing the horizon now, the golden-yellow light turning blood orange. They had, by my reckoning, an hour to launch another assault. The only way they would get it done before sundown would be to jump the ditch and charge.

I walked along the ranks of my men, sharing jokes with the ones I knew well, nods and handshakes with the ones I didn't. They were mercenaries to a man, loyal to their purses before me. They wouldn't stand and fight if they didn't want to, or didn't believe they could win. It boosted my confidence to see no trace of doubt in my men as I met their eye; nothing but grim determination.

'Wotan's beard! They're comin'!' a man said, pointing out the obvious as the Batavians advanced at the canter towards the ditch. We all held our breath in suspense as in one fluid motion, nearly five hundred horsemen leapt over the obstacle. Time seemed to almost stand still – just the fading memory of the sun and my thudding heart remained – and in slow motion they reached the peak of their climb into the air and inevitably came crashing back down.

With a noise like thunder, hooves slammed onto the grass the other side of the ditch. Horses stumbled and men toppled from saddles; I watched one thrown rider take another man with him on his sharp drop to the hard and unforgiving earth. The grace and beauty of their flight was shattered with the snap of bone, the howl of trampled men and the screams of injured beasts. My men cheered, loud and strong. I joined with them, seeing the sun continue its descent towards the horizon.

Our joy was short lived, as it appeared the tribune was thirsty for our blood before he turned in for the night. He rallied his remaining men, forming them into line and cantering on to our position.

'Get ready, lads!' I hollered, mainly to cover my own growing nerves. That's the thing about being the leader, the feared warrior who men look up to and follow. You can't ever show them you are scared. I was, of course. I have been before every battle or skirmish I have ever fought in. Everyone is and that is the reality of it, but you cannot let it show. I hauled my sword from its scabbard, the only man in my front rank not to be armed with an axe. To be honest, I have never mastered the weapon – too top heavy for me. I thrust the sword in the air and bellowed '*Ravensworn!*' at the top of my voice. My men joined me; the clamour was deafening.

We watched as the Batavians hurdled the next two sets of pits, losing more men on the way. One row of 'lilies' remained only ten paces to the front of our line. When they landed from that jump, they would land not on grass, but on a wall of men, wood and iron.

'Step back three paces,' I ordered, seeing the danger.

The Batavians were galloping now. The ground shook furiously, as if Hel were trying to escape from her underground prison.

The enemy approached the final pit, and in horror I suddenly realised that my men armed with only short-handled axes would be horribly outmatched against this tidal wave of armoured horse flesh. 'Spearmen to the front, spears to the front!' I bellowed in near panic, though my men responded quickly. With no more time for thought or doubts, I watched in awe and terror as the famed Batavians leapt the last pit; hooves flailed in the air, helmeted men screamed and snarled as each picked a target for his lance. I sucked my teeth, set my face in a savage grimace and hefted my sword.

I was Alaric, Lord of War. Nothing but victory awaited me.

8

The first man to meet my blade died with a foot of iron through the back of his mouth. The next had half his right leg cut off as I stepped over my first victim and swung a savage backwards slash that cut through his saddle and into his mount. It is difficult to describe the first engagement in a battle. Thrilling? Bowel-clenching terror? Probably a bit of both. The din of combat filled my ears: iron met iron with an ear-splitting clang; blades chopped through spear shafts like a sickle through barley; horses whinnied in fear and men screamed in agony and ecstasy. There really is nothing like it.

I had no notion of how the battle went and if my men held their line or their bloodlust had gotten the better of them. The Batavians could have forced their way into our formation; they could even have encircled us and were right then spearing my men in their backs. I wouldn't have known. All I saw was the iron in my hand and the mounted men at the end of it.

I had left my shield wall now and vaguely remember ignoring Baldo as he was yelling at me to get back. Suddenly a horse pressed in on my left flank, and a well-timed pivot allowed me to avoid a piercing lance blow that was destined for my shoulder. I dropped my shield and grabbed the lance in one fluid motion, yanking it hard, forcing the rider to fall from his saddle, and I ran him through whilst he was still struggling to stand.

Another came at me with a snarl, his longsword bared. Our blades met with a mighty crash as he passed. I was still turning when he came back at me. Startled by his speed and control of his horse, I dodged the cavalryman's sword and aimed for the mount. Crouching low, moving with all the speed my armoured body could muster, I slashed at the soft belly and was rewarded with a warm gush of blood that flew from the beast with my blade.

I watched as the animal collapsed, trapping its rider who was quickly trampled by another rampaging horse. It was dark – the sun long gone below the horizon. I staggered as another Batavian galloped past. I was at the ditch now, watching the battle unfold. My first wave of adrenalin had worn thin. I slumped, sword scraping the earth, my breath thick on the night air.

A group of horsemen swamped my shield wall, hooves flailing as lances jabbed at gaps in the murky light, but my men were fighting back. One took hold of a saddle, causing the rider to sway. The second rammed his spear into the man's neck.

Still I watched on as Ruric swung his great axe as if it weighed nothing more than a spoon. He prowled in front of my men's shields, hacking and slashing the butterfly blade at any man foolish enough to get too close. Even as I watched, he lopped the arm off one and the leg from another and his next swing near on decapitated a horse. A centurion in a red-crested helmet kicked his horse towards him, but Ruric merely stood and waited for his moment. He sidestepped the cantering horse and leapt – pirouetting in the air and hacking his axe into the officer's neck on the way back down. It was a beautiful kill, perhaps the best I've ever seen, and I have seen a lot of men die at the end of a blade.

Spurred on by Ruric's prowess, and desperate not to let him steal all the glory, I raised my sword and prepared to charge the Batavians once again. As I did, I heard a piercing howl behind me. It was a wolf's howl, the kind the leader of the pack makes when he spots some easy prey for his family of sharp-toothed savages to gauge on. The howl was followed by another, and soon the night was alive with high-pitched wailing.

My blood was hot, my heart hammering, and every sinew in me was itching to jump back into the fray. But suddenly the hairs on the back of my neck stood up, and my legs wouldn't follow my brain's commands. Fear gripped me, and to my shame I felt a wetness down my leg, a warmth where moments before had just been the cool night breeze. It's not easy for a man to admit he pissed himself, but there you have it. The wolfpack howled again, closer this time. I could almost smell their rank fur; picture their sharp-edged teeth. I sensed their charge, felt the low rumble of the ground even above the cacophony of battle. Within heartbeats, however, my fear had turned to joy.

It was no wolfpack that thundered past me in the darkness. I saw just shadows as wave after wave of black-clad men leapt the ditch, howled their war cry one last time before drenching themselves in Batavi blood.

The Harii had come.

With black shields, black tunics and black skin, they were truly the Einherjar: Wotan's warriors, who had died a glorious death and now feasted in his hall, waiting for the end of days. Shadow warriors, they hurtled the pit in their masses and fell upon the Batavians like a hungry wolfpack on a fat sheep. They were an endless tide, a flood of bared teeth and naked iron. Exhilarated, blood-maddened by their sudden appearance, I howled myself and launched into the fray.

In all honesty, I could not recall to you the events of the next few moments, or hours, however long it lasted. All I can tell you is I hacked and slashed myself a body pile like I had never done before, and not bettered since. By the time we were done, there were but a handful of scurrying survivors. The tribune fell to Ketill's blade, which I remember angering me as I had been carving myself a route to him. I hacked off lumps of fresh horse-meat; smashed my precious blade against so much mail it took me the whole of the next day to clear the iron of notches and dents. I was masked in claret and guts and bone fragments by the end, my long black hair redder than my banner. I stood on that field, surrounded by dead and dying Roman soldiers, and knew I had carved myself another bloody step on the road to legend. Men would sing of my spear fame, and all men would know not to cross paths with Alaric, Lord of the Ravensworn.

I was the battle turner, chief destroyer, Roman slayer. Loki-cunning and blessed by the Allfather himself. There was no man or tribe or army that could defeat me. I was untouchable. Or so I thought.

* * *

A blood sun rose. Fitting, I thought. I knelt beside a great fire built by my men, still drenched in dead Batavi insides. Ketill was beside me, his face running with black sweat from the charcoal he had rubbed on it the day before. We had one of the few surviving Batavians tied up against a wooden stake. He was young, his smooth cheeks pale and soft, his sun-bleached hair like yellow straw. He tried to act the big man to start with, spitting defiance at us even as I heated his own sword in the fire's heart. I saw him recoil in fear as the bright glow of the blade was revealed when I pulled it clear.

I hadn't thought to cover my hands before picking up the blade, and inside I winced in agony at the simmering heat that blistered my palms and sent shockwaves of intense pain up my arms. I managed to hold the sword in front of the puppy's face just long enough to get a whiff of shit over the crispy remains of the skin on my right hand. I dropped the blade back into the fire, cursing myself for being a fool. I saw Ketill's smirk and bit back a retort, instead concentrating my anger on the Batavian. We had established his name was Gerbold and that he came from a long and proud line of Batavi warriors. He was proud, I think, more angry with himself for not dying gloriously in battle.

He had been adamant that he would tell us nothing, but his stern and furious expression had softened in the moments since he had soiled his breeches. 'C'mon, boy!' I said, shaking my burnt hand furiously to no effect. 'Talk, and we'll kill you quickly. Don't talk, and, you know.' I nodded to his longsword, now back in the flame's heart.

'Fuck you!' He spat. 'Curse you to Hel.' His eyes were rimmed with fear, though there was still venom in his tone.

'Oh, I've been cursed before, lad,' I said, chuckling to myself. 'I've had men curse me in front of all the gods in the nine worlds Yggdrasil holds together. They've spat at me, called me a coward, promised me the Allfather will bar me from his hall when I eventually come knocking.' I wrapped my hand in an old cloak I had picked up from the ground and, wincing, lifted the bone pommel of the sword from the flames. 'But, in the end, they've all talked, spilled their secrets and then their guts. Now, don't think you won't do the same, young Gerbold. I know, I know, you're the son of some whoreson who was the son of some other cur. Don't change anything, lad. I lay this blade on your flesh.' I hefted the weapon in my hand. The blade was inches from my face; the heat was intense. I worried it would singe my beard if I let it too close. 'And you'll sing like a bird on a glorious summer's dawn. Ha! Don't shake your head, you will, lad, you will.'

Ketill lifted Gerbold's tunic, laying bare the pale skin of his belly. I lowered the blade, quicker than I wanted to, but the raging heat was quickly seeping through the cloth of the cloak. He had more hair on his belly than he did on his head – and his hair wasn't short. There was a crisp smell as the hair sizzled, and I saw Gerbold's belly tense in fear, heard his gasp of shock and pain. 'I'm going to ask you one more time, Gerbold, and if you don't give me the answer I want, I'm going to hold this blade on your stomach till it burns right through and your guts melt out of your back.' I held his gaze, hoping my own was as vicious as I thought. 'Now, who ordered the attack on me? That piece of shit Trajianus was just a soldier. I want the brains behind this operation, and you're going to tell me.'

I lowered the blade a bit more, and to my satisfaction his skin took on a red glow as it reacted to the intense heat. I met Gerbold's gaze again and knew he was going to crack before he did.

'Okay, okay!' he screamed. 'I'll tell you, I'll tell you everything! Just don't burn me, please don't burn me!' Tears streamed down his bloodstained face, his expression a mixture of shame and relief.

'Good choice, boy,' Ketill said, releasing his grip on his tunic. Ketill pulled a dagger from its sheath on his hip, the curved blade nestling threateningly on Gerbold's neck. 'Now speak, and go and meet your ancestors.'

Gerbold took a couple of deep breaths, trying to calm his

nerves. 'The man you seek is called Fulvius. Marcus Ovidius Fulvius. He is a tribune of the frumentarii, based west of the Rhine, in Colonia Ulpia Traiana.' Gerbold spoke in gasps. His reluctance was clear, his eyes shining with tears of resignation.

I leant towards him, putting a hand on his shoulder. 'You made a good decision, lad,' I said. 'You are one of us. I know you don't think so. Years of slavery and humiliation at the hands of Rome have made you think differently. They've made you think you're one of them, but you're not. You're German! You worship Hercules, Wotan, Donar, just like us.' That wasn't quite true. There were few other tribes, the Harii being one, that still worshipped Hercules in my lifetime. But, I thought, it would do no harm for him to die thinking he was helping the right side.

'You will kill him?' Gerbold asked.

'I will. He has started this, I will finish it.' I snatched my knife from its sheath and put the hilt in his palm. 'Hold it tight, brother,' I said, nodding towards Ketill, who swept his own knife through Gerbold's windpipe without fanfare.

Ketill stood and moved from the writhing form of the dying Gerbold. People think slitting a man's throat a mercy, a quick death awarded to a man you want to spare from pain. I disagree. Gerbold writhed and shuddered for many fluttering heartbeats, dark blood pulsing from the gash in his throat. It was some time before he finally went still, letting out a last, wheezy breath.

'What do we do?' Ketill asked, wiping his blade on the hem of his tunic.

'Find this Fulvius, and kill the whoreson,' I said, showing Ketill my teeth.

9

Two weeks later found me on the eastern banks of the Rhine. It was a glorious summer's night, and moonlight flooded the land as we camped on the banks of the river. I sat there with a stomach full of venison and a skin of good wine in my hand, revelling in the peaceful sounds of the wind whispering through the rustling pine that stood tall and ominously black against the darkening sky. The calming swirl and swoosh of the river's current made me drowsy, the lazy waters kissing the bank to my front. An owl hooted, another replied. I was happy, sitting there in the half light. I loved the land that was Germania: the wildness of its inhabitants, the rugged beauty of the terrain. I thought then of where we were going; to Colonia Ulpia Traiana. I had been there once, many years ago. Roman red brick and slate, multicoloured stone climbing so far to the sky it could almost be a pathway to the gods. But our gods did not live in halls of stone.

What were gods if not the beauty that surrounded us? Were they not there in that whispering wind? Was the rustling of it through the branches not them communicating? They say the

Allfather walked our middle earth once, talking to the humans he met. They say he gained knowledge from us, and spread a little of his infinite wisdom. What would he think if he met me now? Would he curse me for a fool, for seeking vengeance on an officer of Rome? For what hope did I have of attacking this Fulvius whilst he was safe behind Roman stone?

But, I would reply, not only do I possess the wisdom of Wotan, I also have the cunning of Loki, the trickster. Loki, it was told, could take on any form. He could have even been the owl that hooted that night as I lay by the swirling water swigging Roman wine. I recall a story my father told me once, when I had been caught making a young boy on our farm eat cow shit that was still warm to touch – I forget the lad's name now. My father had taken me by the ear and dragged me kicking and screaming to the old barn next to our house. 'Think you're like Loki?' he had spat at me. 'Let me tell you the story of his downfall.'

It was useless, that barn. Any farmer worth their salt knew that in order to make a barn fit to store a winter's supply of grain and cured meats, you had to build it on stilts to stop the damp getting in, let alone the rats. You also had to weave the thatch on the roof tight, letting the reeds thoroughly dry out before you did so. My father, warrior that he was, knew neither of these things. So we stood there, in that damp barn, surrounded by the clamour of scurrying rodents and the odd open bag of sodden grain, and he regaled to me the tale of Loki's doom.

In short, he had tricked Hod into killing Balder. Hod had been blind, and had therefore no real idea what he was aiming at when he launched his spear into his brother's unsuspecting heart. The gods had been devastated. Frigg, mother to both Hod and Balder and wife to the Allfather, had been inconsolable for weeks. Wotan had decided to hold an autumn feast, to help lift the gods' morale. He had asked Donar to seek out the frost giant

Aegir. After some, shall we say, encouragement, Aegir agreed to make the ale. He brought it to Wotan's great hall with his servant, Fimafeng. In a moment of utter madness, Loki unsheathed his twin blades and slew Fimafeng where he stood, then left the hall without a backwards glance.

The gods decided they had had quite enough of Loki and his erratic scheming. They banded together and hunted Loki down to a shallow pool beneath a small waterfall in the lands of the giants. He had taken the form of a salmon. Loki was not concerned when he saw his fellow gods come to slay him, not even when they made a giant net and covered the shallow pool from one rock face to the next. He simply hung in the water, watching the net move slowly towards him. When it was so close he could have kissed the entwined rope, he simply sprung from the water and leaped upstream, away from the useless net and the dumbfounded gods.

Again and again he did the same thing, until eventually when he leapt into the air he found himself smothered in an old cloak and unable to wriggle free. The gods had then taken him to a dark cave under the tallest mountain and left him chained in metal stronger than iron, with just his wife for company.

The reason I tell you this is that I have always considered myself to have the finest of Loki's qualities, always managed to trick myself out of any potential disastrous situation I've found myself in, and there have been a few. And I was about to do it again. Or so I thought.

* * *

We moved out with the dawn. I had left Ketill and his Harii with Ruric and Baldo and the remainder of the two hundred men that had slaughtered the Batavians. With them also were Otto –

another of my captains – and his Hundred. My other two files of Hundred had filtered to us in the days that followed the battle. Like birds flying south for winter, they had known exactly where to find me, as if I had given off some sort of smoke signal for them to follow. Even when we moved on from the battlefield and its stink of open bowels and decay, one after the other the groups of Hundred cantered into sight on the horizon.

With me now I had those two hundred men. I had no hope of taking the stone walls of Colonia Ulpia Traiana by force. Not even with my full five hundred and the might of the Harii would we stand any chance of taking their battlements by force. I would have to sneak in, slither like a snake and be as sly as a fox. I cast aside the bloodthirsty warrior inside me, all thoughts of Donar and his mighty hammer quashed from my mind. Loki was my god now, the only one who could help me.

My two other captains were Adalhard and Gerulf, and they had been devastated to have missed out on the bloodbath with the Batavi and were eager to prove themselves. Both were relatively new in their roles, and in truth I knew little about either man. I was taking a risk, leaving the reliable Ruric behind, and even Baldo had proved his worth in battle, but I had to learn more about my two new captains, and needed to know they could be trusted.

Adalhard was the youngest of the five file leaders. He'd just turned twenty, and his first beard was still sparse and more fluff than bristle. He had short chestnut-brown hair, as he said long hair hindered a man's eyesight in battle, not that he'd had much experience of war. His eyes were small slits, the pupils dark and always moving. A tall man, taller even than me, his torso was packed with muscle, although for a man of such size and strength he was nimble on his feet. On more than one occasion I had seen him train with the sword, and watched spellbound as he danced round his opponent, dodging and swerving cuts that scythed nothing but air. When deep in his cups he would tell anyone who listened that no living man could beat him blade to blade, and only Donar himself could stop him. His name in our tongue meant both noble and brave, and with all the brash confidence of youth he would swagger through his men, gripping shoulders and locking arms, as if his touch alone would bring his men back from the well of fear into which they sunk in the moments before battle. He would learn the truth of that soon.

Gerulf was different. An older head and wiser for it. He had fought for me for many years, and his promotion was well deserved in the eyes of his fellow captains. His bald head reflected the sunlight like polished iron, above a flat face devoid of emotion; a deep scar ran across his nose from a long-forgotten battle, where a hammer had struck him as if his face were an anvil. He was neither tall nor short, not skinny but not brawny either. When he walked through his men, they stood straighter. He had no need for hollow gestures or acts of bravado. In our tongue his name meant 'spear-wolf', an appropriate name for such a warrior.

I rode with the two captains either side of me as we headed north along the banks of the Rhine, the tang of salt strong on the air as we edged closer to the sea the Romans called the Mare Germanicum, simply the Germani Sea. I knew the two captains were curious, that their own officers were whispering in their ears. Why were we going north, when Colonia Ulpia Traiana was to the south? I had kept my own counsel thus far, my mind alive to the risk of there being a Roman spy in my ranks, as unthinkable as that was. We were in the far north and west of our country. To my right as we rode were the marshes and forests that were the old lands of the Batavi, now occupied by Ketill and his tribe.

'Lord, where in the name of the gods are we going?' Adalhard's impatience was seemingly getting the better of him at last.

I showed him my teeth, a savage grin that meant to curb him. It seemed to have the right effect. 'Out there,' I said, pointing out across the estuary to the open sea.

'Lord?' he said, eyebrows fastened together in his confusion. Gerulf coughed a laugh, and I threw him a wink. I was starting to like Gerulf the more I got to know him. He had guessed my intentions, without me having to draw a map in the dirt. 'Where are we going, lad?' I asked Adalhard, knowing the term 'lad' would annoy him.

'Colonia Ulpia Traiana,' he said, 'or so I thought.' He hawked and spat, showing me his frustration. Not always a sensible thing to do.

'Correct, my young apprentice. Now, how would you rate our chances of storming that stone-built fortress from across the Rhine? We have, what, two hundred men?'

Adalhard nodded slowly, his cheeks glowing red. Gerulf did not try to hide his laugh. I sensed these two were not friends, something I would have to fix before we returned to the rest of the Ravensworn. But not just yet. 'And how many men do you think are in Colonia Ulpia Traiana? As well as the Thirtieth Ulpia Victrix, there are numerous auxiliary units within those walls. Now, what did you think we were going to do? Bundle into some barges and sally across the river, scale the walls and massacre the huge army that outnumber us more than twenty to one?'

There was a moment of silence. You could almost hear the weed tumble roll through the dust in Adalhard's mind. 'Well... err...' He trailed off, his embarrassment getting the better of him.

'Exactly, you fool! Now, would you like to know what we are actually going to do?' Both men nodded and edged their mounts closer to mine and I felt their junior officers doing the same. I didn't know those men's names, though I would come to rely on them in the days that followed. Gods, I was bone idle. Expecting men to lead other men into the iron storm; to fight and die for me if necessary, and I didn't even know their names. 'What we are going to do,' I continued, 'is steal ourselves some Roman ships, sail them out into the sea, then turn them round and bring them down the Rhine.'

My master plan. The one I had been working on since I'd first heard the name Fulvius splutter from the captured Batavi lad's lips. With a thousand men at my back, I still could not take that fortress by strength. But I didn't need to. I needed one man dead, and for that I did not need might; I needed cunning.

'The Romans,' Gerulf began slowly, 'will see their ships coming down the river and welcome them with open arms.'

'Open gates I'm hoping,' I said with a wolfish grin.

So we went and pillaged ourselves some ships.

10

When people speak of the great night raid on Ulpia Noviomagus these days, they credit the Chauci for stealing two Roman warships and sailing them from the small port, right under the noses of the dumbfounded Roman soldiers that manned the fortress walls. It fills me with great pride that the raid is still spoken of, and great annoyance that no one mentions the Ravensworn's name – my name alone would suffice.

We approached Ulpia Noviomagus in the depths of a starless night. Gerulf had set his men to building small rafts that we could punt across the river in teams. Five were built in total, one was lost in the dark and haze, but all in all only five men were unaccounted for when we stood shivering in our wet clothes on the western bank. It was a short run north and west from the riverbank that brought us to the city's southern gate.

It was not lost on me that Ulpia Noviomagus was once called Batavorum and had been the stronghold of the Batavi lands. At some point in the distant past, in a turbulent year where four men had fought to call themselves emperor, the Batavi had revolted and been swiftly beaten. As a result of their defeat, they had been ordered from their homeland, moved further west, away from potential allies on the native side of the Rhine. Having just butchered a whole unit of Batavians, it gave me great satisfaction to know I was now going to reap havoc in their old capital.

The walls were manned not by Batavi warriors or Roman legionaries, but men of the Cananefate – another insult to the Batavi, this one from Rome. The Batavi and the Cananefate had long been neighbours, but not friends. Like the Chauci, the men of the tribe had developed a knack for seamanship over the years, and the auxiliary unit of tribesmen based here were the proud owners of two Liburnica Biremises' – Liburnians for short. The Liburnian was a perfect river boat. Short and slim, fast and agile, it held fifty oarsmen in two banks of twenty-five a side. The ships offered scant protection for the rowers, who had just a lattice ventilation on their flank to stop them either plunging into the water or being hit with a spear or arrow. Above them was a simple canopy woven of fabric, held up by tall masts to the front and rear.

I wondered then, and still do now, how the Romans managed to persuade free men to sit at their benches whilst a storm of iron raged above them. German ships were rowed by captured slaves, who were chained to their benches and rarely allowed to leave their post. The oar master of a Roman ship did not use a whip, which again seemed strange, for how else could they possibly encourage the dogs to row faster?

The prow of a Liburnian is gilded in metal, an armoured point designed to smash through the hull of an enemy ship when at ramming speed. Whilst the wooden sides of the ship are painted a light blue or green to help it blend in with the water, and therefore harder to spot by enemy watchmen, the prow is often elaborately decorated with either gold or silver. At

the stern was a giant mast with a red sail, a gold eagle embroi-
dered in the centre. Again, elaborate works of gold and silver
encased the small area, and a modest tent stood erect, ready to
shelter the Navarch or Trierarch that was commanding the ship.

Along with the two Liburnians was a small Celox, both
lighter and faster. The smaller ship was the 'messenger boy' of
the Roman Navy. Messenger or not, I would take it gladly.

We crept up to the southern gate. To my annoyance it was
closed, but that was to be expected. I had left our horses on the
far side of the river, with ten unlucky men whose job it was to
round them up and persuade them to walk and regroup with the
rest of the Ravensworn. We were silent, shadows in the endless
darkness. I took five men and crept right up to the wall, my back
against the timber as I craned my neck to try and spot a
patrolling soldier above. 'You, come here,' I hissed at the nearest
of my volunteers. It was Birgir, who was supposed to be on the
other side of the Rhine with the rest of his Hundred.

'What in Wotan's name are you doing here, boy?' I
harangued him in a whisper.

'Ruric sent me,' he said with a shrug. 'Thought you might
have need of me.'

'Did he now,' I replied with a rueful smile. It was not unlike
Ruric to think of things I had not, but very unlike him to not rub
it in my face. 'What else did he say to you?'

'Try not to get killed,' Birgir said.

'Good advice,' I said, 'however, what we are about to do is
going to be bloody.' I explained my plan in a whisper, and Birgir
nodded when I was done. 'Pass it on to the man behind you, get
him to do the same with the men behind him.' I waited in tense
silence, sure we would be discovered at any moment, but all was
quiet. Finally the whispering and hissing stopped and two men
squeezed between the two of us and raised their shields above

their heads, squatting as they did. I stepped back from the veil of safety of the palisade wall and scanned the battlement. I saw two helmeted heads, facing away from me as they strolled in opposite directions along the walkway. Nodding to Birgir, I set my plan in motion.

* * *

Birgir leapt atop the platform I'd instructed my men to make with their shields. His booted feet planted squarely on the painted black raven and climbed silently atop the battlement. Before he'd even touched the floor I was up on the shields myself, the men holding them grunting and sinking lower than they had with Birgir. I deduced it was because of the added weight of my superior armour, and nothing else. I squatted next to Birgir, who was hunched behind his shield, pointing to the soldier to my left and then at him. Birgir nodded and crept towards the unsuspecting auxiliary.

Taking the one to my right for myself, I made my way along the wall walk, my eyes darting through the dark streets, seeking out movement. I was ten paces from my target when I heard a squeal of pain behind me. Birgir had drawn a long knife from its sheath and had attempted to slit his man's throat but appeared to have made a horrible mess of it. Blood spurted from a deep slash in the Cananefate's neck, but the wound was too far to the left to be a killing blow. Birgir had merely nicked the main artery instead of slicing straight through. Again, the man squealed, and this time it sounded just like a pig giving birth – a rather unpleasant sound a man can grow worryingly accustomed to when living on a farm.

I froze, unsure whether I should finish my man or run and help Birgir, who just stood gaping at the mess he had made. Too late I made the decision to kill my man, for when I spun back around, he was standing with a small bronze horn pressed to his lips, with puffed cheeks as he prepared to sound the alarm call. 'Fuck,' I muttered as I stumbled towards him, suddenly clumsy in my armour and boots. I rasped my longsword from its scabbard, the blade gleaming in the moonlight. The black leather wrapped hilt was a comfort, but it did not stop the sinking feeling in the pit of my stomach.

I lurched with the blade even as the blare of the trumpet filled my ears. The point of the sword ripped through mail and fabric before burying itself high in the Cananefate's left shoulder. Still the trumpet sounded. With my left hand I ripped the instrument from his grasp and tossed it over the battlement. With my right I reversed my sword before delivering a killer blow to the man's neck, and he dropped without a sound. Suddenly my lungs were on fire, my breath came in shallow rasps and my hands were shaking. Some men call it bloodlust – the rush of adrenalin you get in the moments before and after you first engage the enemy. My experience in war has taught me not to waste this, as it is followed quickly by fatigue. Right then, standing alone atop that battlement, I was very much wasting it.

Birgir had finally completed his bodged job of butchering the other watchman; he was covered in so much blood that I thought he must have bled the poor bastard dry. I moved towards him, aware now of raised voices and torchlight coming from within the town. Two more of my men appeared on the rampart, both snarling and with bared blades. I ordered them to follow me, and grabbing a dumbstruck Birgir by the arm, I led them down a small flight of wooden stairs. 'You two, cover us,' I said to the two new arrivals. 'Birgir, let's get this gate open.'

The locking bar was huge and looked as thick as my waist, whilst the gate itself was solid timber beams reinforced with strips of iron. I took the left of the bar and told Birgir to take the right. 'One, two, three... heave!' With all my might I heaved until I was red in the face and in danger of soiling myself. Birgir was also straining with all his might, but being slim he was severely lacking in muscle.

I looked to my two men who were crouched behind their shields. Torchlight edged towards us, as inexorable as the dawn. As the light from the torches grew brighter, I could see aspects of the narrow central street previously hidden by darkness. The shutters of the wine stores, bakeries, blacksmiths and potteries were shut tight. There was the odd wooden bench and a couple of discarded barrels. Beyond them was an army.

'You two,' I yelled at the men still hunched behind their limewood boards, 'come help us, quick!' I had two hundred battle-hardened sworn men on the other side of that bloody gate, but I needed them inside the walls. The two men ran over, discarding weapons and shields as they did. We took a deep breath and lifted as a team. Painfully slowly, the locking bar grated up the iron brackets that held it. I looked over my shoulder, dismayed to see the auxiliaries so close. I could make out their faces in the torchlight, saw their centurion with his red-crested helmet yell a war cry and rasp his sword on his oval shield. 'Donar's balls!' I screamed through gritted teeth, eyes bulging. 'Lift, you whoresons, lift!' With a gigantic effort, the locking bar edged clear of the brackets and we let it fall to the ground. Birgir pushed open the gates and released two hundred Ravensworn into Ulpia Noviomagus.

The wolves were loose within the sheep pen, and the night ran red.

11

There is something inexplicably beautiful about the open sea, with the white-topped waves that launch themselves against the ship's prow. You can feel the gods out here. When the wind whistles through your beard it is almost as if Rán herself is whispering calming words. When the salt spray dries your lips and leaves your skin raw and painful to touch, you feel as if Aegir is testing you, judging your worth as you sail through his domain. Rán and Aegir had nine daughters, nine different waves that could either carry you in serenity to your destination or chop and slash at your hull and send you to dinner in Aegir's underwater hall. I forget their names now, those of the waves, but the tales my father used to tell of Rán and Aegir live long in my memory.

We sailed out of Ulpia Noviomagus towards a glorious rising sun. We had left no fighting man alive in that place, having spent the night stalking the Cananefate auxiliaries through the dark streets with nothing but torchlight to lead the way. I stank of blood and the pitch from the torches. Bone weary, I lay in the tent of one of the Liburnians after telling my men to take the ships out to the open sea.

Gerulf had taken the other galley, Adalhard the small Celox. He had thought it an insult, and in a way it was. He was young, impulsive and reckless; I did not trust him to make the right decisions if we had to fight. The Chauci had ships hugging the coast on the narrow sea; it was not impossible that we would stumble across a patrol.

I woke to the ship's gentle swaying motion on the calm ocean, Gerulf prowling the deck, calling the strokes to the men unlucky enough to be given an oar and bench in the stifling heat. I struggled out of my mail and undergarments and leapt from the ship's side into the endless blue. The cold hit me like a spear point. It ripped through my skin and embedded in my bones, the salt searing in the open cuts from the battle, and it hurt even more than taking the wounds in the first place. I almost froze, down there in the murk, the current taking my aching body as I embraced the icy chill. Looking up, I saw the keen edge of the keel as it tore through the water.

I came back to life slowly. The numbing coldness was replaced by a burning sensation in my muscles. Every kick was like a mile on the march, every stroke like lifting Donar's hammer. Eventually I made it to the light, spluttering my thanks to Rán for sparing me. One of my men threw down a rope and I gingerly clambered back aboard the Liburnian, my muscles screaming with every heave. I was on all fours on the deck panting like a dog when Gerulf threw my cloak around me and raised me to my feet. 'Lord,' he said, a certain reverence in his voice. 'Lord, you swam!'

I had forgotten most men do not know the first thing about swimming, even men who spend most of their lives breathing in the salt air. To be thrown from your ship means certain death; to be sunk in battle means certain death. My father had thrown me into a tarn when I was five years old. My mother had wailed in terror when nothing but bubbles had surfaced and I was lost in the endless shadows. But surfaced I had, with all the grace of a donkey with wonky legs. I had coughed water until my lungs burned like a furnace. My father had stood me up and assured my mother I would live, before throwing me straight back in. Harsh man, my father. But his methods worked. By mid-afternoon that very day I could paddle alongside our hound Fenrir – named for the ferocious wolf, son of the great Loki. By the time the sun set the next day, I could swim the length of the tarn and back, already feeling my chest harden and arms grow with the exercise.

Since then I had swum whenever I could, though opportunity for leisure when you ruled over five hundred cutthroats was rare. 'Yes, Gerulf,' I said through chattering teeth, 'I swam.' Staggering through the central walkway of the deck from the stern to the bow, I nodded to the men on the row benches to my left and right. A rower always faced away from the direction of travel – it was easier to row this way, but also I thought better for the mentality of the rowers, for they did not have to see the endless blue with nothing but the sky kissing the water over the horizon to dampen their spirits.

Slowly my heartbeat softened, and over the roar of the wind I heard the men raising their voices in song. Nothing will fill your ego to brimming point like your sworn men chanting your name.

We were sailing north, and for a moment I was tempted to change direction and sail to see the white cliffs of the island of Britannia. I wanted to see it, the fabled land Rome had conquered, said to be full of druids and giants. Men said that over the northern horizon there was nothing but the ends of the earth. Roman soldiers would say they have stood on the Wall of Hadrian and seen the green landscape roll into the ocean. There was nothing else there; Rome had conquered as far north as north would go. I did not believe that, not for a moment. There were lands to the north of Germania, frozen all year round, the sun not rising above the towering mountains for weeks at a time. I had not been there myself but had traded with men who sailed their ships south and beached on our northern shingle. They spoke a similar language to us, though perhaps even coarser and filled with more grunts. They were tribal, the same as us, and often waged wars among themselves, as one chief sought dominance over another. I had half a mind to sail there, see if I could earn myself some coin. Though the lure of vengeance turned me back south.

We directed the ships as the sun was at its zenith as we rowed back towards the Rhine and battle. Nightfall saw us back in the estuary we had sailed out of. We slowed then, the oars dipping lightly in the rolling waves. We had to sneak past Ulpia Noviomagus like shadows in the darkness. We had killed a lot of men and caused Rome much damage. I did not think there would be more armed men inside those walls, but I did not want to be spotted by chance. My plan depended on witnesses from that slaughter telling whichever legion commander who marched to their rescue that we had sailed north and into the open sea. That way any Roman fleet looking for us would be patrolling the coast, maybe sailing over to Britannia. No one would be checking the Rhine.

We ghosted onto the great river. I had a trusted man in every ship, experienced in these waters, and they steered us masterly through the shallows and past the rocks that had sunk many a good man and his wealth. I had promised them gold if they could just get us safely to Colonia Ulpia Traiana. So far, they had not let me down. We had pillaged the armour, weapons and clothes from the slaughtered Cananefates. I ordered my men to change now, as we would soon encounter Roman patrols. We looked unconvincing to say the least, but I hoped we would not be near a unit of Roman soldiers long enough for them to notice.

I had changed into the uniform of a Roman Trierarchus, and should we encounter any Roman forces, it would be me who spoke with them. I was confident I could pass for a Cananefate officer as my Latin was passable, in truth probably better than many of the German auxiliaries.

The Rhine is a wide river, large enough for our three ships to sail abreast unless we encountered any traffic. There was none that morning, and I found myself enjoying the tranquillity of the journey. I stood at the ship's prow and gazed longingly at the western bank. It seemed so different to the Roman bank to my right. There were no houses, no smoke rising from chimneys. It was just land, an endless green landscape rolling away to the horizon, where it kissed the deep blue of the sky.

I was lost in its beauty when a shout from behind woke me from my daze. 'Ships, Lord!' Gerulf yelled, pointing south down the river. I turned my gaze and saw two Liburnians rowing hard to intercept us. 'You remember the plan?' I asked Gerulf, staring intently into his eyes. They were cool, calm, and it pleased me to see. 'Yes, Lord,' he said, turning to his men, ensuring each in turn knew what was expected.

I ordered Gerulf to return to his own ship and called to Adalhard over the cacophony of the oars hitting the flat of the water and the men readying themselves to fight if need be. 'Adalhard, you know the plan?'

Adalhard just nodded, waving casually in my direction. I felt my dislike for the man grow, to the point where I wanted nothing more than to leap the gap between the ships and run him through with my blade. 'Adalhard!' I shouted again. 'Do you understand what you need to do?' He must have caught the venom in my tone, for he turned back to me, his expression suddenly sheepish. 'Yes, Lord. You needn't worry about me.' Then he turned away, slapping men on the back and gripping others' wrists. Gods, but I hated that man. I vowed there and then that one way or another, he would not last as a leader in my army.

The two ships were close now. They slowed and each turned so their prow was facing a riverbank. They were blocking our path; the only way through now would be to increase to ramming speed and plough through them. It would have been tempting, if I'd had crews of experienced oarsman, and if I myself had any experience of naval warfare. Instead I ordered our ships to slow and took my one forward alone.

'That's far enough!' shouted an officer in a pristine blue tunic. I couldn't make out his face under the dazzling light of his iron helmet, which was decorated with bronze. Great plumes of red and blue sprouted from the top. He looked impressive. 'State your business!' he yelled. His voice carried well over the water.

I breathed deep to slow my heart, rehearsing the words before I spoke. 'My name is Trierarchus Hadrianus Arimnestos,' I said, giving him the name of a German auxiliary commander I had killed in Pannonia a few years ago. 'Commander of the fleet based at Ulpia Noviomagus.' I was taking a huge risk and I knew it. I had no notion of who this commander was, or if he would have any inkling of who the actual commander of the fleet I had stolen was.

'Well met, Trierarchus. I am Tribune Aurelius Castus, on detached duty from The Twenty-Second. We heard you boys were in a bit of a scrap, and I've been ordered north to investigate.' He said nothing more, letting the words hang in the air.

The silence was overbearing, and I sought to calm my thrumming heart, seeking the words that would see us gain passage through their blockade. 'That we have, Tribune. Tribesmen from across the river took Ulpia Noviomagus under the cover of night. My Navarchus is still there, helping the citizens to pick up the pieces. He sent me south with orders to report to the Governor at Colonia Ulpia Traiana.'

Tribune Castus digested this slowly. 'Who were they, the tribesmen?'

I shrugged. 'Didn't ask! Just fought till they were all dead.'

'So none survive?'

I shook my head. 'We slaughtered the lot of them.'

Castus nodded. 'Rumour has it Alaric and his Ravensworn are operating this side of the river. Heard anything about that?'

Gods above! Was all of Rome talking about little old me? 'No, Tribune. I've heard his name spoken though. They say he is... ferocious.' I can't even begin to tell you how hard it was to keep the grin from my face as I said that.

'I've heard that too. They say he has five hundred men, a sizeable force. Rome wants him taken care of. I'll let you through but the governor is no longer in Traiana. He's gone inland. My legate is there though. You can report to him.'

I saluted and ordered my men to start rowing, waving the other two ships to join us. I wanted to be away from this Castus and his men as soon as I could. The two Roman ships parted and I sailed right through the middle, keeping my eyes fixed on the river ahead, and trying not to look smug.

12

Colonia Ulpia Traiana is a fortress, a colossus of timber and stone. From more than a mile away you can see the wooden parapets and the towers that contain the dreaded ballistae. Our small squadron docked on an empty wooden jetty. I vaulted from my Liburnian, trying to feel as confident as I looked about having my feet on Roman land.

Two soldiers with light blue shields that depicted the Roman god Neptune holding a trident in one hand and the reins of two horses that pulled his chariot across the seas in the other approached me along the jetty.

'Why are their shields blue?' Adalhard asked, appearing at my shoulder. 'I thought they were all red?' he asked, motioning to the red oval shield he held in his left hand.

'They are, mostly,' I said absently. 'The Thirtieth are a relatively new legion. Trajan formed them for his war with Dacia. Their patron deity is Neptune, who is the Roman god of the sea. And what colour is the sea?' I asked with all the sarcasm I could muster.

'Blue,' Adalhard said with a sigh, knowing when he was beaten.

'Who's a clever boy then?' I spat at him. 'Now, stand back and let the grown-ups do the talking, all right?' I moved away without another word, swaggering up to the two soldiers.

'State your rank and business!' one of them barked as I got within ten paces of their spear tips.

'Trierarchus Hadrianus Arimnestos, here to see your legate,' I said in my finest Latin, which really wasn't that fine at all.

'Trierarchus,' the soldier saluted. 'I'm Optio Aquila, fourth cohort, second century. Is the legate expecting you, sir?'

'I don't believe so. We have come from Ulpia Noviomagus. We were attacked the night before last by a tribal horde from over the river. My Navarchus has asked me to come and report to the governor, though I understand from the patrol I ran into on the way down here led by Tribune Castus that he is no longer here. I wish to see the legate in his absence.'

The mention of the patrol led by the tribune seemed to visibly calm the optio and his companion, who lowered their shields and eased the grips on their javelins. 'Come with me, sir, I'll see if the legate is available for you.'

I followed the man and his companion through a small wooden gate and into the fortress proper. 'Oh,' I said as if it was an afterthought, 'can a few of my men come in and grab some supplies? Running a bit low, and not sure if we'll be going straight home.' The optio shrugged, removing his helmet to reveal a balding head.

'Course, sir, we're all friends, ain't we?' He smiled and I smiled back. I gestured to Adalhard, who turned and whistled as he walked back to the ships. A troop of men jumped from the boats to land on the wooden jetty. Amphora and chests were passed down after them. The optio saw nothing unusual in this and smiled again before asking me to accompany him.

'Adalhard, you oversee the supplies,' I said with a wink. 'I'll come and find you once I've reported to the legate.'

I followed the optio through a narrow street. The cobbles were smooth beneath my feet and as I gazed up at the red brick on the walls, I longed to be able to build like the Romans. Our wooden halls and thatched roofs would last a lifetime if built right, but walls like these would outlive even Rome itself.

We entered the Principia, the Romans' headquarters building, stationed in the centre of the fortress. Red-cloaked legionaries snapped to attention as the optio and I came into view. It startled me at first, then I remembered I was in the uniform of a Roman officer. I nodded to the men, made small talk as the optio spoke to a clerk, enquiring if the legate was available. 'The legate won't be available for an hour or so, I'm afraid, sir,' Aquila said with an apologetic shrug.

'Fine by me,' I replied. 'Mind if I wait here?'

Aquila seemed confused at my response, as if he had never been asked what he 'minded' by a superior before. He probably hadn't. 'Yes, sir,' he said unsurely. 'There's an officer's mess down the hall, should be pretty quiet this time of day. You can wait there if you wish? I'll make sure the clerks know to inform the legate you are here as soon as he's back.'

I nodded my thanks and moved off down a shadow-filled corridor. I padded slowly, the hobnails of my pillaged boots ringing off the timber floor. I was halfway down when I saw a door open slightly ajar on my right, whispered voices coming from inside. I crept closer, couldn't help myself really. The voices were urgent, and I could see the shadows of frenzied hand gestures as two men argued frantically in hushed tones.

'It's him I tell you!' the first man said. He looked to be tall and slender, his hair long and unbound. Not a military man then.

'How could you possibly know?' came the reply. He was most definitely military; I could tell just from his tone. When I peeped through the gap I saw a man in his early fifties, balding head and a long, strong Roman nose. He wasn't in armour, but wore a standard military tunic, belted at the waist.

'I saw him once in Pannonia,' the slender man said, 'when I was attached to the Fourteenth legion. That's the man that fought under the Raven banner, mark my words.'

'That was a long time ago, my friend, and you saw him but as briefly then as you did today. Many Germans look similar; they have the same build, and all wear their hair longer than yours! Not to mention their beards! No, Suetonius, this cannot be our man, you're jumping at shadows—'

'It's not the shadows you should fear, but what hides within,' I purred, stalking into that room like a lion into a flock of sheep. I knew I had the beating of both men – that if it came to blades, their deaths would be swift and bloody. Both men looked at me with gaping mouths and wide eyes. I rasped my pillaged short sword from its scabbard and showed them my teeth. 'Gentlemen,' I said as I took another pace forward. 'I hear you've been looking for me.'

'It's... it's him!' The man named Suetonius squealed like a wounded pig. I saw him clearly for the first time and he appeared to be every inch the soft aristocrat. His skin was pale and soft, his eyes a light chestnut brown. He had a slender nose and full red lips. He was so pretty that if you put him in a dress, he could have passed for a high-class whore. Suetonius scurried back on his heels, hiding himself behind the other man. 'My name is Alaric, Lord of the Ravensworn. And who might you be?' I asked the question, though in my gut I already knew the answer.

'Marcus Ovidius Fulvius,' the man said, keeping his eyes fixed on mine and his back as straight as a spear. 'What are you doing here, Alaric?'

'What am I doing here? Well, that's quite a story actually. I was called upon to settle a tribal dispute, far to the north of the Roman border. And do you know what I smelt when I got there?' I sniffed the air, grimacing as I did. 'Perfumed skin, oiled hair and gold drenched in German blood. I could smell your trap a mile away. I've spent the last few weeks questioning and slaughtering every Roman I can find. So far this productive enterprise has led me to your door.' I took another step, turning the blade slightly in my hand. It caught the light and iron glimmered into Fulvius' eyes.

'And what do you hope to find here, Alaric?' I watched as his hand crept to his sword hilt.

'Justice,' I said.

'Ha! Justice? Justice for what? For years you and your men have terrorised our borders, killing our soldiers and defiling our women. What justice are you owed?'

'I didn't start this war,' I said. I had moved so close to Fulvius, my beard nearly brushed his nose. 'But you can be damn well sure I'm going to end it.'

'And how did Rome start it, Alaric? What have we ever done to you?' I could sense his grip on his blade now. I *felt* the tautness of his hand as it gripped the bone handle, saw the tension in his shoulders as he braced himself to release the iron from where it slept.

'Twenty years ago, Fulvius. Rome began this war twenty years ago.'

'Twenty years is a long time to hold a grudge,' Fulvius said in a whisper.

'Twenty years is a long time to grieve for your mother. Twenty years of sleepless nights, lying awake, remembering my mother's screams as Roman soldiers took turns to rape her, whilst my father and I were made to watch.' I hawked and spat, right in his face. To his credit, Fulvius didn't even flinch; he just let it settle on his cheek.

'Which legion?'

'The Fourteenth Gemina,' I said. 'Martial and Victorious, I believe you Romans call them.' Fulvius nodded, and an expression I almost took for sympathy spread slowly across his face.

'A fine legion,' he said. 'But even the finest men get... well, over excited at times.'

'Over excited?' I remarked. 'They slaughtered a village of innocents, raped every woman and girl and left the men for dead. It was an unprovoked attack, far to the north of Germania. They had no business there.'

'Now be fair, Alaric. Rome would not have sanctioned an attack out of nothing. There must have been some act of violence from your people towards Rome. What tribe are you from?'

He was trying to delay me, and I knew it. His hand was now fully wrapped round the hilt of his sword, and in the silence after he finished speaking I could hear the whisper of a rasp as he eased it from its scabbard. 'Why are you coming for me?' I asked. 'Tell me who wants me dead and I will make your end quick.' Suetonius squeaked in the background. He was already dead; there was no other exit from the small chamber apart from the door behind me, and there was no way he was going to put up a fight. Fulvius on the other hand...

'Everyone wants you dead!' Fulvius erupted, taking a nimble

step backwards and finally unleashing his iron. 'You raid into our lands, you interfere with our affairs across the border. You are a pest, a *nithing* if what I hear is to be believed—'

That was a step too far. Men can call me Oathbreaker, liar, cheat – fair enough. But a *nithing*? A soft-bellied coward, that I am not!

I snarled as I lunged forwards, my sword slicing the air as I aimed a savage cut at Fulvius' head. The tribune sidestepped neatly and brought his blade up to block. There was a clang of metal as they kissed and then I was spinning away to his left and trying to use the greater reach of my longer blade to get around his defence. I had a vague notion of Suetonius screeching to my right, and for a moment I worried he would alert someone in the building to my presence, so I leapt forwards again, desperate to end the fight before the room was filled with legionaries. Fulvius licked out with his blade, hoping to catch me out with a low lunge. But he was old; I was in my prime and my reactions were as quick as the sharpest cat. I grabbed him by the wrist with my left hand and pulled him to me. With his sword held impotently behind me on my left side, I rammed my own blade home in a piercing uppercut that entered his body below his ribs and sliced through heart and lungs. Blood pumped from his mouth as I dropped him to the ground. I stood atop him as he spasmed, before eventually going still.

Suetonius was on all fours, vomiting his breakfast onto the wooden floorboards. Tears streamed down his cheeks and all he could say was 'No, no.'

'Right then, lad,' I said, kneeling next to him. 'I've got to kill you now, you realise that, right?'

'No, no.'

'I do, and I am sorry for it. But if I leave you alive you will rouse the soldiers before I can get back to my ships, and then me and my men will be slaughtered like dogs. That, I can't allow.'

'No, please—'

'Tell me who is behind this. Fulvius here wasn't the man I've been looking for. He was what, a tribune?' Suetonius nodded. 'I need someone higher than that, the man who's pulling the strings here. I'm sick of dealing with the puppets. Now, tell me the name of the man I am searching for, and your end will be quick.'

'I... I don't know who. But whoever he is he comes from Pannonia, Carnuntum to be precise. Fulvius has been getting orders from him, that's all I know.'

Carnuntum, Pannonia – home of the Fourteenth legion. I'd had many a running with 'The Fighting Fourteenth' over the years since my mother's gruesome death. They were a formidable legion, and their reputation was well earned. I didn't particularly want to go poking that hornets' nest, but it seemed I had no choice.

I sighed. 'Thank you for your assistance, Suetonius.' I did not delay his misery but rammed the point of my blade through his chest. I don't know why, but I held him as he died.

13

Needless to say I did not hang around in Colonia Ulpia Traiana. I fast marched back to my ships, even taking the time to berate two stunned legionaries for the shabby condition of their kit before boarding and ordering my men to row us away as fast as they could.

I kept looking back to those mighty walls as we rowed upriver, sure I would see a sortie of armed men explode from the great gates and give chase. But it appeared they were still all blissfully unaware of the two men I had left dead in the Principia.

I smiled to myself as we rowed. In essence, I had achieved nothing. I was still a hunted man; Rome would still send her legions to claim my head. But I had got a small step closer to discovering who was behind all this; I also had a ship full of the supplies Adalhard had so confidently extracted from their stores. Now I just needed to figure out what in the Allfather's name I was going to do. 'Where to, Chief?' Gerulf asked me. He had insisted on sailing in my ship, leaving his second-in-command of his own Liburnian with his men. *Just in case it all kicks off*, he'd said, as if I was some sort of *nithing* that needing protecting in a fight. Still, I appreciated his loyalty. 'To the rest of our brothers, of course,' I said, flashing him a grin. I had no plan yet, but whatever I ultimately decided on would inevitably lead to blood. I needed the rest of the Ravensworn around me.

* * *

'So, what are you going to do, brother?' Ketill asked me as we feasted on roasted boar. I had killed it myself. Ketill and a couple of his men had cornered the beast between a fallen tree and a giant slab of rock. As Ketill's guest, he had given me the honour of the first spear thrust. Donar had guided my arm as I rammed three foot of ash tipped with iron into the boar's chest, exploding through its ribcage. It was huge, its back reaching almost to my waist. I'm not too much of a man to admit my guts dropped with fear at the thought of the sheer power the beast could unleash. It took four of us to lash it to our spears and carry it back to the Harii's camp.

'Go south, I suppose,' I said through a mouthful of fresh meat. 'Find out who wants me dead and kill them first.' I shrugged – it wasn't exactly a plan the Sly One himself would have considered.

'You've only got five hundred men, brother,' Ketill said. 'You go up against the Fourteenth, plus the auxiliaries they will have camped with them, and you're a dead man.'

'I'm dead if I don't,' I said with another shrug. 'Not like I can just sit back and wait it out. They're coming for me, Ketill. I've got to do something.'

He nodded then, his brow creased in thought. 'You need allies,' he said.

'I've got you,' I said, hoping that was still true.

'Aye, but that's not going to be enough. You need an alliance with one of the tribes, one of the big ones.' I was about to reply when Ketill held up a hand to stop me. 'You can't go back to the Quadi. Areogaesus has just renewed his alliance with Rome, he won't go back on his promise to them again, not after last time.'

I smiled at the thought of all the plunder I had locked away in the chests with my men in their camp. A fair amount of it had come from joint raids with the Quadi and their new king a few years previous. 'He might,' I said.

'He won't,' Ketill said. 'I do, however, know a chief with a daughter in need of a husband.'

Just one look into his wolf-like eyes told me all I needed to know of his plan. 'No!' I shouted, sending morsels of boar meat flying through the air between us. 'No! Not them. How could you even suggest it?'

Ketill held up his hands to protest his innocence. 'They are your tribe,' he said with an apologetic shrug.

'The fucking Chauci are not my tribe!' I spat. 'They're goat fuckers to a man, and I won't go back. Ever! The Ravensworn are my tribe.'

Ketill barked a laugh. 'The Ravensworn are hardly a tribe. Where are your women, your homelands?' He laughed again. 'My friend, if you want to stay alive, the Chauci might be your only hope.'

I rubbed my greasy hands through my hair, desperately trying to think of another solution. The Naristae? No, their chief was no friend of mine, thanks to my previous association with the Quadi. The Marcomanni? Their king had been a close friend once. I had even helped him to ascend to his lofty position. Would he still hold those Quadi raids on his lands against me? The Chatti were a shadow of the tribe they once were. Continuous war had worn them down. They had no real army left to call on. The Chauci were pirates, with a ready fleet of ships suited for either sea or river, plus a trained force to row and fight. I sighed, finally seeing the sense that Ketill already saw. 'Fine,' I said, shoulders slumping, 'the Chauci it is.'

Ketill nodded, rose to his feet and gave me a friendly slap on the shoulder. 'I'll go grab a couple of my lads, send them to the Chauci and arrange a meet.' With that he was off into the night, his battleground voice splitting the close air as he called forth two messengers to ride south. To be absolutely clear, I hated the Chauci, more than I hated the Romans, and that was saying something. But I needed allies, and the chief of the Chauci needed a husband for his daughter.

* * *

The next day found us on horseback, riding leisurely through the marshland that swathed the northern shores of Germania. I had my whole force with me, barring Gerulf and his Hundred. Him I had ordered to man our three ships with his men and row them along the coastline to the lands of the Chauci. I needed options, for I was uncertain at how I would be greeted, even with the tribe being forewarned of my arrival courtesy of Ketill and his two messengers.

I patted my hand on Hilde's flank as we trotted along a narrow path, a nervous tick not lost on Ketill. 'She seems happy to have you back,' he said, motioning to the mare. I smiled, for I have always loved horses, and they me, for the most part.

'She's a good horse,' I said, stroking her neck. 'Perhaps the best I've had.' My hand patted her flank once more, my body betraying my nerves.

'They won't try and kill you, brother,' Ketill said. He reached out and grasped my shoulder.

'How do you know?' I spat.

'Because I asked them not to. And the chief of the Harii is always obeyed.'

I snorted. Even a chief from a tribe the size of the Chauci would be wary of offending the Harii. The thought comforted me, and for a moment I thought how lucky I was to have a friend like Ketill. I even considered telling him. Before I got the chance, a rider came round the bend in the distance at the gallop, his head hanging low and his body flat against his horse. Dust spiralled up in turrets from the dry mud road. 'I think,' I said with a wry smile, 'we may have reached the lands of the Chauci.'

The rider grew closer, his red band of cloth he wore round his left arm marking him out as one of Otto's Hundred. Otto had made all his men wear them after one of his men had killed his comrade in the midst of battle a couple of years ago. It was a good idea. Our men had no uniform approach to their clothing, we did not wear matching-coloured trousers like the tribes, and we had no matching armour and helmets we could all adorn. It would not surprise me to learn more of my men had been killed by their comrades in the heat of a fight, or if I had done so myself.

'Lord,' the rider said as he reined in his horse, 'Captain Otto wishes to report the Chauci have been spotted. About half a day's ride from here, they have camped on the estuary and have two ships and roughly three hundred men.' He kept his eyes fixed on a spot above my head as he made his report. He was young, his skin smooth and free of scars. When he spoke it was impossible to miss his mouth full of gleaming white teeth. I remember envying him then, for I could feel my own rotting away, had even lost a couple already.

I nodded my thanks. 'What's your name?' I asked.

'Ermin, Lord,' he replied, his eyes still fixed on my helmet.

'What tribe are you from, Ermin?'

'The Quadi, Lord,' Ermin said, not able to hide his surprise at the question. 'But I have been with the Ravensworn for three summers now.'

'Why did you leave the Quadi?' I asked. I was convinced there would be spies amongst my ranks, some may even be officers. I made it my business to ask every man their background when I had the chance to speak to them one to one.

'There was a girl, Lord...' He trailed off.

'Pregnant? Angry father? Marry her or leg it? Along those lines, Ermin?' I asked with a grin.

He returned the smile. 'Something like that, Lord.'

I fished in my pouch that hung from my belt, pulled out a silver coin and flicked it at Ermin. 'Keep it in your breeches, lad,' I said. 'And tell Otto not to make contact, to hold his ground till me and the rest of the lads catch up.'

Ermin mumbled his thanks and spurred his horse back into a gallop. I was still smiling as he rode off into the distance. 'Are all your men cutthroats, thieves or hiding from a murderous father and his axe?' Ketill asked me.

'Everyone's running away from something,' I said, gazing off into the distance, as if I could see the Chauci and their horde of blue-trousered warriors over the horizon.

'Well, you're not running any more, Alaric. Come on, let's go meet your people.'

And we did.

14

'Well, well, well. You've got some balls showing your face in these parts. I'll give you that much, Alaric,' said Dagr Fridumarson, Chief of the Chauci. He was a tall man, pale skinned and yellow haired, with serendipitous eyes. They slithered like a serpent, left then right as he scanned Ketill and my captains, who stood resolutely at my back. His great straw-coloured moustache bristled as he smiled at Ketill, who gave him nothing but a look of iron in return.

'It was a free country last time I checked. Thought I'd pop by and see how my old tribe were faring. I see the role of chief suits you, Dagr. Last time I set eyes on you, you were clinging to your father's trousers as he cowered under the length of my blade. You were young then though, what, twenty?' That dark night flashed before my eyes. The night that had changed the course of my life forever.

My parents' farm was on the edge of Chauci lands, far to the north where they bordered with the Cimbri. The Romans had come with the darkness. Their ships sneaking through the choppy waters of the North Sea; the cacophony of the legionaries disembarking and forming into line muffled by the gale that blew from north to south with such force that it was not unknown for thatch to fly from the roof of our small farmhouse.

We knew nothing of the impending attack until the screams began. My father came to me then, crushing me in a great bear hug as he slipped the hilt of a sword into my palm and made me swear to the Allfather that I would protect my mother till death. I was fifteen. My shoulders had started to broaden; I stood taller than most warriors twice my age. I took my father's arm in the warrior's grip and swore to all the gods no man would enter the sanctuary of our home.

I failed that night. I failed as a son, and as a warrior of the feared Chauci. The Romans came. The Fighting Fourteenth in all their glory. It was my first experience with the dreaded 'mincing machine' that had conquered most of the known world. It was also the first time I came face to face with the man who would haunt my dreams for many a year. A man I both feared and hated in equal measure. Silus, first spear centurion of the Fourteenth legion.

'We are not your tribe!' Dagr spat, his hand instinctively going to his sword. 'You betrayed your oath to your chief! You raised your iron and took the life of the one man who should have had your utmost respect and love!'

'And what man was that?' I retorted, my body reverberating with uncontrolled rage. 'The man who left his people to the hands of Rome? Who let his women be raped then slaughtered in front of their children's eyes? The man who didn't raise a finger to protect the lives of the innocent who swear their oaths and pay him tax? Fuck you, Dagr! Your father was a worm, a *nithing*. He deserved the coward's death he got. My one regret is that I finished him off too quickly.'

Before I had even finished my rant, the screech of swords filled the air. Dagr had at his back fifty men at least; I had just five. Not good odds. But my five men freed their blades and lined up beside me, snarling as they dared the Chauci warriors to test their mettle. I knew the men who surrounded Dagr would be no part-time soldiers. They were his household troops, men who lived by the blades they carried. The fact that they owned swords at all would attest to that, for most chiefs would not take on the cost of arming ordinary men with such expensive weapons. They farmed no land, did not work metal over a blistering forge or suffer the stink of fish oil as they cured ox hides to cover a shield. They were warriors, trained killers that lived for nothing but bloodlust and battle glory. If they attacked, we were dead.

'You should watch your mouth, Oathbreaker,' Dagr said through clenched teeth. 'My father was a warrior born, a true descendant of Donar.'

I bent over, howling with laughter at this ridiculous remark. 'A descendant of Donar? That old bastard's flabby arms struggled to lift his eating knife, let alone Donar's hammer!' I made a show of wiping an imaginary tear from my eye, turning my back on Dagr and throwing Ruric a wink. He looked nervous, did Ruric. His eyes gave me a warning, begging me not to provoke the chief further. I ignored him, naturally.

'I seem to remember your mother being the more fearsome of the two. Is it true he only married her because he was scared she would kill him if he didn't?'

Dagr's pale skin went scarlet with rage. He threw off the bear skin that he had worn across his shoulders despite the summer heat and took a step towards me, shoving off his men as they tried to hold him back. 'You want to cross blades with me, Alaric, son of no one? Where was your father when your mother was raped? Where was he when the Romans passed her round like a skin of wine? Did he fight for her honour, I wonder? Or did he sit meekly with his hands tied, whispering worthless nothings into your ear as you screamed in despair as legionary after legionary plied your mother until she bled out on the grass?'

Look at me, Alaric. Just keep your eyes on me. It will be okay, lad. That was what he had said, my father. As we lay face down in the dirt whilst my mother was raped; a black silhouette surrounded by the blazing inferno of our burning home. There was truth in what Dagr said, and that was what hurt the most. The rage got too much, it practically poured out of me as I took a stride forward and bared my teeth, ready to scream the order to charge. To Hel with the fact that I would be killed, or that the good men at my back would have little option but to journey to the Allfather's hall at my back. All coherent thought had gone, replaced by the burning desire to kill the impertinent fool that stood before me. 'Well met, Alaric Hengistson. I see you have lost none of your charm,' said a smug voice from behind me.

I spun on my heels to come face to face with Warin Dagrson, next in line to the Chauci chieftainship. He was short in stature, a fact I knew irked him and one I had previously taken great delight in teasing him with. His straw-coloured hair matched his father's, and I noted curiously that he wore it in a tight topknot, in the way of the Suebi. The Suebi were much more than a tribe; they were an entire nation. More than twenty tribes joined together in alliance, they dominated most of northern Germania. To pick a fight with one of them was to pick a fight with all of them. It was generally agreed amongst the tribes that they were a people best left alone.

'Warin.' I nodded in his direction, my sweat-soaked palm still gripping the hilt of my sword. 'I see you've grown up,' I said with a smirk. Despite Warin's lack of height, he looked a formidable warrior. His broad shoulders were enhanced by a coat of gleaming mail, he wore beige trousers over legs that appeared thick with muscle and a vivid red scar ran down his clean-shaven right cheek. 'Come to save your father from the edge of my blade, have you?'

'Ha!' He scoffed as he sauntered through my men. 'I've come to see you beg for forgiveness, plead to be welcomed back into the arms of the great Chauci. I've come to watch as you beg my father's forgiveness for the shame you put on my grandfather.'

I remember it as vividly today as I did then, standing by the river facing the people I should have been able to call my own. I'd been met with no resistance as I barged my way through Fridumar's hall. I had a discarded Roman short sword concealed within my cloak; the two useless bastards guarding the chief's hall had not even thought to search me. Men had nodded to the hairless youth as he slithered through the throngs of men that feasted and drunk on their chief's benches. Up the steps to the dais, past another useless warrior. Finally, face to face with the chief himself. I remember Dagr then, five years my senior, muddled with mead and more courageous for it. I remember the words he spoke in front of that packed hall, the insult he threw my way, before I had even told of the attack on our farm and my mother's prolonged death. It is what happened next that will haunt me to my dying day.

'Beg? Plead? I've come here to put my seed in your sister, boy. You'll hear no begging from me.' I spat on the floor in front of his booted feet, then showed him my back as I faced his father. 'Where is she then?' I asked with a sneer. I had a vague memory of Saxa, but she could not have been more than six or seven when I previously laid eyes on her.

She had been a small bundle of skin and bones when I had

last had the misfortune of crossing paths with Dagr. It was at a meet of all the heads of the biggest tribes that had lands bordering on the Rhine and the Romans beyond. I had not been invited as such, but had tagged along with Ketill, mainly to see what mischief I could get myself into.

Saxa had been a child, just an unremarkable girl, I hoped she had grown into something more substantial. I did the maths in my head, reckoned her to be about fifteen now. I was, well, in my thirties for sure; it was a normal match up in terms of ages. Some Roman senators I knew, well into the winter of their lives, married girls who had just awoken to their first bleeding; this marriage almost seemed normal compared to that.

'She is on her way,' Dagr said, motioning for one of his men to bring forward his daughter. I saw the flicker of doubt cross his mind, the lump in his throat when he swallowed nervously. Not for the first time I wondered as to his intentions; I was no friend of his, so why was he giving me his little girl?

Men parted behind Dagr, and I could just make out a set of small booted feet, stepping carefully through the throng. I felt a new sensation then, in that heartbeat before I set eyes on the girl who would become my wife. I worried about my appearance. Don't think I ever had before, don't think I have since. But right then, in that moment, I was scared to Hel that she would find me unattractive. It did not matter if she did, of course, the poor whelp would be stuck with me all the same. But still I found myself removing my dull iron helmet, running a hand through my long mop of unruly dark hair. I stroked my beard, hoping it wasn't sticking out to form whiskers either side of my mouth, which it had a habit of doing. I wore the torc around my neck that I had taken from chief Wulfric of the Fenni – another man still very much on my hitlist, as he was balls deep in the charade that had got me caught up with Rome in the first place. But we shall get to him in due course.

Saxa shuffled forwards to stand next to her father, who put a comforting hand on her shoulder. She was short, slim, still the bag of bones I remembered. Mouse-coloured hair atop dull brown eyes, a short-pinched nose and thin lips and high cheek-bones on pale skin gave her a pasty look. Her lips quivered as she sized me up, taking in my bulk and expression. 'My lord,' she said meekly as she dipped her head in respect. Dagr squeezed her shoulder then; I thought I saw the hint of a tear in the corner of his eye.

I was about to reply, The Trickster himself only knows what I was going to say when a voice from behind cut me off. 'So, this is the famous Alaric, Lord of the revered Ravensworn men whisper about in quivering little voices.'

I turned to look upon the most beautiful woman I had ever laid eyes on.

15

Surely in all of the nine worlds there had never been a creature so beautiful. She had long locks of flowing black hair that shone a dark purple in the sunlight. It curled down past her shoulders and rested on a pair of heavy, rounded breasts. Her lips were full, luscious and comely. 'Kissable', Ketill would have said, if he were not as dumbstruck as me. She glided forward, walking through the five men at my back, who stood with their eyes glued to her form. A light scent of jasmine followed in her wake, a trail on which I could walk forever.

Her nose was as straight and broad as a ship's prow; it suited her rounded face. Her cheekbones were high and defined, but where that gave Saxa a gaunt expression, it only enhanced this woman's beauty. But her most captivating feature was her eyes.

Bluer than the cleanest water, purer than a glacier, they gleamed in the light of the day; truly a marvel to behold. I was lost in those eyes, dazzled by them. 'You're not very talkative, are you?' she said with an arched eyebrow. By the gods, what a beautiful eyebrow. They say Freya is the most beautiful of all the goddesses, but I would have wagered all my chests of silver and gold that she did not have a patch on the vision that stood before me.

'Wh... who are you?' I finally managed to croak out, all too aware I was making a fool of myself in front of the one man I really didn't want to. I could feel the arousal growing under my woollen trousers. I wished they were not so tight.

'Allow me to introduce Ishild, my wife,' Warin said with as much pomp as he could muster.

'Ishild.' I didn't so much say, more breathed it, savoured it on my tongue like a fine wine. 'Your what?' I snapped, suddenly waking from the spell she had me under.

'My wife,' Warin said, moving to her side and patting her arm. He patted her arm! Like he was showing me his new war horse. Says everything you need to know about Warin. 'She is the daughter of King Agnarr of the Suebi.' That explained the topknot, I thought. Dagr had gone to bed with the Suebi, I presumed in a vain attempt to keep the land-hungry nation off his turf. I prayed to The Trickster it would not work. An alliance between the Chauci and the Suebi did not suit my plans at all. I wanted Dagr to need me, to want me and my five hundred Ravensworn at his back. If he was in bed with the Suebi, my five hundred men would be nothing to him but a speck of dust on the breeze.

'Maybe we should return to the matter at hand,' Dagr said. I assumed he was reading my mind, seeing the desire that must have been plain as day on my face. 'Maybe the women should leave us? We could talk over a midday meal? I've had fires prepared.' He spoke urgently, loudly, competing for my attention with the beautiful woman who stood before me.

'Yes, of course,' I muttered, having to pull myself away from Ishild. I turned towards Dagr and his daughter, who stood lost as a lamb at his side. I saw the pain in her eyes, the shame at my open attraction to her brother's wife. But what was I supposed to do? Saxa was a child, too thin and small to capture my attention. Ishild was a woman grown, with voluptuous curves and eyes that dazzled. Saxa had no chance, and she knew it.

* * *

'Get yourself together, man,' Ketill rasped in my ear. We walked through the Chauci camp; men stared at me through narrow eyes. 'Oathbreaker, chief killer.' I heard it muttered through clenched teeth as men hawked and spat in my direction.

'I'm fine,' I said, though I knew I wasn't. The sweet scent of jasmine still filled my nostrils; those eyes still blinded me. 'Wotan's eye! You ever seen a woman like that before?'

'Never,' said Ketill without hesitation. 'But you have got to forget about her, Alaric. We're here to marry you to Saxa. You need this alliance, remember? You're a hunted man, brother; you need allies. Don't fuck this up.'

Wise words, I thought as we were guided to a huge fire in the centre of the temporary camp. A circle of swordsmen stood around the perimeter. They parted to make way for their chief and his retinue. The glorious smell of fish sizzling on flames wafted up my nostrils; I wanted the scent of jasmine to return. Dagr pointed to a spot of dewy grass, gesturing for me to sit.

'Hungry?' he asked as I sat, immediately feeling the damp earth seep through my trousers. I noticed he sat on a small cushion, so his arse would be dry when this was over. Just another little insult from the cursed man and his tribe that had once been my own. I sat to his right, in silence as I devoured four fish. I rubbed my greasy hands down my trousers when I finished and drank greedily from a jug of dark ale.

'So,' I said, smacking my lips together as I savoured the taste of the ale. 'You're in league with the Suebi these days?'

'We are,' Dagr acknowledged, considering me with those slithering eyes. 'You have a problem with that?'

'No,' I said. I shot him a quizzical glance. 'Though I am interested as to why you would allow me to marry your daughter. You must have some sort of treaty with king Agnarr? What need have you of me and the Ravensworn?' I have always been rather blunt and forthright. No point beating around the bush, as they say. If I had something to say, I just said it.

'You command a formidable force. It is known across the land that one of your warriors is worth five of the average tribesman. You keep them well armed and armoured at all times; no other chief can say the same. I respect you. I may not like you, but I certainly respect you.'

I was impressed, I have to say. There are not many chiefs who would treat me like an equal, let alone praise me to my face, especially since I had killed his father. I felt some admiration towards him, a glimmer of hope that this could actually work.

'So, what do you want from me?' I asked cautiously. I was wary of making promises I had no intention of keeping. After all, I had enough enemies.

'Saxa's weight in silver will be the bride price. Apart from that, I want us to be allies. Your enemies will be mine, and mine yours,' he said. It concerned me that he would not look me in the eye as he spoke.

'Got many enemies, have you?' I could not think of a single tribe that the Chauci would be likely to go to war with. They had an alliance with the Suebi; no other tribe in the area had the strength to take them on.

'Not right now. King Agnarr sees to that. But...' He trailed off, casting a wary glance at his son, who was locked in an arm wrestle with Ketill. Only one winner there, I thought. 'I don't know how far I can trust Agnarr. He has bewitched my son, or that daughter of his has. As each day passes I feel I lose a bit more of him. It worries me.'

An eruption of cheers announced that Ketill had finally finished teasing Warin, who now lay in the mud clutching his arm to his chest. So Dagr thought his son might betray him to the Suebi. Interesting. I thought of what a war with the Suebi would mean to my men, how many of them could trace their lineage to the wild plains to the east. My brow furrowed with my concern.

'And what of you, Alaric? What enemies would you have me bare my iron against?'

I smiled then. One of those evil grins that show nothing but black holes where there should be teeth. 'Only one, Dagr. Rome.' I saw the lump in his throat as he gulped.

16

It was dark in the depths of my mind. Cold, silent, lonely, like the heart of a mountain, blanketed in stone and winter snow. I sat on the dais of a newly built hall, surrounded by drunken men full of ale and banter and kinship. I smiled to them, joined in with the odd joke, cheered with the crowd when the inevitable wrestling bouts began. But I was dead inside, lifeless, as cold as a Spartan baby that had been left in the trees for the wolves.

My new wife sat beside me, her belly already beginning to show the first signs of the offspring that grew within, though even her presence, or that of my firstborn child growing right in front of my eyes, could not awake me from my gloom.

We had married just three days after that glorious summer's day I had met with Dagr and his weasel son Warin. And Ishild.

The reason for my sombre silences, my disinterest in the world around me. Ishild. Beautiful, enchanting Ishild. Oh, to hear the strings of that husky voice once more; to look upon the endless wonder of her crystal-blue eyes. Merciful Gods, I was a mess. Unfortunately for me, our Gods were not known for their clemency.

Dagr and I had formed a steady alliance in the few days I had spent with his men. In fact, he had laughed with genuine amusement when my men appeared high on a ridge to our south, and Gerulf had guided my three ships to blockade his in the estuary. 'Always have an exit strategy,' I had said and shrugged. For all I had known, things could well have turned to swords very quickly. They nearly did.

My men had feasted with his, and for two days and a night we had drunk and ate till our stomachs rebelled, only to start once more the moment our guts had finished churning. I have never had the displeasure of dining with a Roman, but I'm told their high classes dine whilst reclining on a couch and will often eat until their bodies repel the rich meals their slaves have prepared them. Now, I'm no stranger to emptying my stomach in the nearest bush, bucket or serving girl's lap – whichever happens to be closer – but I can't ever say I have particularly enjoyed the process. I certainly would not want to do it every day.

I sat there, staring into the bottom of my ale cup, trying to find the energy to get it refilled. My head was muggy, clouded, as if thick fog shielded my thoughts from me. Saxa stirred to my right, and I felt vaguely annoyed at the prospect of her trying to strike up a conversation with me.

A commotion on the peripheral of my vision; Ketill politely asked Saxa if he could have a moment alone with me. I moaned into my empty cup, all too aware I was about to be on the end of a tongue lashing from the chief of the Harii. 'What in all the nine worlds is wrong with you?' he hissed as he sat beside me.

He and his men had stayed on with mine after the wedding, his men even helping to build my grand new hall, plus smaller roundhouses for my men. We had built on one of my favourite campsites, the conflux where the rivers Elbe and Saale merged. We had so far left the old Roman fort untouched, but I had plans on restoring it to its former glory. It was good land to build on, soft but firm. The rivers would protect our backs, woodland to the north and marshland to the south. It was east any attack would come from, unless it came from the river itself, but we would prepare for that by building walls come spring.

'Winter,' I said, my mouth still covered by the empty cup. It gave my voice a hollow ring, which I thought appropriate. 'Every winter is the same. Stuck in some hall or other, listening to drunkards tell the same old stories, breathing in the stench of unwashed pits and rotten bowels. Bring on spring, brother; it can't come soon enough.'

'Aye, brother, I get that,' he said, settling down and pouring himself some ale from a jug. Ketill was a warrior born, a man built for the iron storm, much like myself. He too would have spent more than one gloomy winter waiting impatiently for the ground to thaw and wind to stop its howling, sharpening his blades all the while. 'But we're in *your* hall, with *your* new wife who's pregnant with *your* child.' The way he put the emphasis on 'your' every time he said it really ground at my bones; I chose not to react. 'If you can't be happy now, brother, you never will be.'

Ishild. She could make me happy. If I had to fight Hel herself and all her minions to get her, I would leap into the fray in a heartbeat. 'I just need some action,' I said, trying to distract myself more than anything.

Ketill snorted. 'I know just what sort of action you're after, Alaric. Thought you'd be getting plenty of that, being newlywed and all.' We both laughed at the cheap joke. It was good to laugh and mean it. 'Why don't we go out for a ride tomorrow, get some fresh air. Will do us both some good, I think.'

I nodded, my spirits already rising. It was good to have friends like Ketill. Ruric and the other captains were all good men, but they weren't my friends, not the way Ketill was. They took my orders, fought with me side by side in the shield wall, revelled in our victories, and I knew each of them would die for me. But none would come and talk to me the way Ketill had when they saw the thunder in my eyes. They just weren't brave enough. Too scared of losing face in front of their men or favour with me. They avoided me when the dark clouds raised a storm in my mind. Lurking in the shadows, waiting for the light to return.

I felt lighter already, the way you feel when you clamber from your blood-drenched mail after a battle and sit in the sun's waning light and rejoice in the fact that you're alive to see it. Tomorrow was a new day, a new dawn, and I would greet it with a smile nestled in my great dark beard.

'Lord,' a man said, pushing his way through the throng of men that crowded the hall's benches. 'Lord, there are riders outside, from Dagr.' It was Birgir, and I was about to comment on the steady thickening of his fluffy beard when I saw the concern in his eyes.

'What is it, Birgir? Who is it? Why have they come?' Dark tidings, that was my first thought. Why else risk braving the winter's wrath unless it was to bring dire news? What else would drag men from the comfort of their hearth and the warmth of a good woman? 'Birgir,' I said again, 'who has come?'

'She has, Lord.' He wouldn't meet my eye as he spoke; his foot made circles on the thrush-covered floor. 'Ishild, Lord,' he said in a quiet voice. 'Ishild, wife of lord Warin is here. She is asking for you, Lord.'

I looked at Birgir, then turned slowly to lock eyes with Ketill. I guessed my expression was just as dumbfounded as his. Ishild was here, and I think Ketill knew before I did that we would not be going out riding tomorrow.

* * *

As it happens, I did go riding the next day, but only as Ishild commanded it. I was like a playful puppy, bounding round its mother as it clambered for attention with its brothers and sisters. Whatever Ishild wanted, she got. She had demanded a bench nearest the hearth the moment she stalked into my hall, her dark locks sodden with melted snow, comely curves on show where her wet dress clung tight to her striking figure.

She had effortlessly commanded the attention of everyone in that room, as gracious as a swan. She had ignored Saxa completely, a fact I should have been acutely aware of and deeply unhappy about. I wasn't; I hadn't noticed.

We rode through a winter woodland; bare trees arced towards the dark clouds. The ground was a mixture of mush and ice. There had been no snow the previous night, the first night without in a long time. Yuletide was nearly upon us; the time of the Wild Hunt when Wotan would lead his warriors across the sky, spears held high as they looked for some fair game.

'What ails you?' Ishild said. She had slowed her mount to a walk, so my horse walked alongside hers. I had been so lost in thought I hadn't noticed.

'Nothing,' I said absently. Hilde snorted and tossed her head, causing me to lurch in the saddle. She didn't like the great stallion that Ishild rode; she grew skittish whenever he was near. 'I fear these two will never be friends,' I said, just for something to say.

Our morning's ride had been mainly silent. She was taking in the land, the sights and the smells invigorating to her, energising her. I had spent the morning thinking of intelligent things to say, hence the prolonged silence.

'It would appear not! That mare is very defensive of you. How long have you had her?' Ishild asked, reaching out and stroking Hilde's flank, tantalisingly close to my leg.

'Seven years or so? She was still a foal when I bought her. And she should be defensive of me! She has been treated well.'

'Bought?' Ishild said, arching an eyebrow. 'I thought Lord Alaric of the Ravensworn took whatever he wanted? Broke every oath he made and lived as if he was a Roman king? The more time I spend with you, Alaric, the more interesting you become to me.' She gave her horse her heels and cantered off into the bare forest. I watched her hair sway with the rhythm of the horse and wondered what stories she must have been told about me. Was it so shocking that I actually bought a horse? Truth is, I hadn't; Hilde's previous owner had declined the gold I'd offered him and said I'd only take her over his dead body. So I did. But I wasn't going to tell Ishild that though, was I.

I cantered up to Ishild's side, heaving in a lungful of bitter air before asking the question I had not been brave enough to up to this point: 'Why did you come here?' It came out all wrong; my voice croaked like a frog with a sore throat.

'Why do you think I came?' she said. Her mouth was straight, but her eyes laughed at me.

'I... I don't know. Did your husband send you?' I spat the word 'husband', not able to disguise my hatred for Warin.

'No,' she said through a laugh. 'In fact I did not tell him I was coming here.' She threw me a wry look, her eyes full of mischief, lips puckered into a soft pout.

'Where does he think you are?' I said as my heart hit my

ribcage so hard I'm sure my mail shook. The swelling under my woollen trousers was back, and I regretted the extra layer of animal skin I had wrapped atop my breeches.

'I said I was going to see a friend, so it wasn't a total lie.' We had reached the huge lake that lay sleeping below a thick sheet of ice. Ishild dismounted and walked cautiously towards the ice, trepidation written all over her face. 'Will the ice hold if I walk on it?' she asked without turning to look back.

'Friends, are we?' I asked as I dismounted Hilde, I gave her nose a stroke as she grumbled about being left to stand in the cold. 'And yes, it should hold. Shall we find out together?' I asked, holding out a hand for her to grasp.

Her hands were like silk as they brushed the calloused skin of my palm. Now we were away from the horses the scent of jasmine hung on the air, the rich aroma intoxicating after inhaling the bland taste of winter.

'I think we can be friends,' Ishild said, taking careful steps on the blue ice. It was as clear and pure as her eyes, and if you looked hard enough you could see the darting shadows of the fish as they scuttled through the water. 'Sure,' I said, wanting to say so much more. I felt a twang of guilt for Saxa, who I had left behind in our new hall. She had tried so hard, been nothing but appreciative and accommodating in the months since our wedding. But she just could not compete with Ishild and her seductive beauty. I was about to pull her in close, to put my arms around her and take what it was I so desired, when a spear arced from the low hanging clouds and thumped through the ice in the small pace between Ishild and me.

She screamed as I tore my hand from hers, spun on the balls of my feet and hauled free my sword. I had nearly left it at my new hall, only picking it up on my way out as an afterthought. I had my spear with me, but that was tied to my saddle and Hilde and my would-be attackers were now between me and my mount. I sent a swift prayer to the Allfather that I'd had the sense to put on my mail, even if it was only to add an extra layer between my torso and the cold.

Two men stood on the edge of the lake. They were clad all in black; charcoal darkened their faces and hands. Both had shields, round and black; one still held a throwing spear whilst the other had just a sword. I edged forwards on the ice, wary now of the groaning that greeted every step. I knew that if I walked carefully back across it would hold my weight no problem, but if I had to fight on it... That was a different matter.

The man who still held a throwing spear took aim and let loose. I stood confused as the spear flew far over my head and was about to shout a ribbed comment on his aim when Ishild screamed and the leaf-shaped iron point tore through the side of her cloak. There was a dash of red that gleamed in the dull light, then it was gone as Ishild bent over and covered her cut arm with her hand.

The furies were with me then, the battle rage pumping through my veins as I bounded across the ice, heedless of the risk I was taking. The first man met my flying charge head on and our swords clashed with a scream of iron, sparks flying through the air. We rebounded off each other, me landing like a cat and him stumbling on the sodden ground. I wasted no time – I leapt with my sword held high and whilst my attacker was still finding his footing, I drove the blade through his skull, warm brains spattering my face.

The second man stood stock still, transfixed at the sudden savagery he had just witnessed. I snarled and charged him and he didn't even move as my sword cut through his neck, arterial blood gushing like a waterfall from the grievous wound. He sunk to the earth like a stone in the sea.

I stood panting, my breath steaming on the bitter air. I stumbled and slipped my way back to Ishild, who held her wounded arm to her chest. 'Are you okay?' I managed to say through my laboured breathing.

'Fine, I'm fine,' she muttered, though her lips were blue and she shivered like she'd just swum in the northern ocean. 'Come on,' I said, putting my arms around her, 'let's get you home.'

17

'The two men, did you see their hair?' Ketill asked me as we reclined by the hearth in my hall. Night had fallen, and I had spent the remainder of the day since the attack scouring the lands around my new home, searching for any further attackers. I had found none.

'Their hair?' I said, slurring my words as I wiped ale from my beard. 'I was too busy killing them, Ketill, I didn't stop to look at their fucking hair.'

He smiled, then looked around to make sure we could not be overheard. 'They wore their hair in topknots. Like the Suebi,' he said in a hushed voice.

I was raising my cup to my lips as he spoke; I slowly lowered it when the implications of what he said hit me. 'Donar's beard, brother. You're right.' We both sat in silence for a time, each gathering our thoughts. 'You think Agnarr sent men to kill his own daughter?' I asked.

Ketill shook his head. 'No, I don't think so. I mean, I don't know the man, have no idea what his relationship is like with her—'

'Or Dagr and Warin, more importantly,' I cut in, my mind already whirling. I had been shocked when Dagr had agreed to let me marry his daughter. Flabbergasted when I had learned he was now a puppet of the Suebi. He had spoken so easily of his relationship with the land-hungry tribe when we had met in the summer, as if life could not be better. I had a horrible feeling in the pit of my stomach that something was afoot, that Dagr may have need of my Ravensworn sooner rather than later. 'Ketill, find Ruric and send him to me. And have your men ready to ride at first light. We have questions that need answering.'

I was already rising uncertainly to my feet when Ketill grabbed my shoulder and dug his nails in. 'May I remind you, *friend*, that I am the chief of the Harii and not some new beard you can order around, even if we are in your hall!' He kept his voice light, but I saw the underlying anger in his eyes. I had offended him, and he was a man whose support I could not afford to lose.

'Sorry, brother,' I mumbled, suddenly embarrassed. 'I spoke without thinking. But we may be in real danger here. Those men were all in black, as if they were from your tribe.' I held up a hand, halting the protest of innocence I knew was coming. 'Someone has once again tried to pitch you against me, and we need to find out why. If something is happening between Dagr and Agnarr then we need to know. Are you still with me?' The sudden fear that Ketill might round up his troops and head home hit me like a spear to the guts.

'Of course, brother. Your enemy is my enemy, always.' We locked wrists, the warriors' embrace, then he stalked off through the noise of the hall to ready his men.

I stood still and breathed deeply, methodically, trying to slow my heart and clear my head. I scanned the hall, searching for Ruric, but locked eyes with Ishild instead. She sat on the top table, a cup of wine in her hand. Her left arm was heavily bandaged, and even in the dull light of the flames I could see she still looked pale. She had sobbed all the way back to the hall, mumbling incoherently to herself. But her eyes still glistened in the glow of the flames, dominating the room and casting me back under her spell. I barely registered Saxa at her side, or paid any heed when my wife rose and left the hall without a backward glance.

* * *

Ten days we rode through everything the winter had to throw at us. Snowstorms, blistering winds, hail and rain were our constant companions. I had with me my whole force, five hundred battle-ready men who grumbled and moaned every step of the way. Ketill had one hundred and fifty of the Harii, and each day I marvelled at how quickly they were ready to march, how efficiently they set up camp each night. How little they moaned into their fur-lined cloaks. My men were hard, dangerous and as I always claimed, the best fighting unit outside of Rome. For the first time I was starting to doubt if they were the toughest.

I wore all my finery, which was rare for me. A beautifully crafted iron helmet trimmed with bronze sat atop my head. It was Roman, and even still bore the white horsehair crest that had adorned it the day I slaughtered its previous owner. The neck guard was too long for my taste; it dug in my back whenever I raised my head. I had done away with the leather chin straps that were designed to hold it in place, but my long, wild hair seemed to be enough to hold it firm atop my head.

My finest mail sat snug around my torso. I had cursed the winter for forcing my lack of exercise the first day of the march;

three of my men had had to help me pull it over my growing belly. I'd sworn them to secrecy on pain of death. The mail was long sleeve, which added more weight and wasn't my normal preference. But the small iron links were intertwined with silver and it gleamed on even the dullest of days. It may not have been the sturdiest or most practical bit of armour I owned, but by the gods I looked good in it.

I had even added fresh leather to the hilt of my sword. I owned many swords, most finer than the one that sat on my hip. But that blade was mine, as much a part of me as my beating heart; I would never be without it.

'Are you going to tell us where in the Allfather's name we're going in this pissing weather?' Ruric grumbled as he cantered up to my side. He looked old, did Ruric. He seemed to have aged a decade since our fight with the Batavi in the summer, and I'd thought him ancient then. His pale-green eyes shone almost grey in the cloud-filled sky; strands of grey hair wisped from under the hood of his cloak. His hair had thinned with the summer; by the time the sun finally thawed the last of the winter snow, he would be almost as bald as the day he was born.

'East,' I said. 'Not much further now.'

Ruric moved his horse closer to mine, leant over on his saddle. 'We're not going to the Suebi, are we?' he asked in a cautious whisper.

I flashed my teeth and leant towards him. 'Sound scared, old man. You sure you still got the stones to be my Second?' I winked as I spoke, but was quietly apprehensive as to his reply.

'Fenrir's teeth, lad, but you've got some front!' he exclaimed, sucking the remnants of his teeth. 'You have just made peace with the Chauci, sworn an oath to their chief, not to mention impregnating his daughter! And now, just a few weeks later, you're going behind his back to his master? You know what they call you, right?'

Oathbreaker. At least he had the decency not to say it. I revel in my enemies whispering obscenities about me when they think I cannot hear. The looks I get from chiefs and kings when I stalk into their halls. But my own men talking dirt behind my back? Well, I can't be having that.

'The men are worried I'm breaking an oath to Dagr? That my actions may lead to war?' I tried to think rationally, put the emotion to one side. It was only reasonable the men would be whispering; the weather and forced ride I had made them endure would not have won me any popularity.

'There have been mutterings...' Ruric said. He would not meet my eye as he spoke.

'Tell the men,' I said in the calmest voice I could muster, 'that I have reason to believe Dagr might be about to betray us. The two men that attacked me dressed as Harii warriors. Their hair, though, was in the style of the Suebi—'

'So why are we going to the fucking Suebi?' Ruric spat. Clearly we had reached the crux of the issue.

'To find the truth, my friend. Why else?'

* * *

'Alaric! Alaric, wait, come back!' My father bounds along the path behind me. I hear the crunch of a twig then the sharp intake of breath as the old man snags his foot on the undergrowth and falls to the floor with a crunch.

I turn, autumn's rich aroma filling my nostrils. It had rained in the morning. The freshly cut harvest from the fields that surrounds the small patch of woodland I stand in radiates a smell which reminds me so much of my childhood. The moist earth; grain a golden yellow;

a hint of woodsmoke that resonates in my nostrils. 'Go home, Father,' I say, turning back around, fighting the urge to help the old warrior to his feet.

My mother is dead. And with her died my childhood. I have no need of this place, this poor farm that sits on the northern edge of nowhere. My father had such fine dreams for what we were going to achieve the day he hung up his spear for good and swapped it for a plough. The sad truth is, ten years later he has not even bothered to give the place a name. Just a rundown house with a sodden barn, surrounded by a crop of trees and marshland. It is worth less than him, and that is saying something.

'Alaric, son,' he says, rising slowly to his feet. Despite myself, I stop and turn; a smidgeon of sympathy remains in my wintry heart.

'Whatever you have to say, make it quick,' I say as I stand stock still and try to make myself look bigger than I am.

'Where will you go?' he asks as he approaches, holding out a hand to grasp my shoulder to pull me back toward home.

'What's it to you?' I say. 'You've always thought me weak, never showed me a shred of respect for the man I have become. What do you care what I choose to do with my life?'

He has the nerve to look hurt then. I fight the urge to give in, to fold myself in his arms and cry more tears for the ashes of my mother.

'I always cared, son,' he says, taking another step towards me. 'Why do you think I was always so harsh? This ain't Rome, lad, you'll get no grain ration where you're going. Our country is a hard one, wild, and you'll soon learn people don't often play fair. All I have done is to get you ready, equip you for the challenges you will soon face.' His head is a handbreadth from mine now; he speaks in a whisper, both arms locked around my neck. 'I love you, Alaric, maybe more than you'll ever know. I just want you to be ready.'

I stand and control my breathing, trying to ease the furious shakes building in my bunched fists. Is that what he was doing when he threw a five-year-old boy into a freezing lake? Or when he threw a ten-year-old a spear moments before a charging wolf ripped through his throat, after he had trapped them together in a pen? 'Thank you, Father,' I say in a voice that portrays nothing but hurt and anger, 'for the lessons you have given me. Thank you for making me strong, for giving me the skills to survive in this harsh world. I will remember your lessons, always.'

I turn and walk away. Orange and brown leaves flutter to the ground, the wind picks up and the strong smell of pine wafts through me. I pull my cloak closer and take my first steps to a new beginning.

'Alaric, at least take this,' my father says, holding out a sword wrapped in an old cloak. A black pommel protrudes from the top.

18

The rain tore through my skin like flying spear tips. The wind was ferocious, howling and wailing as I crashed through the thick undergrowth of the forest. I panted as I paused, scanning the trees that swamped me. Nothing but the murk and shadows, my vision made blurry by the viciousness of the winter storm. My hair was drenched with rain and sweat, my throat dry and chest heaving as I fought to control my breathing.

A shout to my rear, the cry of a hunter bearing down on his prey. A glance showed me bared teeth, a speck of white in the blackness as the hunter leapt a fallen tree trunk. BANG! A crash of thunder was preceded by a flash of light. More men were illuminated in the flash, all with spears to hand. I showed them my back and hurtled down a narrow track. My feet were in tatters, blisters forming on both heels. I sucked in air and kept my head down, my spear caught on a hanging branch as I ran and fell from my grip. I had no time to stop and retrieve it.

The bark of the hounds sent shivers down my spine, the sight of their fangs a horrid picture in my mind. The thud of their paws on the sodden earth, the beat fast and angry, as if

Fenrir himself was on my tail. Somewhere, Loki laughed in spite. Out of the trees now, the giant pines parted to reveal a small clearing that seemed to dazzle in the half light.

I saw it then, not twenty paces from me: safety. With renewed energy, I pumped my legs and felt the tired muscles respond. The heather was up to my knees, the smell rich and invigorating. Men cheered now, some for me and others raised their voices in anger. A sliver of red; the first hints of daybreak battled through the cloud on the horizon behind it.

Closer now, no more than twenty paces, the flag billowed in the blistering chill. I reached out my arm, close now, so close. A hound barked behind me, so near I could hear its breath as it strained with all its might to reach me in time; longed to feel the break of my skin beneath its fangs, the metallic taste of my lifeblood on its tongue.

With a lurch I reached out and took hold of the flag, pulling it from the tree as I collapsed in a ruined heap on the wet heather. I gasped in great lungfuls of air, spread out flat on my back like a sacrifice to the Allfather. The hounds were on me now, snarling and drooling as they circled me, each deciding what bit to eat first. A sharp whistle, harsh on my ears, and they dispersed, tails between their legs.

A man approached, swathed in shadow. He wore a great bear skin that could have kept three average men dry in the storm; he filled it and more. His hobnailed boots dug into the earth as he approached; from the corner of my eye I saw the faint glimmer of a spear tip as it was lowered to my throat. 'I'd heard you had The Sly One in you, Alaric, but I didn't believe it till today.' The spear was raised and I grasped the offered hand, allowing myself to be pulled to my feet. 'You have earned the attention of King Agnarr, young man, and now you may tell me why you are here.'

* * *

Two days later I sat in the king's hall, drinking too much bitter ale and all the better for it. I had passed the test. Earned myself an audience with the king of the biggest union in Germania. The Suebi were a collection of tribes, a coalition of people all pulling together in the same direction. There was something very unique about being in a hall with a mixture of tribesmen and for there not to be blood splattered up the walls. To my right was the chief of the Sideni, in quiet conversation with a warrior from the Avarpi. Opposite them was an emissary from the Tevtones, clinking cups and drinking ale with the chief of the Lemovii. None of this was right; these tribes were all neighbours and should therefore be at each other's throats. It was of course preferable to be on friendly terms with the tribe in the next village, but it was rarely the reality.

I had met Agnarr on a wide plain, just south of a stronghold called Viritium. My scouts had reported he was wintering there with the bulk of his men, and sure enough a small army marched out to meet us as I approached with the Ravensworn. Ketill had snuck off into the forest the night before, taking his men with him. We had agreed that it might be prudent to keep part of our force secret from the king in case it ended in battle. I had been confident it would not, that the king would welcome me to his hearth and listen as I asked my questions. I hadn't expected to have to prove myself by avoiding capture in a night hunt through a deep pine forest.

At the time I thought it was all innocent fun. Now I think he would have really killed me if I had not made it to the flag before the hounds got me. Anyway, water under the bridge now, as they say.

True to his word, Agnarr had listened as I fired question

after question his way as we sat by a small fire under the very tree I had grabbed the red flag from. What deal did he have with Dagr? Did he have any contact with his daughter? Was there any reason why he would want his daughter dead? Or me, for that matter. Long into the night we talked, the howls of wolves and squawks of hunting owls surrounding us. He met my eye with every answer, showed genuine horror when I spoke of the attack on his daughter and the wound she had taken. It was clear to me he loved her very much and was less than impressed with her husband. I had been sent away when my questions were asked. Told to wait until he had time to reflect on what I had told him. I had not seen him since.

'Lord Alaric?' a young warrior asked. I had not heard him approach, my senses dulled by the ale and the general cacophony in the hall. 'Hmm,' I said as I staggered to my feet. I looked the warrior up and down; he was tall and broad, his arms thick with silver rings that marked him as a killer. But his face was young and pure, he had no beard and was free of scars. Large, blue puppy eyes looked at me in awe as he took in the leader of the most feared army in the land.

'Can I help you, lad?' I slurred, staggering on unsteady feet. I grew suddenly conscious of the roaring hearth behind me.

'Sorry, Lord. King Agnarr requests you attend him, in his private quarters. Follow me, Lord?' he asked. His voice was high and squeamish; it didn't suit his height and build. I followed the warrior with the girl's voice through the throng. I was known here, feared. Men whispered as usual; some had the courage to meet my eye and nod a greeting.

We moved through a door at the rear of the hall and entered a small corridor. There was a strong smell of livestock and damp hay. Agnarr clearly wintered his animals in the huge hall, making me wonder why he didn't have a separate barn built. I pinched my nose and breathed slowly through my mouth. Pig shit, horse sweat, sheep's urine – it was all there, hanging in the air. We passed a busy kitchen, sweat-soaked slaves rushing around large pots that sat atop cooking fires.

Finally, we reached a small door at the end of the corridor. To my left now was the animal pen, packed so tight with life it was a wonder any of them had room to drop their guts. My girlish-sounding escort knocked once on the door then stepped to the side, gesturing for me to enter.

I pushed open the door and entered a tiny bedchamber. For a man who ruled large swathes of land, with kingship over numerous small tribes, it was sparse and void of any decoration. I had seen slave quarters with more possessions, small roundhouses that had more colour. The king sat on a small straw pallet, wearing nothing but a faded Roman tunic and woollen trousers. He looked tired, worn out. I closed the door behind me and nodded, fighting the urge to stand to attention as if I was some new recruit on parade.

'Alaric.' The king nodded, rising to his feet and gripping my arm. He honoured me then, treating me as if I was an equal. He sat back down and motioned for me to sit on a small wooden stool next to the bed. I studied him as I did, taking in his tired features. His hair and beard were as grey as the winter; age lines scarred his face. His eyes were a dark brown, like bottomless pits. His nose was small and bunched, as if it had been flattened by a shield boss one too many times over the years. Knowing the man's reputation for violence, I assumed it probably had.

'Lord King, I trust I find you in good health?' I asked once I had sat, noticing the yellowing of his complexion.

'I'm fine, Alaric, just old is all,' he said, running a fat finger through his beard. 'I have been thinking on our conversation the other day, planning my next course of action.'

Silence. It hung in the air like woodsmoke trapped against a thatched roof. I did not know whether to speak or wait for the king. He ended my indecision. 'I took Dagr and his tribe into the arms of the Suebi because I'm old, Alaric. I rule over many tribes, many chiefs, but none of them have the strength to rule when I am gone, to keep the alliance together and the people strong. I had been hoping Warin would be that man. It appears I was wrong.'

I didn't speak, was unsure if I was meant to. I had an inkling as to where this conversation would end: war. 'I have not been idle in the days since we spoke, after you proved yourself to me in the hunt.' I shuddered. My muscles still burned from my night run through the forest; I could still smell the warm breath of the hounds, the image of their fangs still keeping me up at night. 'I have a spy in Warin's guard. Ten men sworn to protect him till death, though only nine are loyal to him. He sent word of his jealousy of you, and my daughter's feelings towards you. It would appear he let his emotions get the better of him and tried to have you both killed.'

I felt my cheeks colour, wished I had not drunk so much ale that my wits had deserted me. 'I spoke to your men, Alaric. Earlier today you were too deep in your cups to notice. Ruric stammered his way through your defence, the rest of your captains feigned ignorance and one even threatened to kill me!' Agnarr said, his face splitting into a grin.

'Baldo?' I asked, arching an eyebrow.

'Yes! Quite the warrior, I think.' Luckily for me, Agnarr was still chuckling. The laughter caused him to erupt into a coughing fit. When he was done, dark blood was spattered over his hand. He wiped it on his trousers. I could see the shake in his hands. 'As I said, Alaric, I have no *legitimate* sons; my wife was always barren. Sure, I had lovers and they bore me sons, but can

I leave my people with a bastard? When I am gone, I need someone I can trust to rule my people. That man could be you. I see a lot of myself when I look at you, the man I used to be.'

I sat there, mouth open, tongue drooping to my chin. Me? Rule the Suebi? 'I... err...' I couldn't speak, couldn't think clearly.

'Your men love you, Alaric. If I knew nothing else about you, that would be enough. But I also know your enemies fear you and hate you for it. I know your men are the most formidable force this side of the Roman borders. And I know that you love my Ishild.'

I went to speak, to protest my innocence, but Agnarr's raised hand silenced me. 'I know, I know! You haven't touched her, you're married to Dagr's daughter, she's having your baby. Spare me, Alaric. You love her, and she loves you. That is all that matters.'

I felt sick. The heat from the small fire in the room was suddenly overbearing. 'What are your plans for the spring?' Agnarr asked, wheezing now; another coughing fist was imminent.

'I have business in the south,' I said, still trying to gather my thoughts.

'Rome,' Agnarr said. It was not a question, but a statement. 'They want you dead. I received a messenger, a frumentarii agent last spring. Said his name was Trajianus, offered me gold for your death. Like I said, your enemies fear you. What will you do?'

'I don't know yet,' I said with a sigh. 'I was hoping Dagr would help me on that front, hence I married his daughter. But I can't sit idle and wait for the dagger in the night. I must take action.'

Agnarr nodded. 'You must, I agree. I'll make you a deal, Alaric, Lord of the Ravensworn. You go south and deal with

Rome, and I will clear the path for you to be my successor and give you Ishild's hand in marriage.' He spat on his palm and offered it to me. I did the same and gripped his arm. I was going south. Rome would feel my wrath and my sword would sing a bloody song as it cleaved through the skulls of my enemies. And when I returned, I would be king of the most powerful tribe in the land, with the most beautiful woman as my wife.

PART II

19

Late summer of the following year found my small fleet and me on the River Danube, cruising under a star-filled sky. It was the tenth year of the reign of the Emperor Antoninus Pius, a man who had won great battle fame in northern Britain, even extending their borders beyond the wall of Hadrian, to the 'Vallum Antonini', or 'Antonine Wall' as it was to be known, without ever setting foot outside Italian soil.

Nor would he, if the rumours were to be believed. The divine Hadrian had named him as successor towards the end of his reign, though from what I gather he was most undeserving of the reward. Hadrian had been a man I would have liked to have met on the field of battle, an adversary I could respect. He ruled for more than twenty years, scouring his lands and boosting his troops' morale wherever he went. Despite his preference for boys, he had seemed a military man to the core, someone who knew that his soldiers were the most important people he ruled. Sadly for Rome, none of that seemed to have rubbed off onto his protégé.

Rome was at peace; the 'Pax Romana' ruled in all corners of the world, if the merchants coming north from the empire were to be believed. There had been no widespread publicity for my raid on Ulpia Noviomagus the year before, my capture of three warships or my assassination of two frumentarii agents. Not to mention the fact I had snuck into Colonia Ulpia Traiana disguised as a Roman officer and butchered two men there. I had an ego, still do to be honest, and that ego needs to be stroked, caressed and teased until my head feels so big my back might collapse under its vast weight.

It hurt, the lack of recognition. The raid on Ulpia Noviomagus had been credited to the Chauci, which really pissed me off. No mention had been made of the missing ships. Rome's pride, their hubris, was about to cost them dear. No one challenged us as we casually sailed through waters that were officially 'Roman'. People waved from the southern bank, smiled and cheered as we laughed and waved back.

Getting our boats onto that river had been no easy task, but I was determined to have them for what I was about to attempt. We had rowed them down the River Elbe, from the North Sea at its top to its very end in southern Germania. The last miles had been absolute hell, rolling the great ships over felled tree trunks through hilly terrain and marshland. It had been a Roman auxiliary unit that had first given me the idea, for I had seen them do the very same thing when fighting on the north coast. Granted, they had had the full might of a cohort to help with the pushing and pulling, not to mention the constant chopping down of fresh timber. But my men had done their job well, and all three ships made it in one piece.

I had three hundred men crammed onto the ships with me. Ruric led the other two files of Hundred, his own and Baldo's, on the northern banks of the river. I'd given Adalhard the smaller vessel again; he had admittedly grown quite attached to it, and as we sailed through the night, I could hear him and his men argue over what name they were going to give it. With me I had Otto and Gerulf. Gerulf commanded the second Liburnian whilst I was aboard the other with Otto and his Hundred, men I had not spent enough time with over the last year. They were good, disciplined and efficient, as I would expect of any of my files, but I had not yet seen them fight.

We had entered the river just east of the Roman town of Lauriacum, an administrative town that was home to some auxiliary cohort or other. The River Enns drifted lazily off the Danube and deeper into the Roman Province of Noricum. It was not Noricum I wanted to be in though; that small auxiliary cohort was not my target. I wanted Pannonia and the Fourteenth Legion.

I had learnt the previous year that the order for my death had come from Pannonia. There were two main legions based on Rome's northern border in that province: the Tenth at Vindobona and the Fourteenth at Carnuntum. The Tenth legion were an unknown quantity to me, though only a shadow of the legion they had been when Caesar led them to victory in Gaul. The Fourteenth I had far more knowledge of. Not only had they been the legion that raided my home and murdered my mother, but I had fought a few skirmishes in southern Germania with them in the years that followed. They were deadly, well trained and well led, and not to be taken lightly.

I knew deep down that the man I sought could be found in Carnuntum, hiding behind those rectangular shields emblazoned with the Capricorn. I had no evidence to prove it, but I just knew it.

'You okay, Chief?' Otto asked me. I must have been staring off into the night. My eyes had glazed over, and I had to shake my head so they regained focus. 'Thinking of the baby?' he asked with a knowing look in his eye.

Saxa had given birth to a boy in the spring. Little Ludwig Alaricson had been born on a cold and cloudless night. He weighed less than my sword; I instantly fell in love with his small button nose and scrunched-up eyes. His skin was as pale as his mother's, but his long arms and legs promised a physique like his father; at least that's what the old crone who had helped deliver him had said. She had given me the creeps, that woman. Claimed to be close to the gods, claimed to be able to see men's futures. I saw through her charade. Only the three spinners can determine a man's destiny, and she was most certainly not one of those.

'No,' I said, bringing myself back to the present. 'War.' Otto studied his boots for a time, then finally said, 'You know my men can be counted on, don't you, Chief?'

I started at the question. True, Otto was something of an anomaly to me, a man I had spent little time with. He had been appointed to his position on Ruric's recommendation two years ago. In that time we had seen very little action, and what fights there had been Otto and his men had not been a part of. 'You really think you would be here if I didn't?' I asked, both shocked and ashamed that he would feel the need to ask.

'Sorry, Chief,' Otto replied, still studying his boots. 'Just don't see much of you, is all. I know we might not be your favourite men, the ones you always chuck in to the fight first. But my men are good, Chief. You give us the chance and we'll show you what we can do.' A tumult of growls and cheers greeted this as his men echoed their captain's confidence. I gave them a rueful grin. I had been unaware our conversation was being overheard; it did my heart good to know the men were eager to show me their prowess.

'When we reach Carnuntum, if it comes to a fight, I promise you boys will be the first in line, and I'll be right there with you.' I hauled my sword from my scabbard and thrust it towards the stars. A great roar echoed in the night, a loud rasp as one hundred men bared their weapons to the gods and roared their war cry.

Somewhere, the Allfather stirred. Surely even he did not command better men.

* * *

'The bridge, Lord. The bridge on the horizon!'

I was dozing at the steering oar. Too many late nights and hot days had gotten the better of me. I snapped from my torpor to see a long wooden bridge on the horizon, spanning from Carnuntum on the south bank over to the lands of the Quadi on the north.

I had not told my men what I had planned for when we reached Carnuntum. Mainly because I had no idea myself. Somehow, I had to get in there. Somehow, I had to find the man that wanted my head and remove his before he had the chance to take mine. The one small issue was that I was completely clueless as to how I was going to get that done.

A full-frontal assault was completely out of the question. I had no siege equipment, no ladders or artillery. There were five thousand battle-hardened legionaries behind those high walls; even if my men managed to scale them, I didn't fancy our chances of living long enough to tell the tale.

Getting in by disguise would prove much harder than it had at Colonia Ulpia Traiana. Too many men there knew my face, officers especially. Somehow, I needed to lure the legion out, get them over that cursed bridge and into Quadi lands. Then my five hundred men and I could force an entry and fight off the few men left to guard the fortress.

'Otto, pull the ship over on the north bank. Behind that island there, we'll disembark and regroup with Ruric and the rest of the men.' Slowly, the threads of a plan were coming together. I watched on as my two other ships followed our lead and rowed over to the north bank. The River Danube is vast in width as well as length, so that islands appear sporadically along its course. Some big, some small, all just patches of marshland covered in dense bush. I knew they were despised by merchants and Roman warships alike, as they narrowed the river temporarily and caused traffic to slow to a standstill at times as two ships argued over who had the right of way. But to me, right then, they were a gift from the gods.

The island we were behind ensured we couldn't be spotted from Carnuntum. I knew if I could see through the dense greenery I would see walls, red-tiled roofs and a busy market down by the small harbour. But that view was hidden from me, and I was hidden from them.

We leapt from the ships and waded through the shallows and the reeds to clamber up onto the northern bank. Birgir stumbled from the water just behind me, dragging a reluctant horse from the water. 'Hates the ship, Lord!' he said cheerily as he saw me. 'And I hate him! Right bastard he is!'

'Why do you have him then?' I asked with a raised eyebrow.

'Because he's a demon in a scrap and he's fast as the wind!' he said as he vaulted onto his back. 'I'll be off to find the others then. See you at nightfall.' And with that he was gone.

I clasped hands with Gerulf and Adalhard as they made it on to dry land, and waited impatiently as the men were formed up in their units on a flat patch of grassland.

'You going to tell us what the plan is, Chief?' Adalhard asked.

I had pretended to ignore them as my three captains had a hushed argument as to who was going to ask the question. I smiled to myself, prolonging the tension with the extended silence.

'Today, my friends, we're going to start a fire, a big one.'

20

That summer was glorious. Too glorious. Each day the sun scorched the earth, shining down on crops that wouldn't grow, and fires would burst into life within the dry scrub and drought-stricken fields of grain. I had already heard of several farmsteads that had seen their crops ruined, burnt to nothing more than dust. It would be a hard winter for many.

I knew that to lure the Fourteenth from their lair I would have to do something remarkable, make such a storm that those red shields would have no choice but to march across their wooden bridge and seek me out.

Any old fire would not have achieved that. The Romans would have merely watched from the walls and laughed as their enemies were plunged into further plight. No, I had to start such a blaze that the Fourteenth would have no option but to come rushing from their fortress, swords sheathed and water buckets at the ready.

There was a small fort on the north side of the bridge, a lookout post, a small fence and a gate. I reckoned there to be no more than a century posted there at any one time, so no more than eighty men. That fort symbolled Rome's only power our side of the river. Its sole purpose was to give advanced warning to the rest of the legion of any impending attack. That day, I think, would be the first time the men stationed within would have been called upon to see out that duty. Happily for me, they failed as miserably as I had been expecting them to.

The grass had grown long around the small wooden barricade that enclosed the lookout tower. There was, I was sure, a parapet on the far side of the barricade, though no soldiers were patrolling it. Nor were the lookouts in the watchtower giving the northern horizon the slightest glance. As I crept down the defensive ditch that surrounded the fence, I could hear the cries of glee and anger as a small circle of legionaries played dice in the shade. The clunk of the bone dice in the wooden cup was audible as the men held their breath and prayed to Fortuna for the numbers to fall their way.

A horse whinnied and pawed a hoof on the dry ground as I leaned up against the barricade. I could see it through the gaps in the wooden beams, its ear flicking to listen for trouble. Again it whinnied, snorted and stamped. I panicked momentarily, fearful the noise would alert one of the lounging Romans who would spot me through the gaps in the barricade. I need not have worried; the only reaction it sparked was for one soldier to launch an apple at the noisy beast, who was happy to take the treat in exchange for quieting down.

Birgir scrambled up the earthwork behind me, a mischievous glint in his eye as he drew his flint from a pouch on his waist and grabbed a handful of yellow grass. The first sparks came to nothing, and with each one I flinched, certain I would see a helmeted Roman appear at any moment.

Another strike of the flint and this time the spark caught. Light smoke drifted from the small orange flame, which Birgir carefully lowered to the base of the barricade. We slowly added fuel to the fire; more dry grass and an array of twigs. It caught quickly, the flames rising higher and the base spreading along the floor. With a wink I slapped Birgir on the shoulder and silently gestured for him to retreat with me.

As we ran we heard the first cries of alarm; saw the great bloom of orange and yellow as the beacon fire was lit in the tower. I grinned savagely. Right now there would be pandemonium within the fortress over the river, men scrambling into armour as centurions struck them with their vine sticks.

Birgir and I rounded a sharp bend in the landscape and ran into my wall of German iron. The Ravensworn were formed up for battle, five hundred of the finest warriors in the land. It brought a tear to my eye seeing my men in all their battle glory. It was not often I had the time or space to bring them all together and practise combat manoeuvres. But still, each man knew their place in the 'cohort', as I liked to call it, purely as a means of mocking the Romans, although there were similarities between the two.

A Roman cohort was made of six centuries of eighty men. My unit had five units numbering a hundred each. Ruric and his Hundred held the right flank. It was considered the position of honour on the battlefield; the place where a General would assemble his best troops. Gerulf was next, standing in the front rank of his men with a single-headed axe in one hand and his shield in the other. Adalhard held the centre with his great longsword held two-handed, his head free of a helmet so his long locks swayed with the breeze. Baldo stood with his back to me, haranguing one of his men for what I am sure was a slight misdemeanour, while Otto and his men were on the far left. He raised his shield to me as I ran closer. The black raven on the red background gleamed in the sunlight.

'Men!' I bellowed in the loudest voice I could with burning lungs. Running any distance in armour is no joke, especially in that heat. 'I need you to make enough noise to awaken the Allfather in his hall! I need Donar to hear you in the far north. I want him to pause and cup his ear, and know the Ravensworn are roaring their battle cry! Can you do that?'

'Yes!' was the immediate reply.

I slotted into the right wing next to Ruric, taking an offered shield and hauling free my sword. Ruric stood holding a great spear, the shaft longer than him. 'You do know you are quite mad, don't you?' he said with an expression that offered not the slightest bit of humour.

'Oh yes,' I replied, a stupid grin fixed on my face. 'Come on, old friend, admit it. Life would be dull if I wasn't around.' I winked at the men around us, hoping to calm a few nerves.

'That's true, Chief,' Ruric said, 'although it might also be a damn sight longer.' I erupted into laughter, slapping him on the back so hard he nearly fell into the man beside him.

'Cheer up, you miserable old goat. Let's get through this, and I might just find you that nice little farm you've been thinking about.'

There was an eruption of noise from our left flank, who could see further round the bend than us. Birgir came haring across our front line; he wore just a tunic and his feet were bare; he ran as if Hel herself were chasing him. 'They're coming, Lord!' he said in a breathless voice. 'The bastards are coming!'

I took a long, slow breath as I tried to calm my fraying nerves. The unmistakable sound of tramping hobnails could be heard through the trees to my right as five thousand men marched for my blood. I could see the dark smoke smudged against the pale blue sky. They must have quashed the fire quickly, or maybe it had not spread as far as I had hoped.

My men stood ready, blocking the muddy track that passed as a road this side of the Danube. Each captain knew the plan, which should have been passed to each warrior by now. We just had to see it through.

* * *

It took an age for the Fourteenth to attack. They approached us in a column eight men wide. As we watched, each century swung either left or right from the central path, showing their disdain for us by trudging slowly to their allotted position. It was so calm, organised, and not for the first time I wished for the command of a force so disciplined. My men were better than any in our land; they would hold their formation and fight as a unit, to start with at least. But once their blood was up I knew some of them would break ranks and charge. The fighting would become disintegrated, impossible to manage or follow.

Not that the battle would be my problem today.

After what felt like a month but must have been half an hour at most, the Fourteenth were ready for battle. The first cohort of the Fighting Fourteenth were laid out in all their finery. Their segmented cuirasses gleamed in the sunlight, scarlet cloaks billowing in the breeze. A golden eagle stood in their centre; I must admit that even I was momentarily caught up in its splendour. A huge man prowled their front ranks; his feet rumbled the earth like an ice giant from legend, legs thicker than the tallest pine tree, arms thicker than a cow's waist and clenched fists the size of hams.

Well, okay, but he was *big*.

First spear centurion Silus, primus pilus of the Fourteenth legion, barked command after command at his men. His voice carried clearly over the tumult of men readying for war, each command cutting the air like iron. He turned to face our line and I saw the shimmer of his pure blue eyes from a hundred paces. There were not many men I feared in all the nine worlds Yggdrasil holds together; Silus though, was certainly one of them.

A horn sounded from somewhere behind the Roman line and without the slightest sound or protest, each man put his left leg forward as one. There was a rumble in the earth – and in a few of my men's bellies, I'm sure.

They were magnificent as they approached. A solid wall of red shields, standards held high. All you could see of each man was the top of his iron helmet, the straps of his sandals and the tip of his spear. I racked my mind for something – anything to say to my men to boost their courage. I drew a blank.

Fifty paces off and the low rumble of cavalry filled my ears. My men held a narrow front, with woods either side to protect a surprise attack on our flank. Even so, I shuddered just thinking of the carnage the long lances could carve up. 'Shields!' I yelled, finally finding my voice. My men raised their own red shields, showing the Romans nothing but a row of black ravens.

Thirty paces, sweat already blinded me. My left arm shuddered with the weight of my shield, and my sword arm dropped lower, lower. 'Steady now, boys, we know what's coming,' Ruric said, as if commenting on a passing rain cloud. I felt the men around me group closer together, seeking the protection of their neighbour from the hail of iron they were about to receive.

Twenty paces, and across the Roman line the trumpets blared and men got ready to unleash their spears. Pila, the Romans call them. Long shafts of wood topped with deadly iron spikes, fitted to the pole with a long iron shank. They would tear through our shields, rip through our mail and condemn us to die a sad and lonely death, with us screaming for our mothers as our sword brothers fought on around us.

A loud grunt, followed by a slow whistle, and then blissful silence. I stood transfixed as five hundred spears arced through the air towards us. The sky went black; even the carrion birds that circled patiently, waiting to feed before sundown, were gone. It was beautiful, in a funny kind of way, almost like a dance.

BANG! With a wet crunch the spears hit home, finding gaps in the shield wall and tearing my men to pieces. The screams were harrowing. A man to my right took one through the eye. The spear went through his head and exploded from the back of his helmet. Bone and brain matter spattered the side of my face, covering me in blood. Before we had time to recover there was another loud grunt and once more the spears cut through the air.

I remember very little of the battle that followed. The shield walls clashed and for a time there was nothing but the shoving match that decides most battles. I fought next to Ruric in the front rank, who hacked and sliced with a short-handled axe, always probing for an opening. He caught the rim of a shield early on, tore it down and I hacked through the neck of the legionary behind it. I remember taking a blow to the shoulder, then one to the ribs, but because of my sturdy mail I'd only see some bad bruising from them.

For the majority of it I just leaned into my shield, roaring incoherent abuse at the Romans and trying not to get killed. I felt the pressure slacken on my shield and risked a glance over the rim to see my opponent had slipped on some blood. Without hesitation I raised my shield, lunged out underneath it and stabbed the legionary in the groin. His arterial blood was almost black as it swamped the mud underfoot. He collapsed with a scream, convulsing in agony. Within heartbeats there was a new shield against mine as another nameless Roman took his comrade's place in the line. I resumed my position, keeping my head down and waiting for another opening.

'Reckon it's time you were off, Chief,' Ruric said as he hacked with his axe over the top of his shield. 'We'll hold them here.'

I said nothing. Risking a brief look across our line, I saw our men holding their own. We had given no ground, which pleased me. With a nod to Ruric, I gestured for the man behind me to take my place.

I grabbed Birgir by the arm, and in turn summoned the other twenty men who were to accompany me. With barely a backwards glance, we ran from the battle, deep into the woodland that guarded my army's right flank.

21

The quiet in the forest was unsettling after the roar of battle. There was only the echo of the song of iron; distant screams muffled by the density of the trees. We ghosted through the darkened woodland like shadow walkers, our feet light and silent on the earth. For a time I wished Ketill and his men were with me, for there were no better warriors at this kind of work than the Harii. But my men did well. Each man had been chosen for his lightness of foot and his ability with the sword; they were good and loyal men, who would die for me if my plan went south.

Suddenly we were leaving the darkness behind us; the gaps between trees grew greater and the bridge was in sight, and as I had hoped, it was barely guarded. The Fourteenth had trampled across the wooden boards, so intent on the enemy to their front it had not crossed their minds that they could be attacked from the rear.

Eight men lounged around the open gate. One tent party, or *contubernium* as the Romans would call it. None looked in our direction as we streaked from the forest. I had told my men not to make any battle cries, so our silent charge went unchecked till the moment we were upon them. My ribs ached from the blow I had taken, and the second wind I was hoping would come was slow in arriving. I more lumbered than charged into my opponent, who would have dispatched me with ease if he had been looking my way. As it was, he was studying his sandals, his back turned to me. With one clumsy sword stroke beneath the neck guard of his helmet, I almost cut his head off in one blow. Without so much as a grunt he sunk to the earth, his lifeblood pumping from his mangled neck.

As I stood hunched over, panting and trying to ease the stitch in my side, I saw with satisfaction the other seven legionaries had all joined their friend in death. Sucking in a great lungful of air, I set off across the bridge, not waiting to see if my men followed.

It felt strange, running into a Roman fortress. As we arrived on the far bank of the river, we ran across a road paved in stone. It was flat, perfectly laid, and superbly maintained. The whole landscape was different; all around was order. The land either side of the road was partitioned off into perfectly squared sections, each presumably owned by someone different. There was a ludus, a gladiator school set just off from a giant amphitheatre where the slaves would be forced to fight to the death. I grimaced as we passed, thinking of all the free German warriors who had not been lucky enough to die on the battle-field, sold into slavery as a spoil of war and forced to fight their comrades as thousands of greedy Roman bastards cheered on and put money on their favourites. There really was nothing likeable about Rome.

Past the amphitheatre, we raced through the small buildings that surrounded the fortress. The east gate was wide open, not a sentry in sight. I sent a swift prayer to the Trickster, thanking him for watching over me and my daring endeavour.

We crept through the arch of the wooden gate, the walkway high above us casting a deep shadow in the small courtyard. It was deserted, eerie, nothing but the odd gust of wind and the distant bark of a dog.

'Where to, Chief?' Birgir asked in a hushed tone.

For the first time I began to doubt my plan, for I had no real idea where to go myself. 'The Principia,' I said with a shrug. The Principia was the legion's headquarters, where the main administrative offices were to be found. And, I hoped, the answers to my questions.

We darted down the Via Principalis, the main road that ran from east to west. To both sides were lines of identical barrack blocks that were the home of the five thousand legionaries that had signed up to serve for twenty-five years under the eagle. We reached a small open square outside the Principia and still found no one to challenge us.

We crept through the wooden archway and up a small flight of stone stairs. In the shade of the colonnade we could see a small courtyard with plain flagstones sitting void of decoration in a flood of sunlight. 'I don't like it,' muttered one of my men. 'Where are the bastards?'

'Getting killed by the Ravensworn, that's where,' another replied, to a low rumble of laughter.

'Quiet now, lads,' I muttered, an eerie feeling creeping over me. My man was right; where *was* everyone? Surely they hadn't left the place completely unguarded?

We crept down the walkway, the only sound the scuff of our boots on the flagstones. All the doors to our right were closed. I guessed they were offices of some description. One, though, was just held ajar, light flooding in through the long thin crack.

I slithered up to it, as soundless as a snake through long grass. Leaning against the wooden door, I heard the faint mutterings of a man cursing as he slammed shut the wooden frame of a wax tablet. I pressed my eye to the thin line of light, seeing the man for the first time. He was tall, broad and his torso showed the beginnings of someone slowly letting himself run to fat. He had a mop of red hair that became seeded with grey as it trickled down into his beard. He snatched up another tablet as I watched, grunted then threw it onto the growing pile on his desk.

Silently, I drew my sword and used the point of the blade to push open the door. 'Who's there?' came the startled reply from the man within. I stepped in through the pool of light; slow steps, menacing, my booted feet now a loud clap on the cobbles beneath.

'Ave, Roman,' I said in the most unpleasant tone I could muster. 'How are you on this fine summer's day?' I swaggered into the small office, my men filing in behind me.

'Jupiter's cock! What is going on here? Who are you?' the Roman exclaimed as he clambered to his feet. He reached for an imaginary sword on his left hip, then grimaced as his hand struck nothing but the folds of fat bursting from the side of his oversized belly.

'My name, Roman,' I said slowly, teasing the words out, 'is Alaric. Lord of the Ravensworn. And who, pray tell me, might you be?'

I watched in pleasure as the Roman's mouth moved but no sound came out. 'I am Felix, Camp Prefect of the Fourteenth legion. How did you get in here?' he eventually stuttered.

'Through the gate. How else? You appear to be a bit light on men, Prefect. I hope my lads aren't causing your legate too much grief over the river.' I turned to Birgir, a mirthless chuckle in my throat. For a moment I was confused and angry that he hadn't joined in with my merriment, then I realised I had been speaking Latin and he and the rest of my men had no clue what had been said.

'Your men?' Felix asked. He moved towards me, around the side of his small wooden desk. 'Why are you here?'

'Someone is trying to kill me,' I said, not beating around the bush. 'And I want to know who.'

Felix stopped in his tracks. His eyes narrowed and he licked his dry lips. 'You're *that* Alaric?'

'There are others?' I said, raising a sarcastic eyebrow.

'He wants you dead. We have orders to kill you on sight,' Felix said, again fingering an imaginary sword on his hip.

'Who, Prefect? Who wants me dead?' I was desperate to know. I reverberated with the burning desire to find the man who had put a price on my head.

'Th... the senator...' Felix trailed off. His lip quivered and there was a twitch in his neck. Clearly, he was going to be reluctant to give the name up.

'I need a name, Felix. Give me a name and I promise you will live. No one need know I came here today.'

'Mars, give me strength,' Felix muttered. He brought himself up to his full height, thrust out his shoulders and looked down his nose at me, the pose all Roman officers seem to be so good at. 'You shall have to kill me, you barbarian piece of filth. You will get no name from me.'

He meant it, I could see it in his eyes. To betray Rome was unthinkable to a man of his stature and position. He was the Camp Prefect, the highest rank a man could rise to without having the privilege of being born to the cream of society.

'Very well,' I said, raising my sword. I had to kill him. He was going to give me nothing, and I could not let him live and spread word of my appearance on the Roman side of the river, let alone the home of the Fourteenth itself.

Just as I raised the blade for the killing blow, there was a disturbance at the door behind me. A clerk burst through the threshold, a bundle of tablets in his arms. He screamed and sent them flying as he caught sight of the twenty armed barbarians surrounding the prefect.

'Gods above!' he wailed and went to run out the door. One of my men grabbed him by the neck and steered him towards me.

'Well, well, well,' I said with a smirk. 'What do we have here?' The clerk was young, I'd wager not yet twenty, with pockmarks over pale skin and a scruff of light brown hair atop his head. 'Who are you, boy?' I spat at him.

The clerk shivered, writhed in my man's arms and let out a whimper of terror. 'Longinus,' he said. He nearly added 'sir' at the end but stopped himself.

I smiled. Nothing like a shit-scared kid to give you all the information you need. I raised the point of my sword to his neck and pushed just hard enough for a trickle of blood to run down onto his tunic. 'Well met, Longinus. My name is Alaric Hengistson and I'm after some information. Do you think you can help me? If you do, I'll let you live. Don't get any fairer than that,' I said.

'W... what do you want to know?' Longinus asked, his voice quivering like a child's who had lost their mother at the market.

'I want to know the name of the man who is trying to kill me. Frumentarii, you ever heard of them?' Longinus nodded. 'Are any of their people here?' He shook his head. He tried to look down at my sword tip, still resting at the base of his Adam's apple. 'Where?' I asked, my voice an icy whisper.

'There's a villa, a mile or so south of the fortress. That's where their base is—'

'Quiet, boy!' Felix roared. I spun on my heel and whirled my sword in an arc, the flat of the blade landing flat on Felix's nose. He slumped to the ground, crashing into his desk as he fell.

'You were saying?' I said as I turned back to Longinus, trying to appear relaxed when in fact my heart was pumping like I was still in battle.

'A... a mile south of the fortress...' Longinus trailed off, peering around me to look at the unconscious Felix.

'Go on, boy,' I said. I was so close to finding out what I needed, I couldn't let the boy get distracted now.

'On the right of the road, just over a small ridge. There's a big wooden gate. It has white walls and red tiles on the roof. There's a huge water feature as you enter. I've been in there once.' A solitary tear rolled down Longinus' cheek as what I took to be thoughts of his own mortality raced through his mind.

'And the name? Whose villa is it?'

'Tacitus. Publius Cornelius Tacitus.'

22

I did not kill either Felix or Longinus, though I very much felt like it. I figured the Legate of the Fourteenth legion would be pissed off enough as it was when he returned to Carnuntum, without having a dead camp prefect to add to his woes.

I sent my men back north across the river, not wanting them to be caught on Roman territory when the legion marched back across. One man, I thought, would stand a better chance of remaining undetected.

I walked slowly down the cobbles of the Roman road, begrudgingly admiring its fine state of repair, the evenness of footing and the smooth surface of the stone. Damn the Romans to Hel, but is there anything they cannot do? I saw only a few travellers on my stroll, which suited me just fine. I had stolen a dull brown cloak on my way out of Carnuntum. It was plain, ordinary, thin and well worn, the type of cloak any Roman slave would wear. As the gentle slopes to either side gave way to woodland, I hopped behind a tree and removed my sword and armour, burying it deep in the undergrowth. I carved an X on the side of the trunk where my kit was buried with the tip of my sword before burying that too. I paused then, scouring my immediate surroundings, but I saw no one.

Re-joining the road, I walked for perhaps a quarter of an hour before a great wooden gate appeared between the trees on my right. It was maybe ten foot high, certainly too high for me climb, for there were no hand or foot holds on the rough timber. To each side was not a wall but thick hedge, stretching out around the perimeter. I paused at the gate, again keeping a sharp eye on the road. Could this be the building Longinus had been referring to? I judged it roughly a mile from there to Carnuntum but had not seen one of the mile markers the Romans seemed so fond of. Well, I thought, only one way to find out.

The gate was out of bounds, but I managed to fight my way through the hedge to the right of the gate. I cursed the full summer bloom then, wishing it to be the depths of winter and the hedge to be bare and therefore more assailable. I cursed too my lack of weapons, wishing I had kept the long knife I wore tucked into my left boot. No, I thought then, it would be far worse for me if I were caught here armed; at least unarmed I could try and talk my way out of danger.

Finally I wriggled through the last of the biting thorns hidden beneath the fine greenery and fell to the hard ground on the inside of the compound. I lay there for a while, spitting prickles and trying to gauge my surroundings. I was in a huge garden, bigger than I could have credited from the outside. The grass was short and well maintained, and a huge stone water feature rose from the ground directly to my front just as Longinus had told me, hiding my presence from the main building.

The building was all white-washed stone with a sloping, red-tiled roof. I nodded in satisfaction, confident I had found the right place. Looking around, I could see no one, which instead of calming me set my spine tingling. I was walking into the home of a very powerful man, of that I had no doubt. How could there possibly be no guards at the gate, or patrolling the perimeter of the compound? Or maybe there was, I mused, and I had just fallen through their defence at the right time.

That thought spurred me into action and I clambered to my feet, crouching low behind the water feature. Looking past it, I studied the villa: it was single storey, and small square windows dotted the perimeter, their shutters open. I tried to peer through the open shutters into the villa but from such a great distance I saw nothing but shadow. I stayed where I was, studying the main doors. There were two of them that appeared to both open inwards. They were made of solid wood, trimmed with bronze, and I had no way of approaching without revealing myself to whoever was inside those open windows. There was of course a good chance I could reach the doors unobserved, but on the other hand, I could be mobbed by armed guards halfway to the villa.

Still I did not move, my indecision rooting me to the spot. There is nothing worse than a leader of men who is indecisive at key moments in a battle; he leaves his men vulnerable, gets them killed.

Casting my doubts aside, I rose just as the doors swung open. With a shudder of fear, I leapt back behind the water feature and curled into a ball. There was no way I had not been seen, surely? Sometimes you get a feeling that the gods are with you. Hiding behind that water feature, letting the gentle sound of the trickling water sooth my throbbing heart, I knew the Sly One still had my back.

Two men, both armed and armoured, strolled past me down the main pathway that led from the main gate to the great double doors. They paused briefly at the gate, one man sliding the locking bolt from a small door built into the gate itself and holding it open for his comrade to pass through before following after. I heard snippets of their muted conversation but could not quite make out the Latin over the gentle tinkle of the water. Once I had heard the locking bolt slide back into place on the small wooden door, I peered back towards the villa. The great doors had been left ajar. Clearly, the two men were not planning on being gone for long. If I was to enter, I had to act now.

A short sprint brought me to the door and I crept through, closing it behind me. Looking around, I found myself in a dark but spacious reception room, or 'vestibule' as the Romans call it. It was void of decoration, with brown tiles on the floor and bare plaster on the walls. I had always thought the upper classes of Rome spent lavishly on decorations for their homes, just so they could show it off at banquets with their fellow rich citizens – clearly the master of this villa possessed no such vanity. I crept through, seeing and hearing no one. I passed through another set of double doors into a light and airy atrium. Above me was a sloping ceiling, angled down until it ended with a small square hole, directly above a shallow pool. It was called a *compluvium,* I knew, and the small pool was known as an *impluvium.* The water that fell from the sloping ceiling and drained through the pool would be transported through an assortment of underground pipes before ending in a giant cistern, which would be situated above a roaring fire, somewhere in the slave quarters. Steam that rose from the cistern would be transported back underground through more pipes for underfloor heating in certain rooms, and the heated water would be for the master's bath. But who was the master? Who was this Tacitus? And what did he want with me?

I strolled through the atrium, admiring the detailed mosaics on the floor and the paintings that adorned the walls, all appearing to glorify some long-dead Roman general. I found myself looking out onto a small courtyard dotted with fruit trees; another striking water feature was the centrepiece. Turning right, I strolled down the shaded colonnade, trying to appear as if I belonged. My stolen cloak covered my face and was so long it concealed my long leather boots. I wondered if I should have stolen myself some leather sandals, for I feared the boots would give me away, but it was too late now. Peering from beneath my hood, I saw all the doors that surrounded the courtyard were closed, bar one.

The door directly to my front sat ajar, and instinctively I made towards it. I paused at the threshold, once more turning to survey the courtyard, but there was nothing but silence. Turning back, I gently pushed open the door and walked into a darkened library, lit by nothing but two huge candles as thick as my arm that sat atop silver stands. Shelves of scrolls lined every wall, breaking only to leave a gap for a small shuttered window. A rectangular desk sat in the left corner, an ageing man sitting behind it hunched over a scroll of parchment. One of the candles flickered as I closed the door behind me, and the man looked up with a start.

'Who are you?' the man croaked. It was the voice of a man who had not spoken that day. Phlegm caught in his throat and his words came out in a rasp. He coughed.

'Alaric Hengistson, at your service,' I said as I stepped further into the room.

'Oh,' the old man rasped. There was not the shock or fear I had expected, just mild curiosity in his dry, narrow eyes. 'You do, I presume, know who I am?' he said as he rose shakily to his feet. Despite myself, I had to fight the urge to approach him and give him my arm to lean on.

'Publius Cornelius Tacitus,' I said.

The old man nodded, taking an uncertain step towards me. He moved further into the flickering light of the candles and for the first time I saw him properly. He was old, that was for sure. I would have wagered he had seen more years than any one man had the right to see. His head was bald save for a few lank grey hairs that wisped from his scalp. His narrow eyes surrounded a long and strong Roman nose. 'You know my name, but do you know who I am?'

I shrugged, not wanting to let on how much I did not know about him. I had nothing but a name, and I had killed a lot of men just to get that. I was not going to let all that work go to waste now. 'I am indeed Publius Cornelius Tacitus, and I am a senator of Rome.' I nodded at that, for surely only a man who possessed as much power as a senator could have caused me the trouble I had been through. 'Not that I have seen the floor of the senate house in many years,' Tacitus said with a sad smile. 'There was once a time that I dined with emperors, had their ear and was able to influence the direction of our great empire. Alas, those days are long gone.'

'Why do you want me dead so badly?' I was not interested in the ramblings of an old man; I had not come this far to listen to his tales of youth.

Tacitus laughed; it was a dry laugh that caused him to erupt into a coughing fit, which at one point I thought would finish him off. 'Straight to the point, eh? I like that. But then you Germans never did hold much stock in intellectual conversation.'

'Known many of my people, have you?' I asked with a scoff. I did not think it likely that a high-born senator would have had much doing with us 'barbarians', as they were so fond of calling us.

'I have indeed, Alaric, I have indeed. You know I once wrote a whole book on Germania and her people? Fascinating.'

I paused, unsure whether the old man was either mocking me or just buying time. I thought then of the two men who had left via the gate. How much time did I have? 'Why,' I said again, 'do you want me dead so badly?'

'Very well,' Tacitus said, holding up a hand in defeat, 'I shall tell you what you want to know, although you will not like what I have to say. I am just sorry I will not be there to see your downfall, Alaric, for I feel it will be a story all of its own.'

He padded past me on soft feet to a small side table in the opposite corner of the room. He poured himself a small cup of wine without offering any to me, and then reached into his robe and produced a small leather bottle that hung from a length of string around his neck. He opened the bottle and poured its contents into his wine. 'The things you have to do when you reach my age,' he said, motioning to the cup. 'Anyway, where exactly would you like me to start?'

'At the beginning,' I said. Tacitus moved back past me and returned to his seat behind his desk.

'Very well, young man. I am a senator of Rome, as I have already mentioned. I once sat at the side of the great Trajan, although my first consulship was during the short reign of Nerva. I married the daughter of the great Julius Agricola, the conqueror of Britannia, and held a proconsular rank myself as Governor of Asia. But it is as a writer and an orator that I have carved my fame. Go to Rome, ask anyone who sits on benches of the senate; they will tell you they know me. Alas, that now all seems to be in the past. Now I am nothing more than a puppet master, trying to keep the *Pax Romana* alive across our northern border.

'I control the frumentarii agents that operate in Germania,

and have done for some ten years now. From here I read their reports and proposals, naming a king here, changing a chief there, all to keep the tribes focused on each other, and not on rebellion, of course.'

I scowled at this and made to speak, but Tacitus shut me off with a raised hand.

'You knew very well the game we play, Alaric, let us not pretend otherwise. It is a game that was begun long before we were both born, and it will still be being played when we are nothing but dust. Now, in recent years I have been receiving more and more concerning reports about a man thwarting our plans. We place a new chief in a tribe, a week passes and that chief is killed, his tribe swallowed by another. We pitch two tribes against each other in war, and instead of destroying each other, one tribe wipes out the other and becomes stronger. I could name more examples: cattle raids, raids against the empire herself, but I fear we would be here all day if I did. And do you know, Alaric, all these disturbing reports, all brought in by different agents, do you know who they all lead to?'

'Me,' I said with a savage grin.

'You. You and your Ravensworn, as you like to call them, are a constant thorn in our side. Your meddling allows certain tribes to grow stronger, get bigger. Rome cannot allow one tribe to get too big, too powerful. It could undermine everything we have achieved thus far. You understand why, I presume?'

I shrugged. 'You let one tribe get so strong it engulfs the others, then before you know it you have another empire in the making knocking on your door. As it stands all you have is a collection of individuals that all hate each other as much as they hate you. Only if the tribes unite can they pose a real threat to Rome.'

'Precisely, dear Alaric, spot on. Now can you see how your

meddling has caused us a few issues over the years? Why, just look at the Marcomanni and the Quadi and how powerful they have become. You had no small part to play in that.'

I shrugged again. 'I work for whoever pays the most,' I said. 'Never concerned myself too much with the outcome.'

Tacitus chuckled and swirled his wine cup. 'I do like an honest man. Now, up to about this time last year we were prepared to leave you be; you do, after all, only command five hundred men and therefore pose no real threat to the empire itself. But we were approached by someone, someone you know, someone close to you, and asked if we could assist in bringing about your downfall. It was an interesting proposition, one I was not prepared to let go.'

'Who?' I asked urgently. Someone close to me? 'Who was it?'

Tacitus did not reply at first, he just smiled and drained his cup in one. 'Now, that is the question,' he said, wincing as the wine regurgitated on him. 'Someone long forgotten, someone who shares your blood. She will be your doom, Alaric, not I, not Rome.'

I wanted to grab him then and shake him till he stopped his riddles and gave me the answers I so badly needed. But I never had the chance. I realised all too late that the small leather bottle Tacitus had emptied into his wine must have been poison, as the old man spewed vomit over the flagstones and fell to the floor in a heap. He shuddered for a short while, writhing, white foam bubbling at the corners of his mouth.

And then he passed from this world.

23

I walk through a small town. Children dart around my knees, entangled in a frantic game of tag. The smell of fish oil is strong on my nostrils, causing a burning sensation as the rank smell invades my senses. I can taste it on my tongue, its presence so strong on the air it makes my eyes burn. I blink back tears and try not to think of the lake by my father's farm, the one he had thrust me in and watched as I writhed and flapped in the endless blue. I used to love fish as a child, but since that horrid day anything to do with water just brings back the pain of betrayal I felt as I slowly drowned, sinking into the silent depth of my doom.

It was autumn when I left, and now the first signs of spring are in the air. It had been a tough winter. Scrounging and stealing food, sneaking into barns after nightfall and praying to the gods the owner didn't appear at the threshold with a drawn blade and send me on my way.

Every morning I started with the resolve that this day would make me stronger. Each night I lay on a cold hard bed and cry for the loss of a mother taken before her time. I wondered how my father was, if he had been able to survive a lonely winter without the comfort of his wife or only son to keep his hearth roaring and stomach full. Thoughts of him turn my mood to ash; my eyes harden and my resolve doubles. Whatever the fates have in store for me, I will not go grovelling back to that bastard. I will not set foot on that lonely farm and admit I was wrong, that I am too weak to survive on my own. He is dead to me.

There is a commotion to my front, people streaming past me, forming a giant crowd on the edge of something I cannot see. More people rush past, their breath steaming the air with their excited gasps and shouts. I push forwards, barging my way through the throng. I am forced to a standstill and result to craning my neck over the bobbing heads, trying to catch a glimpse of what has caused the excitement.

I see nothing, but the people at the front of the crowd appear to be looking down. I stare around in confusion. Atop the streets of mud and debris, there is a collection of huts. Up the top of the hill to my right is a great hall; they say that is where the king lives. The Marcomanni are a big tribe, and their king rules over a great swathe of land on the Danube border with Rome. All winter it had taken me to get here; I was disappointed to find it was not what I expected. Where were the great buildings, the flagstone roads and high-walled towns they talked of in the north? The tribes on the shores of the great grey sea talked of the Marcomanni as if they are legends of old. A tribe taking the fight to Rome, standing their ground and even forcing the emperor to pay them off with chests of silver. I see no evidence of such wealth. When I look back to the front, the crowd has begun to disperse. I move forwards, squinting my eyes in my eagerness to catch a first glimpse of whatever has gripped the population.

A pit. At least eight feet in depth, four mud walls forming a near-perfect square. There are two men within: one standing, drinking greedily from a jug of ale. The other is dead. My eyes widen as I take in the spectacle; two men are in a pit, and they have just fought to the death.

The victor is a big man, young, looks to be about my own age. He has a great mane of red hair and a bushy beard clotted with blood. His eyes are dark and ferocious, his nose wide and flat. The man on the floor is bigger still, broad and powerful. At least, he was. There is a gaping hole in his stomach, half his guts splattered on the floor. Blood still oozes from the horrific wound, thick and black like a snake slithering from a dark cave. I stare in awe and disgust. Why would two men choose to do this? What possible purpose could there have been? I am no coward, not like my bastard of a father. But when I choose to fight, it will be for honour, for glory. Not for coin or the enjoyment of a town of bloodthirsty peasants.

'Balomar, hey, blacksmith, you hear me?' The red-haired man looks up, ale dripping down his beard. 'Here's your winnings, low life.' The speaker throws a small bag into the pit. It chinks as it hits the floor. 'The king says you are to fight again tomorrow, and not to win so quickly this time. You're meant to be the entertainment; ain't no one entertained by a fight that's over before it's got started.' And with that, the speaker walks off, lost in the crowd.

The man named Balomar bends down and picks up the small bag, weighing it in his palm. I am still watching him when his head jerks up and his dark eyes pour into mine. There is a challenge there, visceral and violent. I snap my own away so as to avoid any confrontation. They are drawn to the body on the ground, the giant death wound in the torso. I look into the dead man's face, trying to get a measure of the man he was. I nearly yelp when his eyes snap open and his lips mouth the word 'Help.'

* * *

With the deed done, I crossed the river by paying a fisherman for use of his boat with the money I had taken from Tacitus' purse – I figured he would have no more need of it – and went in search of my men. It felt an age since I had left them on the battlefield valiantly holding off wave after wave of Roman attacks. I met Ruric at the edge of a thick forest. We clasped arms and as I went to move back from the embrace, his grip tightened on my wrist. 'We lost men, Alaric. A lot of men.'

He let go and as I stepped back, I saw the pain in his eyes. He hated me. Right then, in the shade of those trees, he hated me for the loss of those men. For the pain they went through as they hunched behind their shields and stood against the inexorable tide of the Fourteenth legion. A twang of guilt hit my heart like a spear point. Ruric had been with me since the beginning. I had been nothing when I met him, just a lone traveller wandering the land. I fought the odd battle in the pits the tribes make. Men made wagers on me losing; I could hear them jest and laugh as they pointed, wondering how many rounds I would last till I was speared in the guts or lacerated with a blade. I proved them all wrong, every single one of them.

It had been Ruric who had first sworn his loyalty to me, Ruric who had installed the belief in me that I could change the fate the Norns had woven and lead men into battle. I saw the fire in his eyes then, streaks of red where there should have been white. Some wounds men take to the body, others they take to their soul. I had wounded Ruric, a wound that could not be cured by any surgeon from Rome or any priest from the sacred groves in Germania. I had betrayed him, betrayed my men, just to get my vengeance.

'What happened?' I asked in a small voice.

Ruric hung his head and shook it from side to side. He had a great bruise on his crown, visible through his thinning hair.

'They broke through,' he said. He sighed; tears welled and then his breath came in shuddering gasps as he fought to hold the tears back. 'They broke through,' he repeated. 'It was carnage. Murder. Horrible.' After some probing I learnt the second cohort had succeeded where the first had failed and forced a hole in the centre of our line. Adalhard's Hundred had fought valiantly, according to Ruric. Wave after wave of attack they had beat off, but it had been Adalhard himself who had caused their downfall. 'He fell for the feint,' Ruric said. His voice had steadied now. 'The second retreated, appearing to be in disarray. You know the old trick – pretend to run away, then when your enemy break ranks form back up and charge them. They formed a wedge, a boar's snout as we would call it. It tore our men to shreds.'

I could picture it, clear as I could see Ruric's slumping form in front of my eyes. Adalhard whirling his sword above his head, screaming his battle cry as he saw his enemy falter and stagger from him. His men, their blood up, joining in with the frenzy and leaving the safety of the shield wall for an all-out charge. Oh, the glory, the glee of seeing the backs of your foe. I could see the triumphant glint in Adalhard's eye as he charged. His eyes lit up with the silver his battle fame would inevitably gain him. I could picture his smug face as he stood before me and regaled the tale of his heroism, his gallantry in battle. How his men would have cheered when I honoured their captain. 'Who else will lead us when old Alaric is gone?' they would say over the rim of their cups. Surely the Gods had blessed them to be serving in the great Adalhard's Hundred?

'He dead?' I asked in a gruff voice. Ruric nodded; he clearly did not have the words to reply. I clasped Ruric's shoulder, gripping it tight. 'It's not your fault, old friend,' I said, lowering myself so my eyes were level with his. He was sitting now, hugging his knees.

With a start he rose to his feet, throwing my hand from his. 'Is that what you think is wrong with me?' he roared, as ferocious as any lion in the amphitheatres across the empire. 'You think I blame myself for his death, his and so many others?'

I took an involuntary step back, for Ruric was a dangerous man. I am skilled with a sword, a deadly foe in combat. But I would not choose to cross blades with Ruric, no matter how old he had become.

'If Adalhard broke ranks then the blame lies with him,' I said. I hated the defensive tone I used.

'The blame lies with you, Alaric!' Ruric roared in my face. 'You! You who left us on the battlefield, you who abandoned your men to their deaths so you could scamper off and seek some sort of petty vengeance. Those were your men, not Adalhard's, yours. They fight for you, take your coin and swear their loyalty to you.' He stopped, his chest heaving. It seemed he had run out of anger, or was at least too exhausted to carry on.

'How many men did we lose?' I asked in a shamed whisper.

'One hundred and twenty,' Ruric spat. 'You lost one hundred and twenty.'

I felt a great weight come crashing down on me as the force of the truth Ruric spoke struck me true. When had I become so blind, so selfish? For years I had known men followed me because they knew I was one of them. Come from nothing, born to no king or war chief. A new resolve washed over me. Never again will I put my interests above those of the Ravensworn. Never again will I leave my men to the iron storm whilst I scamper away and see to my own ends. I would change, become the leader they deserved.

I staggered away from the shadows, into the glorious light of the summer sun. It did nothing to rid the chill that ran down my spine, or stop my shaking hands. I slumped to the ground, thoughts of my long-lost mother filing my mind. She would be so ashamed, embarrassed, to see the man I had become. My father would have understood, and that thought just enraged me all the more.

A commotion stirred me from my dark thoughts. There was the thud of hoofbeats and the clinking of armour as a man rode up to me. Turning, I saw he wore the colours of the Suebi, and his long hair was tied in a topknot as was their fashion. 'Lord Alaric,' he said as he dismounted without ceremony. 'I come bearing dark tidings.' *Dark tidings?* I thought, surely things could not possibly get any worse.

'Speak your message,' I said.

'Warin has murdered King Agnarr and claimed the throne of the Suebi. He has captured your wife and put a ransom on your head. People say he is colluding with Rome.'

Your doom will come not from Rome, Alaric of the Ravensworn. But from where you least expect it. Tacitus' words ran through me. The shiver in my back turned to stone-cold ice.

'Saxa? My son?' I asked, not wanting to hear the answer.

'Alive and well, when I left. There are men in the Suebi who would fight for you, Lord. They have no loyalty to this Warin, see him for the *nithing* he is.' I nodded, trying to regain my composure.

'You come from these men?'

'I do. I also send greetings from Chief Ketill of the Harii, who is still camped nearby with his men. He urges you to come north with all haste. With luck, we may be in time to save your wife and children.'

I turned from the messenger, looking over the faces of my men who had gathered to hear the news. The fierce expressions

I had seen when I first met with them earlier had evaporated with the morning dew. There was a softness there now, sympathy mixed with resolve. They would follow me, I knew it in my bones. I thought there no serious danger to Saxa, who was Warin's sister, after all. But my son could be seen as expendable by the new king of the Suebi. And then something occurred to me. 'Children. You said children?'

'Why, yes, Lord,' the messenger said, his eyebrows raised. 'Your wife, Lord, the Lady Saxa, is pregnant.'

24

I was a whirlwind of emotion as we rode north at the gallop. *Why, yes, Lord. Your wife, the Lady Saxa, is pregnant.* I could not get my head around it. She had only just given birth to Ludwig; how could she possibly be with child again? Just once we had lain together as man and wife since the birth; it had been brief, and painful for her. Dark thoughts swirled within me, growing with every thump of Hilde's hooves on the turf. Could the child really be mine? Had Saxa been disloyal whilst I had been away in the south? I thought of my wife then, the timid child I still thought her as. I couldn't bring myself to believe she would have summoned the courage to stray. Not to mention the ring of armed men who would have been surrounding her day and night. I had left twenty men to guard her and the child, so surely if one of them had thought she'd played me false they would have sent word.

I felt rather than saw Ruric approach my flank. My face was a mask of iron. All thoughts I'd had when returning to my men of my selfishness and my newfound resolve to be better had vanished like morning mist. I knew I would throw more of my men's lives away if I had to, that there was nothing I would not do to see my wife and child safe, and to have Warin's head on the end of my spear. Deep down, I would never change. It wasn't down to any great love of my wife that drove me north faster than a winter gale. It was pride and stubbornness.

How *dare* Warin make a move against *me*. Who did the snivelling little bastard think he was? Even with his father's support, did he really think he could get the better of *me*? I was Alaric, Lord of War. Battle-turner, Loki-cunning; there was no man or army in this land that could bring me low. I was invincible; Donar rode at my shoulder. When I entered the arena of death, men's courage deserted them; they prayed to their gods and begged for their mothers even as I ripped the guts from their bellies. Men knew me, and men feared me. Warin would die; I would be king. Of that there was no doubt.

'I don't like that look in your eye,' Ruric said, rubbing a hand through his bristly white beard.

'They have to die, Ruric. You know that,' I said, not turning my eyes to meet his. I knew I would not like what I would see there.

'I know, lad. I know.' It had been some years since Ruric had called me 'lad'. For some reason it made me feel like a pup again, listening to one of his lectures when I had done something he thought 'improper'. He soon stopped bothering with those. 'But do more of our men need to die too?'

The silence dragged on as I thought of a suitable answer. How could I possibly justify throwing my men back into battle, after what they had just been through? 'If it comes to it,' was all I said. I was in no mood for conversation. 'There is somewhere we must stop on the way,' I said, this time turning in the saddle to face Ruric. 'There's someone who is long overdue a visit from the Ravensworn.' Ruric grinned as he saw me fiddle with the golden torc at my neck, showing me the stumps of his teeth.

* * *

I probably did not look as impressive as I did the first time I rode into the lands of the Fenni. I still rode Hilde, my fine horse, but she was dry mouthed and half lamed from our fast ride north across Germania. I wore still my fine blue cloak, though it was covered in dust and dirt. I was without a helmet, which I had discarded when the beads of sweat running down my head had turned into a torrent. My hair was wild, my beard unkempt; my skin was sunburnt and wind lashed, and my hands were as chapped as my lips.

The village was much as I remembered it. The same brown mud huts, sitting squat in the marshland in the same disorder they had been the previous year. The same half-starved children ran between our mounts' legs, cheering and whooping to see such an army enter their inconsequential village. They would not be so happy when I was done.

I dismounted Hilde and stalked through the huts. The repugnant smell of shit mixed with putrid meat filled my nostrils and almost made me gag. I scowled at the pale, skeletal men who backed away from me, creeping into their hovels, hoping to hide until I was gone. Cowards. *Nithings*. I reached the centre of the village and drew my sword, standing stock still, waiting for the man I had come to kill.

'Lord Alaric,' a small voice said from behind me. I spun on my heels to come face to face with Wulfric, chief of that worthless tribe. 'How... how good to see you again, Lord,' he said, bowing his head.

Gods, but that man really was pathetic. There he was, the

chief of an actual tribe. And there was me: the outlaw. Chief of a tribe that didn't exist. A warband of cutthroats and thieves, oath-breakers and life takers. Wulfric had every right to show his outrage at my impudence, baring a blade in the centre of his own village. He just lacked the courage, even then at the end.

'You know why I'm here?' I said. It was not really a question; we both knew it.

'Y... yes, Lord.'

'Why?' I asked. That really was a question.

'Lord?'

'Why did you sell me out to the Romans? I had no quarrel with you, or your people. Don't tell me it was just for gold?'

He paused, did Wulfric. His lips moved, as if he was trying to shape the words, before he finally let them out. 'She made me, Lord. Said she would wipe the Fenni from history if I didn't comply. I didn't want to, Lord, I swear. But my people, I couldn't protect them from her.'

Her? That was unexpected.

'And you think you can protect them from me?' I spat. I had moved closer to him, our faces just a hand's width apart.

'No, Lord,' he said, sobbing.

I sighed, a hint of sympathy creeping through me for Wulfric, for clearly he had been put in an impossible situation. 'Who is she?' I asked. 'Who has been collaborating with Rome to see me dead?' The words of Tacitus sped back through my mind. He had mentioned a woman, and something about sharing my blood; I had not made much of it at the time. *She will be the end of you*, he had said. What else had he told me? It all felt so long ago now, not the couple of weeks it had actually been.

'You really don't know?' he asked me, his expression almost mocking. 'Half the tribes are talking about her.'

'Talking about *who*?' I bellowed, spittle flying from my mouth to spray his face. I was raging, confused and vulnerable. Not my favourite emotions.

'Why, Ishild of course.'

I stood, dumbstruck. *Ishild? My Ishild?* The woman who haunted my dreams? Strong willed, luscious curves, eyes bluer than the deepest ocean. Ishild. She was plotting to have me killed, this whole time.

I have only a vague memory of my sword licking out and carving into Wulfric's skull. Vaguer still is the memory of Ruric and Baldric hauling me to the ground as I howled in rage and slaughtered every member of the Fenni I could get within sword's reach. Men, women, children; I killed them all.

The only thing I can truly remember is the curse. Wulfric's wife, standing over the bloody corpse of her husband, arcing her fingers into claws and calling on the Gods to witness her words. She spat and put her thumb to her forehead, before speaking again: 'I curse you, Alaric, son of Hengist. I curse you before all the Gods. May you never rise to the heights you desire; may your men all be slaughtered at the hands of your enemies. But may you live, Alaric. May you live long into your winter years, your heart void of joy and filled with bitterness and regret.

'Your death will come many years after that of the dogs that serve you; the son of your greatest foe will be the one to strike the telling blow. With the Norns as my witnesses, this shall be your fate.'

25

The rest of the journey north was made mainly in silence. My men had watched in horror as I had butchered a dozen or more innocent people then been the recipient of a foul curse. I remember regretting that I hadn't killed the old crone whilst she was in full flow, but I had never paid much heed to witches and curses and was therefore quite nonchalant about the whole thing.

Men though, they are superstitious. Particularly poor men who come from nothing and have no education or clue as to how the world works. They simply find a lord and follow his orders. Gods, I could never be such a man. I did, however, have three hundred and fifty men at my back, all who came from nothing, all who lacked any form of education – or common sense, for that matter – and they were superstitious, very superstitious.

I could hear the whispers all around me. I rode in the centre of our marching column, trying and failing to appear happy and cheery to the men within earshot. They gave me guarded looks; put their thumb to their eye and spat in the hope it would keep off the curse that had befallen me. I worried, in those days as we passed through the empty countryside, whether they would still follow me into battle. I had more need of those men then, than I had ever had before. Would they still have the courage to fulfil their oaths to their lord? Either way, I was about to find out.

It was Birgir who spotted the figures in the thick forest that lay on our route. He came galloping down the column, his skinny backside bouncing up and down in the leather saddle. 'Warin's men, Lord, in the trees up ahead.' He panted as he brought his horse alongside Hilde, who nipped at the beast when its head got too close to hers. I pulled on the reins, not wanting to create any distance between myself and Birgir and run the risk of men overhearing our conversation. 'How many?' I asked.

'Couldn't tell, Lord. There is a narrow track that leads into the forest. I saw men in cloaks with their hair in topknots on either side. They seemed to be shouting at more men deeper under the canopy, but it was too dark in there for me to make out anyone.'

I nodded, visualising it in my head. 'Good work, Birgir, as always.' The young scout beamed, showing me a set of crooked yellow teeth. 'A good place for an ambush, no?'

'Perfect, Lord. There are banks either side of the track, so although they would have the advantage of both surprise and height, we would be packed so tight together their spears could hardly miss.' I noted with pride that Birgir showed no signs of fear or anxiety as he spoke. He was just a pup, and yet he would gladly die if I ordered him to. Maybe not all was lost. Birgir brought back memories of a lad, Hafdan, who had served me early on in my quest to become the greatest warlord outside the empire. He had been a quiet boy, of no great height or breadth. Ordinary looking, would easily mix in with a crowd. But that had been his great advantage. Never before or since had I had a better scout or spy. The information that lad had brought me had been the main reason my wild venture as an outlaw had been so successful.

'Are you okay, Lord?' Birgir asked, growing anxious at my ongoing silence.

I smiled across to him, a sad smile that didn't reach my eyes. 'Fine, Birgir, fine. Just remembering, is all. We shall set up camp for the night, let those curs wait a day for their carefully laid ambush. Send word to Ruric, will you?' With a nod, the young scout rode off. I slowed Hilde then, steering her off the road to watch the endless file of warriors ride pass.

So much blood. Was it all worth it?

* * *

'This is a fight to first blood. The victor shall receive this bag of gold,' the herald says as he raises a small leather pouch that chinks as he lowers it back down. 'Each warrior will be armed with just a sword. There is no time limit; the fight will end on my signal. Begin!'

I take a deep breath and close my eyes, picturing the beautiful face of my mother as I try to calm my fraying nerves. My opponent moves forward, raising his sword above his head and roaring a battle cry. The crowd cheers. I hear wagers being made and all of them are on how long it will take this brute to best me. He is the champion and on home turf in front of a crowd of his own people. I am a stranger, an unknown quantity. My opponent is both taller and broader than me; he swings his longsword like it weighs no more than one of those vine sticks Roman centurions use to beat their men into line.

I bring my own blade up and kiss it for luck; the feel of the newly wrapped black leather on the hilt brings me comfort. A black sword for a black soul, that is what the tanner had said when I had paid him with the last of my coin for his work. My blade is heavy, cumbersome, and would be the downfall of a weaker man. But I am not weak. I am hardened by training, my muscles toned and responsive. I may not have experience in the dance of death, but I am more than ready to prove to the Allfather that when my time on middle earth is done I am worthy of a seat in his hall. The big man moves towards me and my father's voice rings in my ears: 'Don't watch the blade, boy, watch the eyes. The eyes tell you where the blade is about to strike. Watch the eyes, and you have half a chance. Watch the blade, and you're already dead.'

Those eyes are as dark as the bottomless pit in which I stand. The winter has been harsh and the brown puddles that lie beneath my feet are sheeted with ice. I know this fight is as much about footwork as it is about swordplay. Still, my opponent strides towards me. He really is huge, fearsome; the wolf among the sheep.

With a savage scream, he whips the great sword behind his head and sends it spiralling towards my own. I keep my eyes on his and bring my blade up to meet his savage strike. With a loud snap and clang, the blades kiss and sparks fly through the winter mist. I am forced to my knees with my sword still above my head. With all the grace of a twelve-year-old girl dancing around her mother's skirts, the big man pirouettes on his left foot and leaps from the ground, this time his blade coming in a sweeping arc from low to high. Just in time, I lower my own and once more there is a flash of fire.

He steps back, does the big man, and I am grateful. The two blocks have taken my first wind, and I feel my wrist going limp and my sword getting heavier with every ragged breath. Once more, his dark eyes meet mine. I feel them weighing me, judging my mettle. With a howl of rage and a spark of courage I hadn't known I possessed, I leap to my feet and charge him. A frantic blow to his left then I try to use the momentum of his blade grating on mine to spring the point to the side of his head. There is a low whistle as the blade slices the air and cuts a few stray hairs from his unruly red beard. 'Clever,' the big man grunts as he regains his composure, shrugging off the near miss and rolling his shoulders.

There is no way I can beat this man, I think as I step back carefully, not wanting to slip on ice but also not wanting to let my eyes stray from his. He is too quick, too strong, too talented. I send the Allfather a swift prayer of thanks that this fight is only to first blood; I will not die with my guts spilling from a great wound in my belly, as that warrior had when I had first set foot in Goridorgis. Gods, could I have really been here a year already?

My mind is wandering and once more the big man is on the move. He lets his blade fly in a flat trajectory from right to left, but I have been watching his eyes. He has seen my blade slip from my slack grip, seen my numb wrist struggle with the great weight of the iron. He thinks me weak, tired, beaten. As the sword scythes through the air towards me, I keep my eyes on his. They flick from his blade to my head, and I know where he plans to land his blow. At the precise moment his blade is a whisker from my left ear – so close I can almost feel it piercing my reddening skin and breaking my skull like an egg – I duck and roll towards him. Into the frozen mud my head goes. There is a blinding flash of grey light as I look directly into the dull sky, and then my blade is to my front and I slash it across the big man's calf.

I stay there, on my knees, panting like a dog. I dare not move, or breathe in anything more than a shallow gasp. Silence hangs in the air; the crowd are no longer cheering; no more wagers are being made in loud voices from either side of the death pit. With a huge sense of relief mixed with pride, I see a shallow cut on the big man's calf; the tip of my blade is dark with blood.

I have won.

26

The night was pitch black as I slithered like a snake on my belly, creeping painfully slowly towards the canopy of trees up ahead. I had Birgir and Gerulf with me; the former for his speed and owl-like eyes, the latter for his cool head in a hot mess. I could have brought Ruric along for the jaunt, but I worried the grey-beard would alert the enemy scouts with his creaking joints and cracking knees. Baldo would have suggested a headlong charge at first sight of the enemy; Adalhard was slain and Otto, well, I still did not know enough about him yet.

So, there we were, guided by nothing more than a shrouded moon, edging our way across the open plain, our destination seemingly getting further away rather than closer. I had a plan, or the beginnings of one, but I needed to see the enemy for myself, get a feel for their numbers and positions before I would divulge any more to my captains.

'Wotan's crusty beard,' Gerulf groaned as I signalled the halt once more, 'the sun will be up by the time we get there!' He lay flat on his belly and stretched his aching arms above his head. His neck gave a loud crack as he rolled his head from side to side. If we were not fifty or so yards from a forest full of spears, I would have slapped him on his bald head.

'Quiet,' I hissed, trying to give him my meanest stare, before realising he wouldn't actually be able to appreciate it in the darkness. 'Birgir,' I hissed, 'see anything?'

'Nothing,' the scout said.

'Lot of good you are,' I harrumphed. I wore no helmet and thought I would be safer with my dark hair and face masked in mud, so I raised my head ever so slowly and paused there, my eyes scrunched shut. Ketill had taught me that, along with many other valuable lessons when we were young men. I counted slowly to thirty, then opened my eyes and found with satisfaction they had adjusted to the darkness. I could make out the tree trunks under the canopy now; black figures moved slowly beneath them. I counted up to ten.

'Bollocks,' I muttered.

'What is it?' Gerulf asked in a tense voice. He sounded as though he was desperately trying to hold in a full bladder.

'Donar's pissing hammer, Gerulf,' I snapped in a voice too loud. 'Just piss if you need to, there's no shame in it.' On more than once occasion over the years I had experienced the unpleasant warm sensation of my own urine soaking my trousers and running up my belly. I had once spent an entire night spying on a Roman patrol, with nothing but a couple of stolen wineskins for company. It had not been long until I had deeply regretted downing the both of them.

'Oh, I need to go all right,' Gerulf said with a resigned chuckle. 'But it's not that end that's causing me grief.'

To my left I heard Birgir gasp as he struggled to contain the spasming belly laugh that had taken control of his body and wits. I let out a low chuckle myself. 'On second thoughts, Gerulf, put a cork in it.' Birgir was visibly struggling now, his whole body contorted in mirth. I counted my heartbeats and reached twenty by the time he had calmed down. I was about to raise my head again when a foul smell, pungent like a dead soldier with open bowels whose body has been left to rot in the summer sun, invaded my nostrils, and it was all I could do not to vomit.

'Sorry, Chief,' Gerulf said, and even through the darkness I could see the colour rise on his cheeks.

'What in the name of the gods did you ea—'

'Movement, Lord,' Birgir said, cutting me off. Once more, I braved raising my head and saw for myself a clutch of men holding flame torches, marching together from the safety of the forest, heading right towards us.

'They've made you,' a voice said to my right.

'I think you may be right,' I mumbled, mind racing, seeking a way out.

'I reckon it was you farting that did it. A fart that smells that bad must have gone off like a thunderclap when it shot from your arse. Didn't leave a stain, did it?'

To Hel with the warriors marching out to kill me where I lay. Fuck Warin and his scheming wife, sitting pretty in their hall in the north, waiting for me to hurry on to the ends of their spears. No man, let alone *my* man, spoke to me like that and kept his life. I was about to turn and strike Gerulf right in his round bald head, and then I realised it wasn't he who had spoken...

'How in all the nine worlds did you get here?' I said with an arched eyebrow. I wasn't even surprised, not really.

'Been on your trail for a while now,' Ketill said with a wink. 'Thought I'd wait till I could make a properly dramatic appearance.'

I chuckled to myself, shaking my head. If Ketill had tracked me so easily, then who else knew of my quick march north? 'How long have you been following us?' I asked.

'Following? Oh no, my friend, the Harii do not follow. We have been ahead of you the whole time, making sure you don't run into any trouble.' He winked again, still grinning through his beard.

'And I suppose you have some suggestions about how we may get through that?' I pointed to the torchbearers still making their way slowly towards us. Then the screaming started.

There was a howl and a rush of men burst from the trees, almost invisible in the darkness. They tore through the warriors who thought they had been the predators, preparing to spring the perfect trap. Only now did they realise they were the prey. Men flooded from the presumed safety of the forest, most even without their weapons. As we watched, myself, Birgir and Gerulf all stunned into silence, the Harii butchered the men of the Suebi one by one. It was over in the time it took me to rise on shaking legs, in less time than it took Gerulf to void his bowels.

'Right then,' Ketill said, standing now and shaking the mud and grass from his cloak, 'reckon it's safe to go on now, don't you?'

* * *

At daybreak we moved out. Cautious at first, for we had no confirmation that all of the Suebi warriors were dead. Some could have slipped away under the canopy of trees in the night, despite Ketill's assurances that it was quite impossible.

Bodies littered the ground as we reached the tree line. It was a massacre, an orgy of blood and guts. It was impossible to not tread on something dark and sticky with every step. Ketill looked around in pride as I walked beside him. My men were still mounted and most had already ushered their beasts through the battleground as quickly as they could. I walked with

Ketill and his men, mainly out of gratitude for what he had done for me. 'Remind me never to cross you,' I said as I gazed upon two corpses, men who appeared to have died together. One body lay atop the other; his hand was on the head of the man who lay underneath, as if he had been comforting him in his final moments. It was a sight that stirred great emotion within me, why I could not be sure. I have never exactly been famed for my empathy.

'We are brothers,' Ketill said with a shrug. 'I only do for you what you would do for me.' I nodded and clasped his shoulder, knowing what he said to be true. I did not have many friends; spending one's life as an outlaw made it hard to get close to other people, and equally, fear of being murdered made it hard for me to let other people get close to me. But it is true I would have died gladly for those close to me, my *familia* as the Romans would have called it. Ketill, Ruric, Gerulf, Baldo, Otto, even young Birgir. Saxa would have to be included on the grounds that she was my wife, though the gods knew I felt no love towards her. She did carry my unborn child, and that child and its older brother would most definitely be within my inner circle.

'I fear I owe you more than I could ever repay,' I said to Ketill, my thoughts drifting back to one of the first events that sparked this frenzied period of my life, when we had killed three Romans in Ketill's home.

'Do not worry, Alaric, I have already thought of many ways in which you can repay me,' he said with a smile that told me I should be worried.

We continued our journey north for another four days, stopping only briefly for a midday meal and not halting the march until the last of the sun's rays were lost behind the horizon. We were close then, I knew, so close I could almost smell my son's hair, feel his gentle touch as his tiny fingers explored my beard. On the fifth day we crested a ridge and were met by two of Ketill's men. I waited until my men had moved on and were out of earshot before questioning them.

'Warin is in Agnarr's old capital,' the older of the two spoke. His face was a hard one, his stare cold and unforgiving. He seemed a warrior to the core, but honest if nothing else. 'Not all of the chiefs are with him, but the most powerful ones came over to him as soon as old Agnarr was killed.'

'How was it done?' I asked, meaning the deposing of Agnarr.

'During a feast in Agnarr's hall.' The younger man spoke this time. 'Agnarr was evoking the gods, thanking them for his tribe's continued success when Warin thrust a dagger in his heart. Within heartbeats he was surrounded by the tribe's most powerful warlords, who proclaimed him king.'

'Well planned then,' I said.

'Yes, Lord. It would seem Warin at least had been planning the coup for some time.'

'Or at least his father had,' Ketill cut in.

I nodded, thinking back to my meeting with Dagr, the leader of the Chauci and Warin's father. I had caused the Chauci great hurt when I had killed their old chief. I wondered if this was Dagr and Warin exacting their revenge. 'I killed Dagr's father in his own hall, the same way Agnarr was killed in his. Before I left for the south, Agnarr invited me to his chambers and offered me Ishild in marriage and his tribe to rule when he died.'

There was a period of silence as Ketill digested this. 'Freya's tits, Alaric, why didn't you tell me?'

'I didn't tell anyone, Agnarr asked me not to,' I said, struggling to control the emotion in my voice. 'I was in love with Ishild, captivated by her. The chance to be with her and be a great king was an opportunity I could not turn down. You understand?'

'Of course,' Ketill said, nodding emphatically. 'I was not born to be chief of the Harii; I made it happen, with your help. So Warin gets wind of this and kills Agnarr and makes himself king. That makes sense, but this business with Ishild wanting you dead and corroborating with Rome? It makes no sense.'

I shrugged. I had not told him what Wulfric had told me in the moments before I had killed him, but I wasn't surprised he knew. Ruric would have told him the first opportunity he got. Come to think of it, any one of my men could have told him. 'I've no idea, brother. Guess there is only one way to find out.'

27

'Looks quiet,' I said to Ketill as we lay in the thick undergrowth overlooking Agnarr's old fortress, now Warin's.

'Too quiet, do you not think?' Ketill replied with a grimace.

I agreed, although I said nothing at first. Warin would know we were coming, would surely have planned some sort of defence. I had wanted to go ahead of my men and scout the area for myself before I led them all blundering into some trap. Though from what I had seen so far, it appeared Warin was not in the least bit concerned there was a warband coming for his head.

'Maybe he thinks you are still in the south?' said Ketill, stroking his beard. 'It is possible. We have travelled quickly, and there are no survivors from the battle in the forest. He cannot possibly know we are this close.'

There was merit to what my friend said, and I chuckled at the use of the word 'battle' to describe the bloodbath that was the massacre of the Suebi warriors by Ketill's tribe six nights before. 'It *is* possible, I suppose. But it seems unlikely. If the boot were on the other foot, so to speak, I would have men out everywhere scouting for an approaching warband. I would have spies in every town for fifty miles, and every whore in Germania would have an offer of gold for return of information as to my whereabouts...' I stopped speaking as Ketill's chuckling grew louder.

'There, my friend, may be your problem. You are thinking too much about what *you* would do and not what you think *Warin* is doing. *You* are Alaric, leader of the Ravensworn, a feared and experienced warrior, known for being the turner of battles and slayer of chiefs. *Warin* is a jumped-up little shit who I doubt very much knows which end of a spear is the pointy bit.'

I considered this as I chewed my way through a strip of dried meat. Warin was a pup, inexperienced in war and had grown up with the benefit of his father being the chief of a powerful tribe. He hadn't had to fight for wealth or status; both had been passed down to him. His marriage to Ishild – the daughter of the king of *the* most powerful tribe in the north – had been arranged for him. Would he be expecting me to challenge him? Maybe he did think I would just come begging for my wife and child to be returned. Could he really be that much of a fool?

'No, I'm not buying it,' I said after a time. 'Warin may not be experienced in war or life, but he has men around him who are. Men who won their chieftainships through blood and held them these long years in the same manner. They all know me, know what I am capable of. He will be prepared, I am certain of it.'

'Quite full of yourself, aren't you,' said Ketill with a perfectly straight face. 'Just saying, maybe your spear fame doesn't shine as bright as you think?'

Again, I shook my head. I knew my reputation, and knew it was well earned. I had betrayed men, killed and maimed those who got in my way. I was no hero, that was for sure, but I was known. I was feared. 'He will be ready,' I said with certainty. 'That means we need to be ready. How close do you think we can get?' I asked, pointing my head in the direction of Viritium.

'Why, right through the gates, of course,' Ketill said, flashing me one of his evil smiles.

* * *

'This is such a stupid idea,' I said as we walked through the great wooden gates. Dawn was breaking, the sun glorious, its heat basking. I was sweating like a pig under the thick folds of a heavy riding cloak, the hood up to cover my face.

'You should not worry so much, brother,' Ketill said. His voice was muffled; I could barely make out his face, buried as it was under his own hood. 'I doubt you will see anyone you know.'

'It is not that which concerns me,' I said, trying to keep my voice low and calm, 'it's being seen by people who know who I am!'

Ketill laughed; he was always laughing. 'I thought you were a descendant of The Sly One?' he asked in a tone which promised mischief.

'Well, yes...' I said, trailing off. I knew what was coming next.

'Do you not think this is something Loki would have done? Would he have shit his breeches like you and thought of running away? No, he would have snuck into Viritium, garnered all the information he needed and left without a trace. That, brother, is exactly what we shall do.'

I had my doubts but decided I could not bear to have Ketill poke fun at my perceived cowardice any more. I scanned the surrounding area as we entered the outer ring of Viritium. It was, it had to be said, a mightily impressive defensive structure.

The outer wall was ten feet tall and solid timber. There was no earthwork or ditch in front, but the fortress was built on a ridge and any attacker would have to carry ladders up a steep incline. If the attackers managed to force their way over the walls, they would find themselves trapped in an outer ring, with another wall facing them. That was where I was standing, scanning left and right, looking for a weakness. 'Looks different to when I was last here,' I said. I was still shifting my eyes, trying to work out what had changed. It felt so long ago I had last entered this place, could it only have been a few months?

'You were not planning to attack the place last time you were here,' Ketill said. 'Changes your perspective.' There was merit in that. The last time I had passed through the outer gate I had been mounted on Hilde, trying to look mighty and fearsome on my fine horse with my warband at my back. Now I was sneaking through like a criminal, my hood raised high, face masked in shadow.

'The walls,' I said. They were different. I racked my mind, willing my brain to picture them in the winter. The dark grey skies; howling wind that stung my eyes. Snow, pure whiteness all around. But the walls, they had changed, I was sure of it. I moved towards the inner wall, trying to slow my pace and appear casual, as if I belonged. Never easy trying to pretend you are meant to be somewhere you know you're not. I always get that tingling feeling in my spine; I stand too straight to make it look as though I'm not hiding, even though I know no one stands that straight and appears normal. I smile to people with one of those fake smiles that doesn't quite feel like it fits my face, and when forced to converse with people, I make up some dodgy name at the last moment and give away far too much of my character's personal information. No one cares that a stranger's cousin has lumps on his arse, and that you only came here because you heard the local healing woman has a cream that never fails. Gods, I should have just pretended to be a mute and let Ketill do all the talking.

I didn't.

'You there!' A bearded man with a spear shouted at me from atop the inner wall. 'Lower your hood so I can see your face.' I froze. Sweat poured through my beard; when I looked down, I could see the hair shining in the morning sun. I felt a large drop drip right through and splash onto my boots. Fear. It gripped me like a rod.

Still I stood there, frozen in time like a mountain. People bustled all around me, getting on with their daily routine. I could have stood there for a lifetime, and the same merchant would have whipped the same horse whilst sat on the same cart and never paid the slightest attention to the man slowly turning to stone in front of his very eyes. Still I stood there. Think, *think*!

'Alaric,' Ketill hissed. 'I think he might be talking to you, brother.'

I had no plan, no notion of what I was going to say until I said it. 'Good morning, friend,' I said. 'My name is Adallindis Helmoldson. Could you point me in the direction of your healing woman's home? My cousin has these lumps on his arse, see, poor bastard hasn't had a good shit in three weeks. We heard your healer makes an ointment that never fai—'

'Shut up and lower your hood!' the man called. He thrust his spear arm back, ready to throw. I was in no doubt he would. 'Really?' Ketill muttered in my ear. 'Adallindis Helmoldson?' He was trying not to laugh, and was failing. In our tongue, 'Adallindis' stood for flexible and 'Helmoldson' for helmet – I'll let you put the two of them together. 'Must have been twenty years since I first heard you give someone that name,' he sniggered.

'Seemed funnier then,' I said.

'Are you listening to me, boy?' the man shouted. 'If I have to ask you again you'll be fodder for my spear.'

'Boy?'

'Yep, that's what he said. Let's kill him.' I grabbed Ketill before he became the end of both of us and slowly lowered my hood. I wasn't sure what sort of reaction revealing my face would provoke from the warrior who would clearly know who I was and would have instructions to look out for my face. I was not, however, prepared for no reaction at all.

'No hoods up in this area, friend,' the spearman said, lowering his arm and relaxing his posture. 'Word is there are those who would see our good King Warin in the ground. If you are challenged again, make sure you respond straight away, okay?'

I was stunned, relieved and insulted. Did he really not know who I was? Was he not here in the heart of winter when I made my magnificent entrance dressed in all my finery with five hundred spears at my back? The bastard. I wished I had let Ketill kill him. 'Thank you,' I muttered through gritted teeth.

'You'll find the healer's home at the end of the main street, just before you come to the king's hall. Last house on the right. Warn you now though, her wares don't come cheap!'

I was raging; my hands shook with unbridled anger. 'Can't put a price on a good shit, friend,' Ketill said, clamping my shoulder forcibly. 'Thank you for your assistance.'

And with that, we strolled through the inner gate and into Viritium.

'You got a bit of The Sly One in you, you have,' Balomar the blacksmith says to me over the rim of his ale cup. We sit in the shadow of his forge, basking in its heat and our newfound comradeship.

'What do you mean?' I say, cautious to agree too quickly. He really is a colossus, Balomar. He fills the small domed building the way water fills a lake; his shadow stretches the whole wall behind him, covering it the way night engulfs the day.

'The way you beat me yesterday, more than a bit of luck, that. Took a bit of planning; cunning too.'

'Timing. All down to timing.'

'More than that I'd say,' Balomar says as he refills his cup and offers to do the same to mine. 'You knew where every blow was going to land. You could see it, anticipate my every move. How?'

'Ahh,' I say, sipping my newly refilled cup. 'The eyes, all about the eyes.'

'Care to elaborate?'

'I watch your eyes, not your blade. That's how I knew where you were about to strike.'

He pauses at this, and his face scrunches as he thinks. 'But how can you block the blade? Surely the mark of every great swordsman is their hand and eye coordination? Their ability to plant their own blade where their eyes tell them it must go.'

I shrug, trying to appear more casual than I am. Balomar is a far greater warrior than I could ever hope to be. He is fierce and fearless; strong as an ox and quick as a lynx. I am weak compared to him, and I had spent the entirety of our fight out of my depth. Yet I had won. 'Try it,' I say, 'next time you fight. Don't watch your opponent's blade, watch his eyes. They tell you where he is going to strike. You get an extra heartbeat to react.' I feel my cheeks colour as I become embarrassed giving this renowned warrior lessons in swordplay.

'I will.' He has not laughed and I sense no mocking in his tone. He is serious about his work, eager to learn more of his craft. 'So tell me, young Alaric.' I sense a change in the direction of the conversation. Maybe now he will get to the cusp of why he has invited me into his home. 'What are your plans for the future?'

I wave a hand vaguely; I feel the effects of the ale coupled with the forge's heat start to fog my mind. 'I have no plans, not really. I am without a home, a tribe, friends or coin. I am an outlaw, a wanderer. Who knows what the gods have in store for me.'

'Don't rely on the gods, brother. They rarely take any notice of us here on middle earth. I know a thing or two about that,' Balomar says with certainty. I wonder at what he means but decide it would be inappropriate to press the matter. 'Look at our tribe; we are all the evidence you need of that,' Balomar says.

'How so?' I ask in genuine puzzlement. The Marcomanni are to my mind one of the strongest tribes in all of Germania. They have great swathes of land, a large capital in Goridorgis and a mass of fighting men to call upon should the need for battle arise. They are more organised and regimented than the other tribes in the north, perhaps due to their close proximity to the Danube and the empire beyond.

'Rome, boy. Rome. Can you not see it, smell the arseholes in the air around you? Why, that coin in the pouch that hangs at your waist is filling my forge with their putrid fumes.' He spits and wipes his mouth with the back of his hand. 'They dominate our weak king, tell him who he may fight and who he must keep peace with. They march to our land and take what they want: women, food, weapons, you name it. We say we are free, and proud. Free from the yoke of Rome, outside of their oppression and dictation, able to make our own decisions. It is all lies, all smoke.' A single tear falls down his cheek and I realise how strongly his hatred is for the famed empire. A surge of comradery runs through me, for now I have met a man who may hate the cursed Romans as much as me.

'It is the same where I am from,' I say. 'Even in the north,' I add when Balomar looks at me in surprise. 'Frumentarii.' I spit the word; just saying it makes my stomach curdle. 'They walk among us like they are gods and we are slaves. We cannot touch them; it is advised to not even look upon them for they hold the power of life and death over every soul. It makes me sick.' I am drunk and I know it. In my young years I have not yet mastered the art of drinking large quanti-ties of strong ale. My vision is blurring, and I feel as though I could sleep for a week.

'Your chief, does he do anything to stop it? Has he ever fought back? Our king is weak, merely their puppet. He has no stomach for a fight.'

'It is the same,' I say. A vision of my mother forces its way into my mind, no matter how hard I try to compress it. She is lying there, on her back, legs spread. Man after man takes his turn on her, thrusting and grunting. She is quiet now, defeated. Even in the half light of the flames I can see she has grown pale; her lifeblood is leaving her, taking with it her strength to fight back. I feel tears prick my eyes, and I squint them shut in a desperate bid to hold them back. I fail. 'My mother was killed,' I say. I do not know why I have said it, for it has not been naturally brought into the conversation. And I am not usually a man who shares his inner secrets with a complete stranger. 'Rome killed her. Raped her till she bled out. I watched the whole thing.'

The tears are a flood now, an inexorable tide so powerful it could swamp a mountain. My vision is nothing but a blur; I do not see Balomar approach but feel his bear-like paws grip my shoulders. 'You suffered at the hands of Rome, as have many before you. But surely your chief came to your aid? Surely he fought back?'

I just sob. 'He did nothing,' I manage to squeak eventually. 'I killed the bastard, right in his own hall.'

I should not have said this and I know it. There will be men out for my head; Chauci warriors scouring the land in search of my death. I would be wise not to lead them to it.

'You killed the chief of the Chauci? In his own hall? By the gods, Alaric. I like you even more!' He lowers himself so his head is level with mine. 'If I tell you something can you keep it to yourself?'

I nod. This is the longest I have conversed with someone since I arrived at Goridorgis. Who does he think I am going to tell?

'There is a plan afoot. A plot to overthrow the king and put a new man in his place. A stronger man, one with the balls to fight back against the empire.'

'Fight back? Against Rome?'

'Yes.'

'I would support that man. But he would have to be strong and have a small army willing to fight for him in order to gain himself the throne. Who can garner that much support from the people?'

'Me,' Balomar says, an evil glint in his eye.

* * *

I stood in awe at the woman who walked before me. Her dark hair shone purple in the glorious summer sun; it tumbled down her back, reaching the tip of her perfectly proportioned behind. She wore a fitted dress of deep green, and that familiar uncontrollable force pulled me towards her. I was spellbound once more. Ketill was behind me, trying in vain to get my attention. I registered this but seemed powerless to acknowledge his presence.

All around her were armed men. Well-muscled, armed with spears and swords, they encircled their charge. I had to get rid of them, make a distraction of some sort to prise them from their royal responsibility.

I slowed my pace, putting some distance between me and the green vision strutting her way down the road. 'Freya's tits, Alaric!' Ketill hissed from behind me. 'Are you trying to get us both killed?'

'I have to talk to her,' I said, without taking my eyes from her. 'Make a distraction.'

'Why? What is the point? She wants you dead, remember?'

'I have to know why. I have to, Ketill.'

He sighed, massaged his forehead with his palm. 'Okay. If I do this, do you promise we can get out of here straight after? We have learnt all we can here.' I nodded. It was true our walk around Viritium had been very productive. We had managed to gauge the enemy disposition and morale, their strength in numbers and readiness for battle. We had been about to leave when I had spotted her through the crowd. Now I was going to take a risk, a huge, unnecessary risk.

Ketill skulked off, pulling his hood back over his face. Still I followed her. I could have sworn I sniffed a feint waft of jasmine in the air; it was delightful. I counted my throbbing heartbeats, once more feeling sweat trickle down my face. I raised my own hood when I reached thirty beats, expecting Ketill's distraction to start at any moment. I would not have long, and I had to make it count.

Screams filled the air behind me and at once I knew their origin. 'Murder, murder!' someone shouted, and I slowed my pace and looked in the direction of the panicked cry, wanting to seem as alarmed as everyone around me. As I looked back towards the king's hall where the shouts were coming from, I edged backwards, the scent of lavender getting stronger with every fumbling step. A female voice snapped out a quick order and at once the retinue of armed guards stormed past me. It was now or never.

I did not turn and face her straight away. I edged back three more steps then risked a glance around the edge of my hood. 'Hello, Alaric,' she said in a flat voice.

My heartbeat raced to a rounding crescendo; my palms were slick with sweat and my throat was as dry as a Parthian desert. 'I trust all the commotion that seems to be going on back there is down to you?' Ishild asked with an arched eyebrow. Gods, what a beautiful eyebrow.

I turned, racking my mind for some quick-witted reply; anything to bring those kissable lips curling into a smile. 'Hi,' was all I managed in the end. 'Are you well?' *Are you well?* Yes, that was actually what I said. Ishild, the woman who had been conspiring against me for longer than I would ever know, who held some grudge against me so bitter she would rather go to bed with the cursed empire than stay loyal to her own people. The woman who right then held my pregnant wife and young son captive in the very hall at my back. This same woman, the one I was so hopelessly in love with that some days I could barely function as a picture of her face filled my mind. *Hi. Are you well?* Men really are stupid creatures.

'Quite well, thank you. You? I trust your business in the south was as productive as you hoped?'

'It was, thank you.' *Just kill her. Pull out your knife and ram it through her cold heart.* I should have. Would have saved me a whole lot of trouble in the months to come, and preserved the lives of hundreds of good men. I should have. I didn't.

'Why are you here, Alaric?'

'Why am I here?' I said in the most sarcastic voice I could muster. 'Let me think. Oh yes, that's it. My wife has been captured by some snivelling little shit weasel called Warin – heard of him? Well, he claims he is now the king of the Suebi, no, really! See, his father is Dagr, chief of the Chauci, and he in turn is son of Fridumar, who was chief of the Chauci before him. Now, here's the thing. I may have slaughtered Fridumar one night whilst he feasted in his own hall, so I guess Dagr and his son have some fair reason to want me dead, despite us making oaths of peace between us what, a year ago now? So, that's reason number one.' Ishild pouted and thrust out her left hip, placing her hand against it. Trying to ignore how cute she looked in that pose whilst I ranted was extremely difficult, but I think I just about pulled it off.

'Reason number two: there's this woman that I just can't shake from my mind. More beautiful than Freya, she dominates any chamber she enters. I thought her perfect, and even made an agreement with her father to make her my wife one day. Gods, I was so happy. But, and it's a big but, I'm afraid… it turns out she is also more cunning than Loki, and has actually been conspiring against me for a long, long time. Even going as far as collaborating with frumentarii agents in a bid to see me dead. Any of this sounding familiar to you?' I had not realised I had started to yell. I had lost all control of my temper. I was a bundle of pent-up rage and anger, my pride hurt and ego wounded. I was confused and embarrassed, unable to cope with the conflicting emotions I felt for the woman in front of me.

Ishild sighed. 'Are you done? You are gathering quite the audience,' she said before turning and walking away.

I looked around me and saw that Ishild was correct. People who had just moments before had their attention drawn towards the commotion at Warin's hall had now turned to me. A hundred pairs of eyes scrutinised me; I waited for the alarm to sound as soon as someone realised who it was they were staring out. Praise to Wotan no one did. I scurried along the path, catching Ishild and grasping her arm. 'You have to tell me why,' I said.

'Why what?' she replied. 'Why I paid Rome to have you killed? Why I have longed for your death for more winters than I care to remember? Look at me, Alaric, look at me very closely. What do you see?'

I looked. I stared into those glimmering blue eyes that reminded me so much of winter; a land of ice and snow, as silent as the heart of a mountain. Her pupils were the gleam a frozen lake reflects when the pale winter sun makes a rare appearance from behind the dark cloud. I stared, and for a reason I was unable to comprehend, a shiver ran down my spine. 'What do you see?' she said. 'Is it Ishild looking back at you, or someone else? Someone you once loved and lost? There is a reason you were attracted to me at first sight, Alaric. And there is a reason I avoided your charms and bed. Think on it, will you?'

And with that, she was gone.

29

'Who is that, Father?' I ask as we sit in the shade of a huge oak tree.

'He is Agnarr, King of the Suebi,' my father says, putting his arm around me and hugging me tight.

I am only five years old, but I can already tell all is not well with my father. His yellow hair is wild and dishevelled as he has been frantically running his hands through it since this king and his retinue have arrived. Armed men stand twenty paces from us, hands on sword hilts and spears gripped tightly, and they eye my father with suspicion.

'Why is he here?' I ask. I squeeze my father's hand, wanting to let him know that everything is going to be all right.

'To see your mother, and your sister,' my father says.

'But why? Why does a king want to see Mother?'

My father sighs; he plays with my hair as he thinks on the question. 'Because he and your mother are old friends. They grew up together. He likes to come and see her every now and again, to check she is okay.'

'Does Mother like seeing him?' I ask, suddenly concerned for my mother's wellbeing.

'Yes,' Father says, and tears begin to well in his eyes. 'Yes, Alaric, I fear she does.'

A man walks out from our home. He struts down the wooden steps; his handsome face is set in a satisfied expression. 'Hengist, come here,' he says.

My father rises from his place beside me and, with noticeable regret, makes his way towards the king. In my mind my father is a giant; bigger even than the great ice giants he regales tales of before he sends me to sleep at night. His legs are impossibly long and stronger than iron; his torso is so packed with muscle even Donar would be unable to wrap his hands around it and gain a grip. But when my father stands before this man, this king, I am amazed to see that he is dwarfed. This king truly is a bear among sheep. The top of my father's head reaches only to the king's shoulders. 'I am taking the girl,' he says through a thick, dark beard.

'My lord?' my father asks in shock.

'Ishild, she's coming with me. I will have use for a daughter in the years to come. I will take her with me.' He speaks with finality, leaving no room for discussion.

'Yes, Lord King,' my father says as tears stream down his face. He buries his chin on his chest, a picture of self-pity.

I rise and run to my father, looping my arms around one of his mighty legs. 'You can't take her!' I scream at this king. 'Leave my sister alone!' I reach out a tiny fist and hit Agnarr with all my might. In my mind it is a mighty blow, one worthy of the legends of Wotan and his invincible son, Donar. In reality, I hurt my knuckles on Agnarr's mail and cause the king and his warriors to burst into laughter.

'Why, how tall you are getting, young Alaric,' the king says as he kneels down beside me. 'How old are you now?'

'Five,' I spit with as much attitude as I can muster whilst fighting back tears and cradling my split knuckles.

'Five! Surely you are seven or eight? You are so tall, you seem

almost a man!' Agnarr says as he ruffles my dark hair. The sensation
makes me forget the pain in my knuckles. As I raise my face to meet
his, I note how his hair reminds me of my own; of how his dark eyes
bring to mind my own when I gaze upon my reflection in the crystal
waters of the lake nearby. I stand a little straighter, keen to show this
king how tall I really am. 'One day,' I say, 'I shall be the greatest
warrior in all of Germania.'

Again, there is laughter. Though this time I feel the king does not
laugh in jest. 'I have no doubt, Alaric. Actually, I believe you will
become a great king one day. Men will quake when they speak your
name; every warrior in the land will know the name Alaric, of this I
am sure.'

* * *

'Alaric! Alaric! Wake up, brother, it is time,' Ketill said as he
shook me from my daze. All morning I had been in a state of
disbelief; a lumbering drunk, unable to get myself into my
armour, let alone lead men into battle.

Shaking my head, I looked around at my warband, every
man mounted and in armour. I doubted very much many of
them had managed to fit in any sleep the night before. I had
made the decision to assault Viritium late on in the evening, and
each man would have needed to sharpen his weapons, oil their
mail and see to their horses.

I knew very well my men would find it hard going assaulting
a walled fortress, a form of war we were poorly equipped for, but
Ishild's words the day before had left me reeling. I had to see her
again, had to discover the truth of the forgotten memory that
had dominated my every thought since our encounter.

'Alaric, are you going to be okay?' Ketill asked me in a quiet
voice. He was mounted to my right; to my left was Ruric and my

other captains beyond him. I had told Ketill everything; he was my oldest friend and if you could not tell your oldest friend that the woman you were madly in love with – who was trying to have you killed – was your long-lost sister, then who could you tell?

I could feel Ruric looking at me out of the corner of his eye. The old war horse knew something was up, I could tell. His body language was off. He had been wary around me since I had returned from Viritium with Ketill. But, as always, I knew I could rely on him to do his duty by me. 'I'm fine, Ketill. Any suggestions for the attack?' I asked this question not just to Ketill but to my captains as well, hoping one of them would come up with some inspiration that would see us win the day.

'We can't take the walls with cavalry,' Otto said. I bit my lip until I tasted blood.

'Can we not, Otto?' I replied in mock surprise. 'Do we not have a siege train behind us to help us with that? A few ballistae? An onager or two? No?' No one dared answer my sarcasm. 'I know all too fucking well we cannot take the walls with cavalry, which is why I was asking if any of you curs had any bright ideas? I see I have wasted my breath.'

I nudged Hilde's flanks with my heels and she responded instantly, trotting away from the chastened Harii chief and my captains. I rode away from my men altogether, into the open space between my army and Viritium. I studied the walls as I rode, determined to think of some cunning way to get us through the gate. *What would Loki do?* I thought as I rode, but no fresh inspiration hit me.

But then, in the midst of my gloom and confused emotions, I saw a true sign that I was still favoured by the gods, still the son of Loki.

The gates opened, and out marched Warin and his army.

* * *

I hug my mother tight as Agnarr and his retinue leave. The king himself holds a small bundle in his massive left arm as he rides. It is Ishild, my sister. It makes me sad that I will never see her again, so sad that I sob into my mother's skirt, turning the pale-green colour greener than the sweetest grass. 'Hush, Alaric,' she whispers in my ear. 'This is not the last we will see of her, of that I promise.' She rocks me gently; the gentle flow makes me tired and before I can control it, I feel myself falling into a deep slumber. 'Quick, Hengist. Take him to bed,' is the last thing I can remember my mother saying before the darkness takes me.

'What am I to do, Hengist?' I hear my mother saying as I stir. I feel a desperate, urgent need to empty my bladder, but my curiosity is immediately piqued, and I do not want to let my parents know I am awake.

'Maybe you could start by not allowing him to come here whenever he pleases and have his way with you? Maybe you could just say no!'

'Say no? To the king of the Suebi? If I'd have said no, you and I would have been with the gods long ago. We would have never known happiness; never felt the joy our children bring—'

'OUR children?' my father screams. He is by nature an angry and bitter man. For the first time I feel as if I am starting to see why.

'Yes, Hengist, our children. You knew what you were getting into when you begged me to become your wife. You knew who I was, where I had come from, to whom my heart would always belong.' Between my long locks of dark hair, I can see the sympathy in my mother's bright blue eyes. Sunlight flashes through the open window and her black hair shines purple in its light. She says I have hair to match hers. I like it when she says such things.

'It had been years before Agnarr started appearing. I thought somehow he would have forgotten or decided to leave us alone.'

'He is a king, a great one too. A man like that does not forget those who are important to him. I know it hurts you, Hengist. But when I was young all I wanted was to be Agnarr's queen. That was all taken away from me. You have made me happy, of sorts. But nothing could ever fill the void in my heart that being away from him creates.'

'And what when he tires of you? What if he dies and his heir decides he doesn't want a half-brother living with the Chauci that could one day challenge him for his throne? What then, my love?' I can feel the anguish in my father's voice; the tremor in his tone is audible.

'He would never do that to me,' my mother says. 'Besides, his wife is barren; the king shall have no other children. One day, Hengist, it will be a man of my blood that sits as king in Viritium, mark my words.' I peer at her through one half-open eye and see her pointing at me; blood, glory, power is my future. I must be ready.

30

'Steady, lads. Steady. Hold the line now, do not charge till you hear the signal.' I trotted Hilde across the front of my line, nodded to the faces I knew and shouted encouragement so all could hear. The fog that had clouded my mind had dissipated as I had watched Warin march his men from the safety of Viritium's walls; suddenly my path was clear, and drenched in Suebi blood.

I had roughly three hundred and fifty men left after the battle with the Fourteenth on the north bank of the River Danube. Ketill had just over two hundred Harii warriors; together we made a formidable force.

From my estimates, Warin outnumbered us by around three hundred men. Ketill and I had counted the small roundhouses the warriors were camped in to the west of Viritium from their walls the day before. If there were eight men to a house – which Ketill guessed there were as that was how he housed his own troops – then Warin had just under one thousand warriors at his back.

We had a couple of advantages though: firstly, all my men

were mounted on battle-trained horses. Warin had what appeared to be two hundred cavalry in his ranks, but I would have wagered all my silver that not one of those mounts would be a patch on my own. An untrained horse is a catastrophe in battle. It will shake its head and rear and kick long before battle is joined. The first sniff of blood and it will be off, without paying heed as to which direction it flees. Too many times over the years have I seen a warrior delivered to his enemy on the back of an unwilling horse. It was, it pains me to say, another lesson I learnt early at the hands of the cursed Romans.

It is with no modesty whatsoever that I say our second advantage was myself. I was an old hand at battle, as was Ketill and Ruric. Gerulf, Otto and Baldo were all experienced commanders who had led men independently and were capable of making decisions that could turn a battle to my advantage without waiting to be ordered to do so. Once again, they were my answer to Roman centurions. Gods, I hate them, but they sure are good at war.

It was a small, hilly field that was to be our battlefield. A wooden fence ran along part of the centre, a dividing line between the lands of two farmers. It was mid-summer, and the crops in those small fields were yellowing and within those shoots of barley was where the battle could well be decided. I asked Ketill to take his men forward and down into a small crevice in the field. The dip was no more than eight foot deep, and when the Harii warriors reached the bottom they abruptly turned to the west and hid themselves within the yellow crops. I watched as Warin ordered a hundred of his men into the same ditch to take the fight to Ketill. I smiled to myself in satisfaction when they charged down the slope ready to give great slaughter, only to find it void of men to slaughter.

That, I judged, was where my cavalry would win their first

battle. The Suebi warriors had charged maybe one hundred paces from their ranks and were roughly one hundred and twenty paces from mine. I kicked Hilde's flanks and urged her on as I galloped west across our line to Gerulf, who held the right. 'Gerulf, your men with me, let's go!' I did not wait to see if he or his men followed; I just gave Hilde her head once more and flew into a headlong charge at the enemy.

There was fear in the Suebi ranks, confused leaders and disorganised warriors in no formation; a cavalryman's dream. I had just over a hundred men at my back, and Gerulf had bolstered his ranks with men from Adalhard's Hundred when he had perished in the battle with the Romans. He whirled his sword in a great arc as he galloped up beside me, a savage grin on his usually sombre and considered face. 'No mercy!' he roared as his mount overtook mine. I hauled my own blade free and as always took great comfort from the familiar weight and the black leather grip. The blade was old now, notched and scarred along its great length, but it was still the best sword in the land, of that I was sure.

Gerulf was the first to hit the Suebi warriors. He took a man's head with the first swing of his sword, lopping off an arm with the next. I plunged Hilde between two warriors and she took the first with a flailing hoof, the next I cleaved near in half with my trusty old blade. The rest is all a bit of a blur now. I hacked and slashed, snarled and shouted myself hoarse as the battle fury took me and I could think of nothing but my lust for blood. I do remember a fearsome-looking warrior with a short single-headed axe charging me and coming very close to relieving me of my left leg. Luckily for me, Hilde spotted the danger before me and she sidestepped his swing so he cut nothing but air. I took him in the back as he was at full stretch before he could bring that deadly axe back around.

My arm was dyed red, and my glorious blue cloak that made me look so regal was now a murky brown. Even the great golden torc I had taken from Wulfric the coward had thick blood pouring from the delicate engravings. I had taken a blow to the bottom of my right leg, but had no memory of how and when. The first engagement was all but done as I slowed Hilde to a walk and scanned the surrounding area. None of the Suebi warriors that had charged down the slope would live to tell the brutal tale of this battle. I smirked as I looked out towards Warin, who sat atop his own mount, the indecision on his face clear even from that distance. I signalled to Gerulf and together we rallied our men and cantered back to our starting positions, to much adulation from the others who had sat and watched.

'That was well done, Chief,' Ruric said with a nod as I pulled up beside him. 'You hurt?' he asked as he saw me studying a gash on my right calf.

'Apparently so,' I said absently, marvelling at my own ability to take such a cut and not feel a thing. 'I'm sure I'll be fine,' I said with a shrug. 'Now then, what do you think our friend will do next?'

'I would not be surprised to see him scamper off to the north after that performance. Those men you fought, they were the Avarpi, said to be the fiercest of the Suebi fighters.'

'The fiercest?' I asked in genuine surprise. 'Well, if that lot was the best they have I might just charge the rest on my own and leave the rest of you to make camp!' The jest went down well with the men within earshot, as I had known it would.

'I don't think he will send any men forward again,' I said as I chewed my lip. I was trying to put myself in Warin's position. He had, I guessed, been manipulated into leaving his high walls by the more powerful chiefs among the Suebi. These were the men who had made him king, and he would be relying on them to keep him as king if he survived this bloody day. He knew it all too well, but more importantly, so did they. They were war chiefs; men who lived for nothing more than the savage joy of battle. Not for a heartbeat would they have considered hiding in Viritium and letting themselves get put under siege. If they were to die they would do so on an open plain with a blade in their hands and feast at Wotan's table with their heads held high.

Warin, I knew, would have tried to get them to see his way of thinking. He would have wanted to hold me at Viritium's walls; keep my gaze focused solely on him, until...

'Lord! Lord!' Birgir bellowed as he came up behind me at the gallop. I had sent him north and west four days before, with orders to spy on Dagr and watch his movements. I was convinced the father would come to the aid of the son, for surely it was only natural. The most sensible thing for Warin to do, therefore, would be to hide in Viritium and let me send my men to their deaths as they tried to storm the walls by force. Whilst my gaze and ire would be focused on Warin, Dagr would strike my rear. It was a perfect plan, well thought out and was something I would have considered if our positions had been reversed. What they had not counted on, though, was me being ready for it. 'Dagr comes with all haste! He has five hundred warriors at his back, all mounted and ready for battle,' he said through shallow breaths.

'How long?' I asked.

'They will be here by sundown.'

'Sundown?' I gawped. 'Wotan's hairy balls, Birgir! You haven't given me quite as much notice as I would have wanted!'

'Sorry, Lord.' Birgir blushed. 'Took me a while to find his army. They crossed the River Elbe somewhere to the south and came back north on the eastern bank. Guess Dagr knew you may have someone out spying on him?'

'Yes, I suppose,' I said, though for the first time I felt myself doubting Birgir. Something in his demeanour seemed *off*, something I couldn't quite place my finger on. At that moment, though, I had no time to question him further. 'Right then,' I said with as much confidence and bluster as I could muster, 'we have till sundown to send this lot scurrying off to their mothers.'

'Got a plan?' asked Ruric.

'Yes. Well, the beginnings of one at least. Where are those pesky priests that follow me around? You know, the filthy bastards in the rank old robes who are always harping on about the end of days and have an insatiable appetite for silver.' Ruric smiled. I had never had much time for men who claim to speak to the gods. No one spoke to the gods, not unless they wanted to speak to you. And I could think of no reason at all why the mighty Wotan or any of his offspring would want to spend time with the dirty, old, bearded fanatics who spent half their lives in isolation in caves, hidden deep in the forest.

Still, it seemed I might just have finally found a use for them.

31

'I miss her, Mother. I miss her every day,' I say as I sob into the folds of her dress.

'Hush now, my brave warrior. I know you do, Alaric. We all do. We will see her again, soon I am sure,' she says as she gently wipes the tears from my eyes and pinches my nose clear of mucus with an old piece of cloth.

'But when?' I wail. It has been nearly half a year since we last saw Agnarr, king of the Suebi. The spring that has just begun to blossom will be my sixth, though I feel no joy at its coming. All winter I have been in a state of despair, roaming the lands of our small farmstead wearing nothing but a tunic, desperately seeking my beloved baby sister. I know, of course, even at my tender age, that I will not find her behind the grain barn or sheltering with the livestock, but I like to pretend we are playing a great game of hide and seek, and that one day I will eventually stumble across her and we will laugh till summer arrives in our mirth.

'Soon, my dear, soon.' My mother weeps her own tears and I feel a strong pang of guilt. I may be missing my sister, but surely my mother *is missing her daughter more. I force back the tears and give my mother my best smile. 'I love you,' I say.*

'I love you more, my warrior.' She kisses me, long and hard on my forehead. I feel the tip of her nose on my hair as she breathes in my fragrance. I realise she has shown more affection towards me since Ishild was taken away. That tragic occurrence has caused her love for me to burn brighter than the heart of the fiercest forge, and a part of me is happy at the thought.

My father enters our small one-roomed house and smiles a thin, sad smile as he sees his wife and son embracing. He is ashamed of himself, I know. All winter long he has been outside with his sword, practising lunges and hacking lumps off a large wooden post he has embedded in the earth. He feels shame for allowing his daughter to be taken, and I have overheard him saying he is worried the king will come back and take me too.

The thought of this happening sends shivers down my spine; my parents do not have much, but everything they do they make pay enough to put food on the table for me. Many a night I have been feasting on a thin gruel my mother has prepared in a tiny pot over the hearth; when I ask what they will be eating, they say they will eat when I am abed, but I know they do not. My father petitioned our chief for a small loan of coin to help feed us through winter, but it was rejected out of hand. There is unfinished business between our chief and my father, a burning hatred hotter than Hel's domain, though I know not why.

I will kill him one day, this chief who would have seen us starve in the frozen abyss that was the winter just gone by. I do not know how or when, but with Donar as my witness I swear I will take up my father's sword one day and send him to his maker. It is with these thoughts storming my mind that I fall asleep in my mother's arms.

* * *

Wotan had to hang himself on Yggdrasil for nine days and nine nights before he gained his wisdom, and with it his power. He was wounded in the side by a strike with his own great spear, Gungnir, as he swung from a branch on that immortal ash tree, the rope pulling tight around his neck. He gave gladly one of his eyes just so he could see further and truer, and so his grip on the nine worlds grew tighter.

The Allfather has more knowledge in his mind than any mortal could garner. Through his ravens Huginn and Muninn he sees all throughout our world and more. Thought and memory, we call them. It is my belief that they stand for far more than that. Huginn knows every thought that enters your mind, no matter how fleeting; Muninn can see into your soul. The raven knows what you have been through, the obstacles you have overcome, the people you have betrayed. The raven tells all this to its lord, and The Hanged One remembers, he remembers all. It is my hope that one day, the great doors of his hall will swing open and I will be admitted to feast and drink in his presence. What questions will he ask me? What answers will I give?

'Your eyes have glazed over again, brother,' Ketill said. I snapped from my daze, only then realising my left hand was fingering the golden torc at my neck. The memories flooded my mind; a vicious tide of long forgotten pain and regret. Ishild. Ishild. How could I have forgotten? How is it possible for me to block that dark day from memory?

'I still do not know why she is trying to kill me,' I said.

'Huh?'

'Ishild. I get that we are siblings and she feels she was taken from her home. Forced into a life she did not choose. She feels anger towards me, and I guess she felt a great deal towards Agnarr too, given his recent downfall. But why me? I just don't understand what I have done to her? I was a child when she was taken! What could I possibly have done to make her hate me so?'

'Listen, Alaric. I know you have a lot of confused emotions right now, but... you do realise we are in the middle of a battle, right? And that we have about eight hundred foes to our front and five hundred coming up behind?'

I shook my head of the cobwebs and rubbed my palm over the hilt of my scabbarded sword. 'By the hanged, Ketill, you are right. How are the priests coming along?'

'Looks as though they are nearly done,' said Ketill, nodding his head to our front.

When I looked up, I beheld a truly gruesome sight. Four priests – if that was what the foul retches truly were – had been busy. They were commanded in all things by a Godi, the head of their order and the man closest to the gods, apparently. The four priests had hammered in sixteen spears in an arc, just atop the rise in the valley that the hundred or so Suebi had charged down just an hour ago, only to be slaughtered to the last man.

Once the spears were in place, Ruric had lopped off the heads of sixteen of the warriors we had slain with his great war axe, and now the priests were fixing them to the spear tips. It was disgusting, sickening, and terrifying. And I only had to look at the back of those blood drenched, grey-skinned heads. To Warin's men it would have been truly horrifying. Sixteen of their own warriors looking at them, urging them to come and take revenge. It was a grave insult to those poor men who had done nothing to warrant their bodies being desecrated so. But, if it gave me an advantage, I was willing to see it done.

'So, let me make sure I have all the facts here,' Ruric said, appearing at my left shoulder. 'We need these curs to charge us and give battle. What we really do not need is them scurrying off behind those big walls.'

'Correct,' I said.

'And we did not think the maggots would have the balls to charge us, so what you decided to do was to make a ring of heads, right in front of them. The gory, hollow faces of their own friends, brothers, fathers, and sons staring at them.'

'You really are very clever,' I said, knowing full well where this was going and not entirely sure I had an appropriate answer for the inevitable question.

'So, if we didn't think they had the stones to charge us before, why do we think they will now that we're parading what will happen to them if they do?'

I opened my mouth to answer, then closed it. I frowned, trying to frame the jumbled words that clotted my mind into a coherent sentence. In the end, Ketill came to my aid. 'Courage, Ruric. Courage and honour. See, Warin is a king now. And a king, even more so than a chief, has a reputation to keep up. How can a king rule his tribe if he does not possess the courage to face his enemy in battle? What we are doing here is embarrassing him, showing him to be a *nithing* in front of his men and the gods. If he does not respond, his men will think him a coward. They will see that the gods favour Alaric and that Warin is not a man to follow. A leader is only as good as his reputation, his reputation only as good as his last battle. Warin lost his last battle, about an hour ago in that crevice. He needs to respond, has to, if he doesn't want to have his throat slit in the night.'

I said nothing, just watched on as the Godi pranced up and down behind the fence of heads. I could not hear what he was saying, but guessed from his flying spittle and regular hand gestures towards Warin that he was cursing the king of the Suebi and naming him a coward. A raven squawked overhead, then another. Two of them, circling the battlefield. They circled twice as I watched, then both flew off to the north. Already he would have received warriors into his hall, still armed and armoured in the garments they had fought and died in. Before sunset, there would be many more.

There was a lasting silence when the Godi finally finished his performance and strutted like a war hero back to our ranks. 'I have cursed them,' he said with pride. 'The Allfather knows of this Warin's cowardice and has promised you victory this day, Lord Alaric.' He bowed and waited for my delayed reply.

'Well, that is a relief. You and your men can leave the field now, Godi. You will receive your payment once my victory has been secured.' I said no more to the foul-stinking man. He was stick thin, his legs about as thick as my finger. He wore nothing but a long rag that I could only assume had been white when he first put it on. His dirty grey beard slacked almost to his waist; the remaining hair he possessed atop his head was lank and sparse. In fact, it was so thin I could actually see the lice as he walked past. I think it was only then I realised I had no notion of his name.

But it was too late then to ask the wretched creature; the enemy was charging.

32

They came like a pack of savage wolves. Their war cry was inhuman, nothing like the *barritus* that was common amongst the tribes. They roared their blood fury, spat their defiance and gritted their teeth for the battle to come. My fence of heads had done its work; although for a moment I wondered if it had been a mistake.

Sure, I needed them to charge. I needed them beaten and scattered to the four winds so I could turn and face Dagr, who approached my rear. But what I definitely did *not* need was them so fired up, so geared for battle, that just their sheer momentum could see them tearing through my men like a reaper on harvest day. I had to react quickly.

'Ketill, get back to your men. Ruric... Ruric! You have the centre, make sure the banner stays there, got it? Gerulf, right flank, go, I will be with you shortly. Otto, you're the left. Have your men all mounted and ready to charge. Watch out for Ketill. When he attacks it will be fast and bloody. Baldo, you mad bastard, you're between Ruric and Gerulf. Every man on foot, axemen in front... I know, I know, you know your business. Just make sure the curs hold!' And with that I was gone, galloping across the front of my army, my sword held high, the blade punching the air. 'TO VICTORY!' I bellowed as I rode, revelling in the cheers and savage grins I saw as I rode past them. Gods, I love a good battle.

To my left was a maelstrom of charging men; I spotted Warin in their rear and centre, mounted on a fine white stallion. I sent a swift prayer to Donar that the cowardly bastard would find his way to me in the storm of iron and that it would be my blade that sent him down to Hel. To my right was an endless line of red shields, a black raven painted on the front of each. It was a glorious sight, truly beautiful. Despite the losses we had taken at the battle on the Danube, my warband was still formidable, still almost unbeatable to my eye. The line was perfect, each man with his left foot forwards, ready to shove their might into the wooden boards when the enemy crashed onto them. Gods, I was proud, and not for the first time I wished my father was with me so he could see for himself what a man could become if he put his mind and heart into it. All I'd had when I left that sad little farm was his old sword. I still had that old blade; it sat in my right palm, the black leather grip giving me comfort as it always did. I wished he could see what I had built with it.

'All set, Gerulf?' I asked with a manic grin as I dismounted and allowed Hilde to be taken through our formation. I thought she seemed disappointed that she would not be part of the battle. It amused me that even my mount was desperate to get in on the action.

'We're ready, Lord, aren't we, boys?' A roar of approval that was the sweetest music to my ears rang out all around me. I barraged my way into the centre of the front rank, snatching a shield off a spearman behind me.

'You think your lads can hold them?' I asked Gerulf. He looked hurt; there was a slight twitch of anger in his left eye.

'We'll hold till the end of days for you, Lord,' he said with such calm certainty that I knew he would never let me down. I had not to fear of his men risking a doomed charge on the enemy; Gerulf would not die as Adalhard had.

'You are a good man, Gerulf,' I said and clasped him on the shoulder. 'Ruric is old, ready to find himself some land and settle down. I've a mind to let him have his wish; he has served me well these long years. I will be needing a new second in command when he is gone.' I said no more, just let the offer hang in the air between us.

'I would be honoured, Lord,' Gerulf said. He meant it, I knew. 'I had nothing when the Ravensworn took me in; all I have is thanks to you. I will serve you loyally, always.' We clasped hands, the enemy now just fifty paces from us.

'Right then,' I said, 'let's show these goat fuckers why you don't mess with the Ravensworn! Shields, UP!' And just like that, the men locked shields to a man and hunched down behind them, showing the enemy nothing but the whites of their eyes.

A few of my men had bows, and those now played their deadly tune and the air bristled around me as the slender arrows rained death on Warin's men. Not for the first time I wished I had more men with the skill to take a life at such a distance. 'We have enough spears for a volley?' I asked Gerulf. The German war spear is different to the *pila* used by the Romans. The ash shaft is thicker and longer, it being a weapon more suited for hand-to-hand combat rather than launching at your foe from a distance. But when powered by a man with suffi-cient strength, it will tear through the finest mail and even a stout shield as it hurtles from the sky at terrifying speed.

'Aye, I think we do. Just the one, though.'

'Well, we had better make it count then! Give the order, Gerulf.'

We shuffled aside as the biggest of Gerulf's Hundred strode through and readied to darken the sun. At a distance of a mere twenty paces they sent the heavy spears hurtling into the faces of the Suebi warriors, who could only grit their teeth and pray the Spinners had intended a different death for them. Even I was shocked at the speed at which the spears flew. For a moment they were lost, nothing but a blur between us as they spun, and the sound when they hit with devastating impact on the enemy was sudden, violent, wet and visceral.

Men fell in their scores, gore filled holes where moments before had been whole flesh covered in mail. The screams of the dying were high-pitched and desperate, and a man in front of me went down with a gurgling cry.

There was a pause from both sides as those in the enemy ranks that had survived the storm of spears looked around in horror; our men were reorganising back into lines, the axemen getting their shields back up and ready for the inevitable onslaught. I still had my sword unsheathed in my right hand. My palm was rank with sweat and twice I had to readjust my grip. I felt oddly calm as the rush of blood that had come with my initial excitement of imminent combat had run its course, and I had yet to hit my second wind. I was silent as the grave, my mind as smooth as a summer sea – I was ready.

The first man to hit my shield must have weighed the same as a cow. It was so hard and fast that the rim snapped back and wedged itself between my top lip and nose. I felt one of my teeth crack like a twig and for a few frantic heartbeats saw nothing but the purest white. My legs were like a newborn calf's as I staggered to and from the men to either side of me; I could vaguely hear the cries of fear from the spearman at my back, for he would not want to be the one who was blamed for causing his lord's death. Slowly, very slowly, I came back to my senses. My vision was blurred with tears of pain, but I could just about make out my assailant being struck by three spears and slumping face first to the dirt.

With a tremendous effort I hawked and spat bloody phlegm on the dead man's face, my fragments of tooth landing on his right cheek. Gods, it hurt. I mean, it *really* fucking hurt. Blood welled in my mouth, streamed from my nose, and under my heavy moustache I could feel the long, jagged cut where the iron rim of my shield had driven through my skin and nearly through my skull.

'Lord? Lord?' Gerulf was at my right shoulder still, a spearman frantically covering him as he dropped his own shield to put his arms around me.

'Get the fuck off me!' I slurred like a drunken. The calmness had left me now; I was nothing but a mass of boiling rage. I snarled; I must have looked like a *draugr*, one of the terrible undead that stalk the earth and drag the still-breathing down into Hel's domain. Like a toothless Fenrir I ambled into the fray and hacked and slashed at anything that moved, heedless of whose side they were on. I was a berserker, with no control of my body or mind. I just killed, then killed some more.

I know not how long that bloody melee lasted. I was told the next day I had cleaved my way right through Warin's men. When I had reached the end of that blood-drenched path, I had simply turned around and carved my way back. We won the day, but it was certainly not Alaric, Lord of the Ravensworn who'd led his men to victory. Gerulf regrouped his Hundred and advanced at a steady pace. His men kept their shields locked and as axes ripped down shields, the spearmen pierced through flesh and mail. Ruric and his Hundred stood resolutely in the centre. They did not advance against the overpowering numbers Warin threw against them, but nor did they give any ground. He was quick to tell me that he had suffered the most casualties, with another of his disapproving looks. Baldo had advanced with Gerulf and it had been that mad bastard himself who had eventually tackled me to the ground and held me till the madness had subsided, although by that point I had been as weak as a babe. Otto was nearly overrun on the left; his cavalry had committed too early and left his flank vulnerable, but Ketill had been there to save the day. The Harii were still hidden in the crops, forgotten by even some of my own men. They howled their savage war cry and hit the right flank of Warin's army like a hammer on anvil.

Ketill took great pride in telling me the whole of Warin's force had disintegrated after his men's charge; like leaves caught in an autumn gust, they scattered and went their separate ways. There had been, however, one set back.

'What of Warin?' I asked as I sat and watched the sun set on our day of bloody glory.

'He fled. Some of his men formed a wedge around him and pushed through our lines. Guess he is heading for his father,' Ruric said, wincing as he rotated his old shoulders. 'Merciful gods, I'm not as young as I used to be.'

'None of us are, old friend,' I said. I was feeling the effects of the battle too, though some of my pain I believed I had Baldo to thank for. When I had come to my senses he was sitting on my head, and he is not a light man. 'Get Birgir,' I said to Ruric, 'send him on Warin's trail. We'll soon know where the *nithing* has run to.'

'We have men looking for him, Lord,' Otto said to me. He was, as most of my men were, as I assumed I was, covered in blood. When he spoke, specks of reddened spittle flew from his lips and there was a cut above his right eye so deep and wide a whole portion of his face seemed to flap in the evening breeze.

'For the sake of the Allfather's remaining eye, Otto, please get that cut stitched. I can actually see through your skull to what's left of your brain.' This caused much merriment from my captains, who took it in turns to mock poor Otto. 'Hang on,' I said, only now catching on to what Otto had said, 'what do you mean *looking* for him?'

There was an awkward silence. Gerulf found something fascinating on the hem of his tunic to study, Ruric grabbed himself a clump of grass and rubbed his hands together gently to let it fall gracefully back to earth, and Baldo winced and gave Otto a shrug, as if to say 'got to tell him sometime.'

'Where is Birgir?' I asked again, more urgently this time. I was very fond of the lad, and all there knew it. It takes a lot to get yourself noticed when you live and fight in a band of five hundred bloodthirsty mercenaries. Birgir had done that. Not with any great acts of strength or brutality – things that the men believed would get my attention and my favour; they didn't, ever – but by simply having a unique skillset that no one else could offer me. I have had countless men in the ranks of the Ravensworn over the years, and Wotan himself knows how many now dine in his hall. But when they died, most of them died nameless to me, just another face in the ranks. Birgir was different, special. He had proven his worth to me time and time again.

'Well?' I asked again, my voice pure iron.

'We can't find him, Lord,' Otto said, unable to meet my eye.

'Well, he cannot have gone far, look harder,' I said.

'I've got a couple of my men scouring the field, no luck so far,' Ketill chipped in.

'You mean they are checking the bodies?'

Ketill nodded.

'Ruric, he wasn't with you in the centre, was he?'

'No, Lord. To be honest I thought he was off keeping an eye on Dagr for you?' Ruric looked genuinely shocked at first, then his face set in a scowl and his eyes locked with mine. Birgir was part of his Hundred, but spent so much time away scouting no one would have thought it out of place for him not to be there.

'Otto, was he with your cavalry?' Otto turned and consulted with one of his junior officers. I watched as the young man shook his head as Otto spoke. 'Doesn't seem to have been, Lord,' he said with reluctance.

I kept my own counsel for a few heartbeats, once more considering his behaviour when I had seen him earlier on that day. It had taken him an age to track Dagr and his warband; his body language had been closed and defensive when he had made his report, and he would not meet my eye. Once more I locked eyes with Ruric, the two of us seemingly both having the same thought. He gave me a shrug and tilted his head.

I was about to speak when a rider came haring towards us. A slight figure atop a fine grey mare. As he drew close and dismounted I saw a boy, almost a man, with a crop of light hair and pale, dirty skin. 'Lord,' Birgir said with a half-smile, 'I see you have been busy!'

33

'I was watching Dagr, Lord. I assumed that's what you would want me to do,' Birgir said, all innocence.

'And why would you assume that when you knew full well we had a damn hard battle to fight?' I asked with all the grit I possessed. I did not want to doubt Birgir; I wanted to feel the truth that was written on his face.

'Well... because... well, he was right on our tail! Surely it made more sense to have me watching him?' He seemed surprised, hurt and embarrassed, everything I would want him to be feeling. And yet, something wasn't right, something I couldn't put my finger on.

'Since when did you start making decisions?'

'You were busy, Lord. Preparing for the battle. I thought it better if I just got on with it.' He spoke quickly, almost too quickly. He seemed flustered, his cheeks glowing red, though that could have easily been from his ride.

I nodded. There was truth in his words. I tried to remember our earlier encounter, when he had first informed me of Dagr's approach. As hard as I tried, I could not remember where he had gone once we had finished. It had been a long day.

'So, what did you see?'

Birgir seemed to visibly relax. His posture slouched and a half-smile appeared under the thin wisp of beard he refused to shave. 'Dagr approached even as you were giving battle,' he said. 'It was only the arrival of Warin that halted his advance. They had a brief conversation. Dagr even struck Warin!' This was greeted with much mirth by my captains. 'After a short while they set off east. I came back here then, and here I am,' he finished with a flourish.

I grunted, turning his words over. 'Where will they go? Surely they would head back north and west? To Chauci lands? Why east?'

Silence greeted my open question. Why *would* they go east? Surely there was nothing for them there? The Chauci were based in the north and west; what possible allies could Dagr have deeper inland?

'I shall leave at first light and keep track of them, Lord,' Birgir said, a bit too eagerly for my liking.

'Gerulf and ten of his men shall go with you,' I said.

'What? Why?' Birgir appeared both angry and confused at this. Until now he had always been trusted to work independently. 'I am quite capable of tracking them myself, Lord. And one man stands a better chance of remaining undetected than ten.'

Both valid points, but I had a feeling in my gut. Always trust your gut.

'Gerulf has experience in acting under his own initiative and plenty of experience leading men in combat. You do not know where they are going or what you are going to encounter along the way. He will be in command and you will heed his advice and follow his orders. The ten men will of course be of value if you have to fight, but you can also use them as messengers. I want reports as often as you can. You leave at dawn, we will follow.' I directed the last of this to Gerulf himself; if he was angry at being sent away so soon after a full day of battle he did not show it. He nodded and marched off, already shouting orders at his men. I turned back to Birgir. 'Thank you for your report, Birgir. Now go and get some rest.' Birgir moved off slowly. Maybe he expected more praise, or silver; he was going to receive none of either.

I called Ruric to me and the two of us moved away from the group. For the first time I noticed it was now fully dark. All around me, campfires roared and the air carried the smell of roasting meat. My stomach grumbled; I wondered when I had last eaten. 'Thoughts?' I asked Ruric.

'Something's not right, I don't like it,' he said. He spat and even under the dark sky I could see his spittle was dark with blood. 'Lost another tooth,' he grunted. I grinned at him, showing him my own injury. 'By Hel's teeth,' he said and laughed, 'you were ugly enough as it is!'

'Thanks, old friend,' I said and let out a small laugh myself. As I breathed in through my mouth it made a low whistling noise which had us both giggling like girls.

'Anyway,' Ruric said, wiping a tear from his eye, 'you're right to send Gerulf with Birgir. If he is up to something, Gerulf will find out. I'll go see him now, make sure he understands why he's going.' He made to walk away, then turned back to me: 'Are you going to be okay?'

'What do you mean? I've plenty of other teeth, Ruric. I won't miss a couple!'

'I ain't talking about your teeth and you know it. Gerulf said you lost it today, went charging off on your own. I haven't seen you like that since you got that great scar on your shoulder, many years ago.' Instinctively my hand went up to my left shoulder, where under mail there was nothing but a mass of scar tissue. 'She's got to you, hasn't she, this woman. Don't speak, Alaric, just listen,' he said, showing me the palm of his hand before I could object. 'I don't know who she is or what she has done to you, or you to her for that matter. But you haven't been right for a while now. You need to sort your head out, before you get the rest of your men killed.'

I called his name but he didn't reply. I called again and he turned back: 'I asked Birgir if he saw her today. He said she was riding with Warin when they met Dagr. She's gone, Alaric. But your wife hasn't; you'd know that if you'd even bothered to ask. I gave orders for her to be found and brought to your tent. The gates of Viritium have been closed and are guarded by twenty of my best men to stop the lads from raping and looting. Should have been you seeing to that, *Lord,* not me. She's in your head, Alaric, and you need to get her out of there. Now, I'll see to Gerulf, you go and see your family.'

Ruric walked off into the night; I stayed, isolated in the darkness, rubbing the old wound on my shoulder.

* * *

It feels a long descent as I clamber back down into that pit. My nerves are frayed, and for a moment I panic my courage has deserted me. It has only been ten days since I faced Balomar in this awful place. I leave the sun behind as I descend. Below me is nothing but darkness, nothing but blood and raw hatred. My opponent is already there. He waves his hands frantically at the crowd, and the roar that greets his gesture is the response he is looking for. He is Sisbert, Chief of the Guards of King Roderic, the visiting king of the Quadi.

They have come here in great numbers, the Quadi. Their king is old and infirm. He seeks an alliance with the Marcomanni for his son and heir, Areogaesus. Both tribes are theoretically allied to the empire, but in this world alliances change with the wind. It is no secret among these peoples that both tribes seek the destruction of Rome. To stand alone would be futile; together, they may just have a chance.

Entertainment has been arranged for the king and his retinue: me. This great blond warrior who stands before me is going to beat me to a pulp, show to one and all that the Quadi are a fearsome tribe and worthy of an alliance with the Marcomanni – or so the king believes. It will do no shame to the Marcomanni to see me beaten, for I am not one of their own. I am a wanderer, an outlaw, exile. They would not put Balomar or another son of their tribe into the pit to face this monster for fear of losing face to their rivals. Me? I am expendable.

But Balomar has a plan. He wants me to fight this beast from the east, wants me to destroy him. This is just to be phase one of a blood-drenched day. Phase two is when it will get really interesting. I jump the last few feet from the wooden ladder to the mud. The weather has begun to turn in the time since I faced Balomar; no more is the floor covered in sheet ice. It is mush now, which to my mind is worse.

My boots squelch with every step; I feel them stick and have to yank hard with my hips just to take a stride forward. My opponent in this Hel on earth is once again both taller and broader than me, though he seems to glide across the churning mud. He shows me his teeth, which are as savage as Fenrir's, and when my eye meets his I see nothing but my own doom. Not for the first time, I feel a twinge of regret for agreeing to this part of Balomar's plan; everything hinges on me being victorious.

Balomar himself stands above and behind me. He shouts encouragement and slaps his hands together; the sound reverberates above me. With him is a man called Ruric; an exile like me. He does not speak much, though he gives off an air of confidence and everything

about his stance reads that he is a man of the sword, though I have yet
to see him wield one. I wonder why it could not have been him down
here in this pit, for surely he would stand a better chance.

I turn back to face Balomar, hoping for a small gesture of confidence from the man who has become my leader; when I look up he is
whispering in the ear of a young man named Adalwin, who has
recently been enlisted in the king's guard. I have seen this Adalwin
around Goridorgis. He seems a decent man and is kinder than the
other warriors who dine at the king's own hearth; is he with us? I
have no idea, though it would not surprise me if there was more to
Balomar's scheme than he has let on to me.

A horn sounds and the cacophony around the pit ceases. A circling
crow squawks as it smells blood and the rich pickings of combat. 'My
friends,' the king bellows as he strides to the edge of the pit, 'in honour
of the arrival of our cousins from the Quadi and their noble king and
his son Areogaesus, today we celebrate our newfound alliance with a
show of strength!'

The crowd roars. I look around and see women and children
baying at the prospect of spilt blood; hard men in mail whisper to one
another. There is the odd chink as bets are made and coins change
hand. I try to clear my mind and focus on my opponent. He is a
handspan taller than me with thick muscle dominating his torso, and
he carries a huge single-headed axe rather than a sword. Balomar tells
me this will give me an advantage in reach and with my speed I
should easily be able to avoid his blows. I have my doubts. This is
supposed to be a fight to first blood, but I cannot possibly see how I
will survive if I am hit by that axe.

'Our first entertainment of the day shall be a fight to first blood!'
And the crowd roars again. I get a rush of saliva in my mouth and
have to fight back the overwhelming urge to vomit. 'To my left we
have the infamous Sisbert of the Quadi! A renowned warrior of fearsome courage and whose tales of heroism in battle are known to all. To

my right, we have Alaric the wanderer.' I spit on the mud as the silence hangs like mist on a winter morning. No tales of courage, even of my recent victory in this very pit? Fine. I will show him, show them all. 'Let the contest... begin!'

Sisbert moves with the grace of a dancer, whereas I am stuck hard to the mud. With a heave I free my left boot and rasp my sword from its sheath. I go to step with my right and find I cannot free it from the earth's embrace. I panic, curse and for one idiotic heartbeat take my eye off Sisbert and look down to my stricken leg. I pull frantically but cannot free it, then with a mighty heave I find myself lurching forwards, and with a pop my foot shoots out of my boot, still stuck in the mire.

I stumble forwards, dropping my sword and landing in a sprawling heap in the filth. I see just vaguely a flash of silver in my peripheral vision and feel the rush of air as the axe blade scythes just inches from my face. Desperately, I reach out for my sword with my left hand and roll over onto my back with the blade held before me.

With a look of utter horror I see the blond giant above me. He screams a victory cry and slams the axe down onto my left shoulder. I do not yell in pain, for the sheer agony of the blow has driven all the wind from me. I cannot blink, let alone move as the burning sensation shoots from my shoulder and seems to reach all the way to my toes. Tears well in my eyes as my mother's image comes to mind; she lays there in the darkness, a blackened silhouette in the firelight. She takes her punishment from those legionaries without a sound. It is only now I realise that it is my presence that stops her from crying out. I think for the first time I realise what courage she showed, even as her lifeblood poured from between her legs and her soul was stolen by the legionaries who defiled her body; my mother's dying thought was of me.

I feel a surge of anger, energy driven by nothing but pure hatred. It is not this Sisbert that has stirred such strong emotion, but my

hatred for Rome, for my cowardly father, and for the puny chief that I
had slain as he feasted in his hall. Middle earth is a cruel place, filled
with nothing but pain and suffering. I have suffered enough; it is
someone else's turn now.

I send a swift prayer to the spinners as I vault to my feet and see
that my mail has held. Those three hags surely have a long, lingering
death spun for me, but it will not be today. My left arm hangs limp at
my side, so I have to reach round with my right and take the sword
from my left hand as I cannot move the fingers. My breathing is
heavy, steam fogs the air and for the first time I see a twinge of fear in
Sisbert's honey-brown eyes.

I howl a cry of pent-up rage and charge Sisbert, sending blow
after blow against a boiled leather cuirass I assume he has either been
gifted from a Roman or taken from a corpse. My sword moves quicker
than a darting snake's tongue, licking in and out to land blow after
blow on a dumbfounded Sisbert. I can feel the blood pouring down my
left arm and back and know the fight to be over, but I do not care. The
bloodlust is upon me now and to stop me Sisbert will have to kill me,
though I do not think he has the courage. I batter him to submission
until he is whimpering on his knees and I stand tall above him, my
sword resting on his neck.

Slowly I come back to my senses and, as if waking from a dream,
see we are not alone in the pit. A ring of spears surrounds me, men
from both the Marcomanni and the Quadi. My breathing is shallow
and laboured. I feel the urge to vomit and my head spins like Donar
has struck me with his great hammer. 'Drop your sword,' a faceless
warrior says from behind his shield. I obey, slump to my knees and
spray vomit over Sisbert's boots.

There is a commotion above me on the sides of the pit. I squint and
look up to see the king of the Marcomanni slump to the floor, Balomar's sword still stuck fast in his chest. It is done, I think, and I smile,
even as I pass into oblivion.

34

Gods, I ached the morning after that battle. I had a lad wake me just before dawn and it took all the strength I possessed just to roll off my cot. I landed in a heap on the floor, quite unable to pull myself to my feet. I was still a young man then, though that morning I discovered the difference between still being young and youth. A youth would have vaulted from his cot, breathed deep the sweet air and revelled in the fact he had survived to see the sun rise. He would have eaten a hearty breakfast, drunk deep from a skin of ale and gone about his morning duties with relish. I, on the other hand, cursed profoundly as I struggled into my mail, every muscle in my body screaming in agony. My palms were blistered from wielding sword and shield; my feet were in ruins and my back felt as though I had spent the last year living as a slave in one of Dacia's gold mines. It was clear that I was no longer in my youth.

The cut I had taken under my nose was still open and raw. I stupidly poked it and the rush of surging pain made me wince; as I sucked air in through my mouth, the swollen lump in my gum that had been my two front teeth flared and I cursed aloud in agony.

'Lord, are you okay?' A young warrior appeared at the tent flap, the same one who had woken me. 'Wine,' I managed to croak. 'Bring wine, lots of it.'

I was drunk by mid-morning, and by the time the sun crested the horizon in its slow descent I was a lumbering, slurring mess in mail. I shouted orders, laughed at my own jokes, vomited and drank some more. No one could understand what I was saying, no one would ride at my side, and when I fell from Hilde's back as afternoon was turning to evening, no one approached to help me remount. Ruric had the men form camp around my stricken form. I lay there in the grass, watching the blurry ball of fire in the sky, and quietly soiled myself. I remember feeling a prick of shame at that and when the next urge to vomit had me gagging, I found I was unable to roll from my back, the weight of my armour being too much. I gagged on regurgitated wine, choked on it, and gave myself to the blackness.

When I woke, it was to Ruric and Ketill both standing over me. They were muttering to each other, maybe arguing. 'Wine,' I croaked and tried to rise; the pain in my head was fierce and overpowering. I slumped back onto my cot.

'I think you may have had enough wine, brother,' Ketill said as he lowered himself to his knees. 'How's the head?'

'Oh gods,' I moaned and retched as my stomach convulsed. Ketill didn't move, he just smiled at me. 'I would be greatly surprised if you had anything left to bring up, old friend. I'm certain I saw enough sick leave this tent last night to fill a barrel. Water?'

'Wine.'

'No more fucking wine,' Ruric said. He leant down and

slapped me hard across the face. I tasted the familiar metallic taste of blood and knew he had reopened the cut beneath my nose. 'I told you the day before yesterday you need to sort yourself out! And what do you do? Spend the day drinking yourself into oblivion! You're no *leader*, no *lord!* You're a fraud and a coward, and I'm just about done with you!'

Ruric stormed from the tent while I lay still in my cot, stunned to silence. 'Well, who pissed in his boots?' I scoffed and gently eased myself to an upright position.

'That would be you, old friend. There is some truth in what he says; you should heed his words.'

I made to reply but Ketill cut me off. 'No, Alaric, we need you now more than ever. You may think the battle two days ago was going to be the worst of it. I tell you now it isn't.'

'What's happened?' I asked, reading the grave expression on Ketill's face.

'You need to see it for yourself,' was all he said.

* * *

Painfully, I washed and dressed and with my stomach still churning I mounted Hilde, who had even joined in with the general disparagement of my behaviour the day before by trying to throw me off. I had no idea of where Ketill was taking me or what we were going to find when we got there, though I assumed it was nothing good. I saw Saxa as we rode from our camp. Apart from a brief and joyless reunion the night before last I had not seen her or my young son – well, I might well have done, but not sober anyway. I gave her a feeble wave, and she just looked at me with eyes full of hate and regret. She had not believed me when I had told her that we were only assaulting Viritium to save her and the boy; the lie had been too easy to see through. She was, I knew, torn between her loyalty to me and that of her father and brother. Secretly I suspected she had been left behind just to spy on me and somehow feedback to her family of my movements, though how she would accomplish that I had no idea. I thought again then of Birgir, his strange behaviour and sudden desire to work independently. Was I jumping at shadows? It was certainly not impossible that there were men in my ranks who would betray me for nothing more than a bag of silver. I was all too aware of the calibre of men my banner attracted; proud of it, in fact. But Birgir? No, he was as loyal as Ruric or Gerulf, I was certain.

We rode for half a morning, Ketill setting a rigorous pace and me swaying in the saddle behind him. I asked where we were going twice but got no reply. I was too annoyed and ashamed of my behaviour to ask again, so we rode in silence. We were just coming out from a small crop of trees when Ketill suddenly reined in his horse and waited for me on the road. 'You will not like this, brother. In fact, I hope you do not. I hope it makes your blood boil.' He moved aside and for the first time I saw bright light filtering into a clearing in the trees. For the first time, I saw the bodies hanging from the branches.

Four of my men were swinging in the wind. Four brave sons of the Ravensworn left for the crows. It was an outrage; a savage, disgusting act of cowardice that I knew was aimed at me. Those poor souls had done nothing to deserve such a horrifying and gruesome end. Their only crime was to be warriors under my banner.

As I got closer, my revulsion doubled. The poor men had not just been hanged; they had been disembowelled, their manhood removed and stuffed in their mouths, probably while they were still breathing. There were two of Ketill's men waiting in the shadows; at an unspoken order from their chief, they cut the bodies down, lowering them gently to the ground. I looked on in horror. I did not want to; I wanted to turn away and spray vomit over the thick undergrowth that lined the trees. But I could not stop looking. Their faces were an ash grey with a green tinge. Their eyes told me all I needed to of the anguish they had suffered before death finally released them from their Hel on earth. 'Who found them?' I said, anger slowly replacing the revulsion in my bones.

'My lads did. We had no contact from Gerulf or Birgir all day yesterday, and Ruric and I were concerned. I sent out a couple of lads after you had passed out yesterday evening, hoping to catch them up and discover what they knew. They only got as far as here.'

'So we still know nothing of Gerulf or Birgir?'

'No. But if this is anything to go by, we won't be hearing from them anytime soon, if at all.'

I sank to my knees and sobbed silently. I did not cry for the four dead men at my feet, for if I am being honest I didn't even know their names. They may have had family eagerly awaiting their return at some small village or other, and that wait, it seemed, would last until the end of days. I cried for Gerulf, my loyal captain who I had sent to his death, and Birgir, the scout who seemed would be forever young. How could I have doubted his loyalty, after all he had done for me? I thought back to the fight for Ulpia Noviomagus; his reckless charge and clumsy kill once we had snuck over the walls that had almost got us both slaughtered before we could open the gate and let the Ravensworn in.

I wiped the tears from my eyes and breathed deep, despite the stench from the bodies. 'Bury them,' I said to the two Harii warriors. They turned to Ketill for confirmation, who nodded his assent. That small gesture left me feeling lonely. I commanded the greatest warband in all of Germania – well, what was left of it – and here I was, entirely reliant on my old comrade. As I rose to my feet a thought struck me, and I realised it had been lurking at the back of my mind since I had first sighted the bodies. I looked around at the ground. It was dry and dusty, as one would expect at the latter stages of a summer as fierce as that one had been.

'What *is* it?' Ketill asked, trying to follow my eyes.

'You two, when did you discover the bodies?'

One of the two men looked up. He was young, a shot of dark hair above a pale face. Again he looked to Ketill, who once more nodded. 'Just before sundown, Lord.'

'Anyone else been here?'

'No.' Ketill answered this time. 'I would not let anyone else near this place until you had seen it. The only people who know of this are us four and Ruric.'

I nodded, a frown set on my face. 'What *is it*?' Ketill said with urgency this time.

I looked once more at the light-coloured mud, dry as old timber and dustier than a Roman prison cell. 'There is no sign of a struggle,' I said in a quiet voice. 'Surely these men would have fought. Gerulf certainly would have! Where is the blood on the ground? The odd link of broken mail? Where are the enemy dead for that matter?'

There was a period of silence as each man considered the question. 'Ketill?' I asked as I studied him.

'Leave us,' Ketill said to his two men, who immediately backed away out of earshot. 'You are right,' he said once we were alone, 'something isn't right here. I am angry with myself for not noticing.' He slapped his hand against his thigh and growled. 'What do you think?' he asked me.

'They were not killed here,' I said. I pointed further up the track, deeper into the break in the trees. The sunlight was stronger here; waves of heat broke the air as it rose from the baking mud. 'Look there, there are faint lines in the mud, running directly before us.'

'Or towards us,' Ketill said as he crouched and ran his eye down the path. 'Fenrir's fucking fangs, these poor men were dragged here!'

'Yes,' I said. 'I think they were hanged, their genitals removed; their guts sliced open as they were slowly strangled, but it was not here, brother.'

'If not here, then...' Ketill left the question open. When I looked at him, his eyes were wide and I thought I saw a rare speck of fear cross his face.

'That, old friend, is what we need to find out.'

35

I abstained from wine for the days after the discovery of the bodies. Even the pain of my missing teeth and the wound below my nose seemed to lessen, such was my desire for justice. I rode out in front of the main column at dawn every day and did not return till after dark. We found nothing. Not just no sign of Warin and Dagr, but no signs of life at all. Village after village had been burnt out and all the livestock had been driven from the land. All that was left was smoke and the dead. I could not comprehend what I was seeing. Why would Dagr go to such lengths? I understood the desire to take from the land, for the more livestock he gathered, the less food there was for my men to forage as they marched in his wake. Though, to be fair, we ate well and wanted for nothing. Ruric had emptied the stores at Viritium before we left and there was always a grain barn or two hiding just off the beaten track for us to relieve of its precious contents. Ruric insisted we pay our way with silver taken from one of my great chests, and I did not object when he suggested it, for it seemed we had enough enemies without leaving new ones at our rear.

I was blinded by my fury, a burning desire to see Dagr and his cowardly son strung up at the end of a noose. They would die slowly, I vowed, and I would look them in the eye as they breathed their last. The final thing they would see on this earth was my face, I vowed it to all the gods. Ketill and his men rode with me; we both agreed it would be best to separate them as much as possible from the Ravensworn, for I did not want it to become common knowledge that our scouts had been taken and we were marching blind.

On the sixth day of my fury-driven and frantic ride, I found Ketill waiting for me atop a small ridge in the road. He had with him twenty men, all armoured and armed to the teeth. 'Found something,' was all he said as I approached. 'Let's go.'

Emmerich Fridumarson, chief of Ketill's guard and one of the most fearsome men I had ever encountered, was the man who led us into thick woodland. Giant trunks of pine, oak and ash rose above us, shadowing us from the merciless sun. Ketill's men were silent. Even when Emmerich asked us to tether our horses at the edge of the woods, he spoke in nothing but a whisper. I crunched and snapped my way through the thick undergrowth, much to the disgust of Ketill, who tutted every time my boots hit the ground. 'How do you do it?' I asked him as we slithered between the trees. It was a genuine question; that was not the first time I had witnessed the warriors of the Harii in what they would consider their natural habitat. They trod lighter than field mice and left a smaller trail than a lonely worm. 'We just watch where we are putting our feet,' he said with an annoyingly straight face. For what seemed like half a day or more we crept and stopped, ran and crawled. The forest seemed all but deserted save from the odd bird call. I grew tired quickly, making me more and more frustrated. 'Can someone please tell me where the fuck we are going?' I snapped. 'Feels as though we are going to pay Vidar a visit!'

Vidar was the god of the forest, and more importantly to me: the god of vengeance. It seemed appropriate that we were going to seek our revenge in his domain, presuming that was where we were going, of course. Right then I was, I think, the only one in our party who had no idea of our destination.

Emmerich signalled the halt and scurried down our line until he was beside me. 'Lord Alaric,' he said in a flat tone, 'you are a great warrior and a leader of men, of that there is no doubt.'

'Thank you, Emmerich,' I said in the most sarcastic voice I could.

'But we have left your world, out there in the sunlight. In here, under the canopy of these trees, this is my world. And in my world, you do as you're told. Understood?'

I considered him for a moment. His heavily muscled torso covered in dark blue tattoos and thick arm rings. He had a sword perhaps near equal to mine in length at his waist, though it looked like a toy against his massive leg. His face was a patchwork of thin white scars. He wore no beard to disguise them and had his hair cut short more like a Roman than a German. His eyes were flat, seemingly void of the spark of life. If I fought him in single combat he would kill me within three heartbeats; he knew it, I knew it. I decided it was probably best not to piss him off any more than I already had. 'Understood,' I said. 'But if you could be so kind, Emmerich, feared warrior of the Harii, would you please tell me where we are headed? And why you have made me crawl through mile upon mile of woodland inhabited by no more than the odd field mouse?'

Emmerich sighed, but did not strike me, which I took as a small victory. 'We are headed to a sacred grove, used long ago by our tribe. Now, we are unsure as to who festers there or what god it is they worship. But we believe this is where your men were killed.'

I gawped. 'You think my men were killed all the way in here? Then dragged all that way back west?' It was impossible, folly I was sure. Six days I had ridden like a madman; there was no stone in all of Germania I had left unturned in my search for Gerulf and the rest of my men.

'Yes,' Emmerich said, still looking at me with those dead eyes.

'But there would be signs, surely? Tracks left on the ground, devastation left amongst the trees?' I was going to go on and say that even I could have tracked that, but I did not, as deep down I knew I probably couldn't.

'There has been plenty of what you describe, Alaric. We have been following their trail since we left the road.'

'Oh,' I said as my cheeks coloured. 'Well... lead on then, Emmerich.'

For another hour we crept. We left the sun behind, walking deeper into the dark abyss. After a time, I began to hear noises, faint at first, nothing more than a whisper on the breeze. They grew stronger, more distinct, until I could make out the gentle sounds of chanting. I began to *feel* something in the air around me, something that could not be grasped: something not from this world. We walked into a wall of mist, the rays of the sun behind us now. A cold chill ran down my spine, one so sudden and violent I visibly flinched, much to the horror of the man behind me. I was not the only one in our company to feel as such. Ketill's men coughed nervously and one or two cast anxious glances back the way we had come.

I hurried through the men thronging together until I was next to Ketill and Emmerich. Both men stood as still as stone as they squinted through the mist that shrouded us. 'What sort of Loki magic is this?' I hissed.

Emmerich said nothing; Ketill shrugged and said: 'I do not think this is magic, brother. Listen.'

I closed my eyes and focused on my hearing. I heard nothing apart from the rhythmic chanting at first but after a while, I heard what Ketill did. 'Water?'

'Hmm,' Ketill said with a nod. There was the faint but unmistakable sound of bubbling water. Now my ears were attuned, I heard it trickle and the odd splash where its current was disturbed.

'A hot spring,' I said, my courage taking a boost. This was no witchcraft or magic causing the dense mist – there appeared to be a natural source of hot water ahead of us.

'How many men do you think are down there?' Ketill asked. He looked back at his own men, silently weighing up his options.

'One way to find out,' I said as I silently tugged my sword free of its scabbard. 'Gerulf and Birgir could be there. We have to help them.'

Even as I finished speaking, the chanting rose to a rounding crescendo, quickly followed by a piercing, high-pitched scream of a man clearly in agony. 'That's it, we go now!' I bellowed at the top of my voice, heedless of giving away the advantage of surprise.

I raised my blade before me and charged through the mist; I could see no more than two paces in front of my face, and my boots were nothing more than a deeper shade of black when I looked down. I had no idea what type of ground I ran over; it could have been formed of the very wool used to spin my fate, though it felt more like Fenrir's fur. I had no notion of whether Ketill had unleashed his hounds behind me, or whether I was charging alone; I didn't care. My men were in there, or so I thought, and I was going to get them out.

I ran and ran, charging all the way. It was disorientating, as with every step I expected to meet a crowd of cloaked priests or a huddle of armed men in mail. I met neither, no one. I just kept running until my lungs hurt and I could no longer hold my sword above my head. I stopped, panting, looking around me dumbfounded. Where *was* I? Was it really just mist formed from a hot spring, or had I passed into another world? It was only then I heard it; the distinct clang of iron on iron and screams from men, the kind they only make when they have taken a fatal wound.

I swivelled on the spot, trying desperately to gauge where the cacophony of battle was coming from. I had no idea of the direction I had come from nor what lay around me. Two steps to my left could have been the trunk of a giant tree; two steps to my right could have been my death. I swivelled again, slower this time. That was when I saw it: a flash of scarlet in the world of white and grey. It was so brief I was not sure if I had really seen it. I paused, unsure if I should trust my own instincts, disorientated as I was. But then as I watched, a shadow of a man fell to the ground. Another black figure on top loomed above him and ran him through with a spear. There was no doubting it now. I sucked in a deep breath, adjusted the grip on the black leather pommel of my sword, and charged.

36

I vaulted the body, blood still oozing from a deep wound in his chest. As I leapt above him, I noticed he was both young and pale. He wore an off-white robe spattered with gore. As I moved towards the clamour of battle, the mist seemed to thin and all around me was carnage and death. Ketill was battling two strong-looking men, both with spears. As I watched, he pushed aside a spear thrust from the first man and ran him through with his sword. With his blade still embedded in the first man's chest, he caught the second man's spear with his free hand and pulled his sword free, cleaving the second man's head clean off with a backhand blow. He showed me his teeth as I passed him, the bloodlust fully upon him. 'Thought you had left us to it, Alaric!' he said with a snarl.

'Just giving you a head start, brother, that's all!' A man clad in just tunic and woollen trousers came at me with an axe. He hacked clumsily at my right shoulder. I parried the blow with ease and swiped my sword in a savage arc deep into his thigh. Another man jumped on my back and knocked me to the ground. My head hit a rock with such force I rebounded right off it, and with my ears still ringing, I grabbed my assailant around his waist as he tried to rise. I had lost my sword in the fall but my right hand found a dagger in a sheath at the man's belt. I yanked it free and jabbed hard into the man's chest, feeling it grate on his ribs as the blade plunged into his lung. I left it in there as I recovered my sword and got to my feet.

I staggered for a couple of paces; men streamed past me in all directions, friend or foe I had no idea. I had lost sight of Ketill and could not make out anyone else I recognised as I stumbled deeper into the fray. 'You there!' a man bellowed behind me. As I turned I saw two men coming for me, one armed with a spear, the other with a longsword. 'Come and die, you traitorous cur,' the man armed with the spear growled. It was he who had spoken before, and as he approached I squinted through the mist, trying to work out if I could place his grizzled features. He wore a dark riding cloak, although I could see the gleam of mail underneath. His hood was up, masking his eyes, but I could make out a shaggy grey beard and a toothless mouth. He walked with a stoop. He was slight of build, and a fine-looking bone-hilted knife stuck out from the top of his left boot. His companion was younger, tall and blond. He had no beard and even through the mist I could make out his piercing blue eyes. For a heartbeat they halted me in my tracks, for the resemblance to Ishild was so obvious it almost stopped my heart.

Did she have a son? Gods, did I perhaps have another sibling I had all but forgotten? My mouth was slack, my eyes glazed as I stared at the young warrior. He raised his sword uncertainly, as if this was the first time he had bared it in anger. Judging by his age, it could well have been. The old man circled to my left and gestured for Blue Eyes to go right. I shook my head clear of

Ishild's image and concentrated on the older man. Blue Eyes was no swordsman, that much was clear from the way he held the blade. The older man knew his business though, and as he circled, he dropped to a crouch with the spear point held towards my chest. I tried a feint, stepping in with my blade out to my right and letting it swing with a yell. The spearman didn't move an inch. He had been trained to fight the way I had, it seemed, or his eyes never left mine.

Most men give some sort of warning when they are about to attack. Their eyes will lock on their intended target or their bodies will flinch or shift slightly. There was no hint of either of these before the spear point licked out quicker than my eye could follow and hit me square in the chest. It was a magnificent thrust, one that my assailant would have expected to have pierced my mail and sent me packing to the Allfather's hall. To be honest, as I looked down in panic and saw it pass my guard, I prepared myself for that very end. But I did not die.

The leaf-shaped blade struck my chest, but instead of pene-trating through my mail and cleaving my sternum in two, it struck something solid and rebounded off me with an almighty clang. We both paused, the greybeard and I, and studied my chest. The golden torc, the one I had taken from Wulfric, the cowardly chief of the Fenni, vibrated at the end of its chain. I held it with my left hand and lifted it to my face. If ever there was a sign that I was blessed by the gods, that was it. Wotan himself had saved me from certain death, and by the looks of it lost his remaining eye in the process. There was a small rounded dent in the precious metal, right where the Allfather's remaining eye had been. I kissed it and let it fall gently back into place. 'That was the Allfather himself you just struck,' I said to the spearman, holding my sword towards him. 'You have just made a grave mistake.'

I charged the greybeard, who stood stock still as I cleaved his head from his shoulders. When it fell to the floor, it rolled and his seemingly awed face looked up at me, the spark of life still evident in his eyes. He looked as though he was in the presence of a god, and at that moment I felt as if I was a product of Wotan's seed, for surely I had just cheated certain death. Finally, the spark went out of the eyes, like the last ember in an abandoned campfire.

'Who are you?' I said to the blue-eyed youth, who had not moved throughout the whole encounter.

'I... I...' His mouth blubbered like a trout's; his hands trembled and his sword dropped to the ground with a thud.

'Who are you?' I said again. 'What are you doing here?'

I was dimly aware that the fight was over. Ketill was haranguing his men, forming them up and counting his losses. Emmerich was dunking his head in the hot spring, washing his face free of blood with glee.

'My name is Eghbert,' he said, his eyes downcast.

'Why are you here, Eghbert?' I asked as I studied him closely. The more I looked, the more he resembled Ishild. It wasn't just his eyes; it was the perfect round shape of his face; the high cheekbones that stood out like molehills. His skin was a different tone to hers; he was bronzed by the sun, whereas Ishild stayed as pale as winter. 'What are you to Warin?'

He coloured at this, showing anger in his pale eyes. 'I am *nothing* to Warin, just as he is nothing to me. I am Eghbert, son of Agnarr, rightful king of the Suebi.'

I was stunned to silence at this. All knew Agnarr had no sons; why else would he have wanted me to succeed him when he passed from this world? And then, it hit me like a Donar's hammer. Agnarr did have one son, and he had asked that one son to take up his birthright when the old king finally breathed his last. Me.

A blatant truth that had been right in front of my face. Ishild was my sister, but not just from the same mother; from the same father as well. I thought of the old king then, as he had been on the day he had come to my home and taken Ishild away. Tall, dark haired, well built and all powerful. A thick black beard, piercing brown eyes. I stood, dumbstruck with my tongue hanging from my mouth. All my life I had resented my father, cursed him for being weak and a coward. I despised him for not fighting off the Romans when they raided our lands and raped and slaughtered my poor helpless mother. But that man was not my father, could not be. He was too short, too blonde, too different in every comparable way to me. I was not the son of some poor farmer, destined to end my days with a plough and a failing crop. I was the son of a king, born to a noble line. Agnarr had not offered me his crown just because he thought I was the most suitable man to wear it; he offered it to me because I was his son. Well, *one* of his sons, it seemed. 'Who is your mother?' I asked Eghbert, hoping there wasn't another repressed memory about to surface in my mind.

'Her name was Adelle. She died when I was young.'

'What happened?'

'Same as what I imagine happened to yours, brother. Yes, I know who you are, Alaric, and I know why you are here. He always killed his women, once he had become tired of them.'

'W... what do you mean?'

'Father. He kept women in different places, always on the edge of his territory. Once he grew tired of them, he simply had them killed.'

'My mother was killed by Rome!' I spat. How dare this whoreson speak of my mother, how dare he speak of my *father* like that! I had not known him well, old Agnarr, but everything I had learned of him spoke of a good man, a just king.

'Yours would not be the first tragedy Rome dealt out on our father's behalf. Long had he allied himself with the cursed empire and her red-cloaked soldiers. It was perfect, can you not see? He was hundreds of miles away from the Danube and Rome's borders, no threat to the emperor or any of his domain. An alliance was made, promises swapped and kept.'

'What sort of promises?'

'What do you think? Agnarr gave up certain tribes, allowed them to be raided or destroyed by Rome when their chief got too ambitious or a husband stood between him and a woman he desired. In exchange, Rome got to exert her will on our lands, seemingly burning and destroying whoever they wanted. Our people have lived in fear of Rome for years, but it is not Rome that has been our enemy.'

I thought back to that night: my mother's screams, the heat of the fires. Rome had taken everything I loved in a single night; my whole life from that point had been a battle against the empire and their legions. Turns out, they were just puppets in someone else's game. 'How long has this been going on?'

'Decades, as far as I know. Warin hopes to strike the same deal with Rome. Ishild hopes to secure it for him. One of the conditions for both parties is your head on a spike.'

I scoffed. 'Of course it is. Long have Rome wanted me dead.' But only because of the harm I have caused them, I thought to myself. In so many ways, I had brought this on myself. 'So what was Warin's plan?'

'For you? I think he thought he would destroy you on the battlements of Viritium's walls. He argued against sallying out to meet your army, until he was named a *nithing* by certain war chiefs. He had no choice then but to face you in open battle, or lose face and likely his crown. But there is more you should know.' Eghbert sucked his teeth and ran his tongue around his mouth; he seemed unsure of how to continue.

'What is it?' I asked. Ketill's men encircled us now; the battle was finished and it appeared so had the looting.

'There are traitors in your ranks. Men you would trust with your life will betray you at the end.'

My talk with Tacitus came back to me; had he not said something similar? I had dismissed it then as the talk of an old man who knew his life span measured the next few beats of his heart. But now it seemed a grain of truth lingered in the midst of the old man's ramblings.

'Who?'

'I do not know, truly. But there was more than one, maybe as many as five. These men will be well rewarded when you are dead.'

I nodded. 'So be it,' I said. I turned to Ketill, who wordlessly gripped my shoulder. He, I knew, would never betray me.

'Where is Warin going?' I asked Eghbert; my eyes were still locked with Ketill's.

'East. A place called Parienna, in the lands of the Arsietae.'

'Why there?' I knew the place, had taken the Ravensworn through there once before. It was a small, walled, fortified town, but the Arsietae were a small, peaceful tribe. I did not understand why they would play host to a northern king and the emperor's messengers.

'I do not know. The Arsietae are allied to Rome though, so they may see it as a safe place to meet.'

I visualised the journey in my mind. We were perhaps ten days' hard riding from Parienna; plenty of time to catch Warin and end his wicked schemes. 'What do you think?' I asked Ketill.

'Let us kill this whoreson and then go and kill Warin. Enough schemes, I think.'

I smiled, one of my evil grins that are all teeth. My sword still lay naked in my palm; it was the work of two heartbeats to swing it in a flat arc and send the edge grating into Eghbert's skull. Blood sprayed and seemed to hang in the mist, and my brother Eghbert slumped to the ground and died without so much as a whimper.

37

I do not remember either eating or sleeping for the next five days. I rode with fury in my heart. Seething anger pulsed through my veins; Hilde felt my urgency too and at times it was almost as if she glided across the uneven terrain as we galloped east, always east. Each morning the rising sun blinded me and as it kissed the western horizon on its descent each evening, I basked in the final rays of warmth as I braced myself for a few hours' more riding in the chill of the darkness.

I pushed the men like they had never been pushed before. I jumped at every shadow, found myself fretting with every snap of a twig or clang of armour. I trusted no one except Ketill and his Harii, for he had proved himself loyal beyond measure. If he was going to betray me, he would have done it the year before as I lay under his stinking bed of straw, listening as he entertained a Roman agent of the frumentarii. I was even distant with Ruric, Eghbert's words ringing endlessly in my mind. *There are traitors in your ranks. Men you would trust with your life.* Would Ruric betray me? My oldest comrade in arms, the man who had stood at my side when the Ravensworn had been no more than a fantasy. I did not think he would, but I was uncertain of everyone.

We had had no contact from Gerulf and Birgir, and their continued absence gnawed at my wits. Again I kept thinking of Birgir and his suspicious behaviour before and after the battle at Viritium. He'd owned nothing when the Ravensworn took him in. A runt from the streets of Goridorgis, capital of the Marcomanni, he had grown to manhood in my ranks. I was sure he was loyal but could not shake my doubts.

I thought of what friends remained to me as I rode. Balomar, now of course king of the Marcomanni, would always be in my debt, but I feared the trouble I had caused him in the early part of his rein with my continued raids on Roman lands would mean he would be unlikely to grant me any further favours. I had even raided his tribe on numerous occasions with Areogaesus, King of the Quadi. I wondered if those small crimes would have been forgotten. For all I knew, he too had been conspiring with Rome for my death. Areogaesus I knew was firmly in bed with the empire and flaunted the silver they paid him. His lands were the gateway into Germania for the legions; he knew it and so did they. I did not think it was an alliance I would ever be able to persuade him to break.

I finally got some answers on the sixth day of our hard ride. I was trotting along on a nameless gelding, Hilde being freed of the burden of my weight for the day as I feared her going lame under the continued strain. I saw in the distance a man riding hard, angling straight towards me. I was chewing on some stale bread, washing it down with a flask of warm ale. I wiped my mouth and tossed the residue of the loaf when the rider drew near. I could make him out now, a scruffy youth with tangles of dirty blonde hair beneath a plain iron helmet. He had pale skin and above his lip and round his jawline were the beginnings of a wispy beard. I half-smiled at the sight of him, despite my mixed feelings. Fear and nerves knotted my stomach, and I felt a cold trickle of sweat run down my spine. For this was not just some nameless scout coming in to make his report; it was Birgir.

* * *

'Two days, you say?' I had dismounted the gelding and absently stroked his nose as I thought.

'At most, Lord. With luck, and a little help from The Sly One himself, we could catch them unprepared.'

'Surely they know we are on their trail?' I asked Birgir, still wanting to trust him so badly, but the feeling in my gut stood between me and my scout like a gushing river, keeping him at a distance.

'They have no rear guard, Lord. We have been able to follow them easily; they believe the men they killed a few days ago were all of us. This is the perfect opportunity to strike.'

'And where is Gerulf?' It was the second time I had asked this question. I wanted to make sure his answer was the same.

'He is with his men, Lord. He and five of his men still follow the trail of Warin's army.'

And there it was. Just as it had been when I had interrogated Wulfric in his inconsequential village. The same question asked twice had produced two different answers.

The first time I had asked where Gerulf was, just moments before, he had been trailing Warin with *six* men. Six men would be correct. Ten men had left with Gerulf and Birgir; four had been killed on Warin's order by those inhuman priests in the dense woodland. That would leave six men of the Ravensworn, plus Gerulf and Birgir.

I chewed on this, unsure whether I should challenge Birgir

on this or let it play. I decided on the latter. 'So Warin has reached Parienna?'

'Yes, Lord. As I left, his vanguard were approaching the town.'

'Tell me about it.'

He spoke, and I half listened, his lies weighing heavy on my mind. I knew Parienna, knew it to be a small town of little import. It had a short, wooden palisade that could be taken by a band of children given the right circumstance. I was not worried about fighting my way into the town; it was who I would meet within the walls that interested me.

'Who holds the town? Did you see any Roman banners?' This was my primary concern. Warin would receive no overwhelming support from any tribes this far from his homeland, I was certain. They were Sarmatians, the tribes out here, men who fought almost solely on horseback and despised the western tribes, thinking them all soft and gutless. They came from the wilderness of the eastern steppe, and they loved nothing more than a good war.

'No Roman banners, Lord. Roman agents are within the walls though. They arrived before Warin did.'

I remained silent, the only sound the soft breathing from the gelding as I carried on stroking his muzzle. I fed the horse an apple from the small pouch at my waist, and finally said: 'How many Romans?'

'Two frumentarii agents plus a half century of men from the Fourteenth.'

I made a low growl in the base of my throat as I thought. Birgir was being specific, *very* specific. How could he possibly know there were two Roman agents within those walls? How had he counted fifty Roman soldiers as he sat atop his mount a mile or so away? There was no way he could *possibly* know. Unless...

'How long have you served me for, Birgir?' I asked in a soft voice.

'Lord?' the young scout asked, eyebrows raised in confusion at the question.

'How long have you been with the Ravensworn?'

'This winter will be my fifth under your banner, unless I am mistaken,' he said, eyebrows still nestled under his straw-coloured hair.

I nodded at this, my mind still reeling. Could Birgir possibly be betraying me? Or were my wits so strained that I had sunk to thinking even my most loyal men sought my corpse dumped in an unmarked grave? Birgir had been a runt when he had caught my eye on the streets of Goridorgis. I had been visiting Balomar, had dined in his hall and drunk far too much dark ale. The next day, severely hungover, I had been riding out of the town's great gates when a small street kid with dirty blonde hair had offered to polish my boots for a loaf of bread. I had looked at this child: painfully thin, cheekbones protruding from the flesh of his face like spear tips; twig-thin arms that shook when he held them outstretched as his wasted shoulders were unable to support their weight. He wore just an old white and grubby tunic, despite the icy winter that gripped the land; his feet were blue and his knobbly knees wobbled with every step. No, Birgir would not betray me; it was unthinkable. He was my sworn man, and only death could break that oath.

'Have I... done well by you, in those five years?' I asked.

Birgir scowled at the question. It made him look younger than he was, as if he was that half-starved child again, shivering in the winter gale. 'Yes, Lord,' he said.

'Good, good.' I nodded, unused to feeling this confused,

embarrassed at myself. In truth, I had always taken for granted the support of the men I commanded. I ruled by fear and valour, always exposing myself to the same risks as the rank and file. I thought I led them well, though in truth, it was more than likely that there were many men serving under my blood-red banner who would not be too upset to see me dead before my time. 'I will order the men to speed up the march,' I said with more conviction than I felt. 'We shall proceed as you say, young Birgir. They won't know what's hit them.' I smiled at the lad, hoping it appeared genuine. Birgir beamed back at me, saluted, and made off into the distance. I watched him ride away, tears pricking in the corner of my eyes. Was I being a fool, to trust this man? This fine young man who had blossomed in my ranks, risen to become one of my most trusted companions. *Familia,* the Romans call it. A band of people who were not necessarily family by blood, but they tied themselves to me with their actions. Ketill, Ruric, Gerulf, Otto, Baldo, Birgir, Saxa and of course my son and unborn child. Not all were my family, I wasn't particularly fond of them all at times, but they were my *Familia,* and I would die for them in a heartbeat.

Birgir had made a simple mistake, I assured myself. Gerulf was ahead with six good men, not five. Gerulf would be my loyal captain until the sky fell upon us and chaos ruled the land. Yes, a simple mistake, that was all.

38

Two days passed in the blink of an eye.

We rode at breakneck pace; no men were spared to protect our wagons of food and the huddle of women, children, merchants and general hangers-on that seemed to attach themselves to any body of armed men on the march. We left them to their fate, heedless of the consequences.

My spirits were soaring in those two days, all doubts quashed from my mind. We would reach Parienna, storm its feeble walls and slaughter every man inside. Then I would be free. Free of the schemes of Rome, free of Warin and my bewitching sister Ishild. Dagr too would die under my blade, as his father had before him.

I rode with Ruric before dawn on the third day. We had all the men up and in the saddle well before daybreak, determined to make the most of our surprise. 'It is going to be a fine day, old friend,' I said with a wide grin. I could just make out the darkened shadows of Parienna's walls in the eerie light of pre-dawn.

'If you say so,' Ruric said, his head swivelling as he tried to keep track of the men riding recklessly around us. 'Should we not slow the pace? We're going to lose men and horses riding at this speed in the dark.'

'Don't be such an old woman!' I chided my longest-serving warrior. He grunted before allowing a slow grin to spread across his face. I studied him then, taking in every scar and wrinkle. The man truly was the greatest thing that had ever happened to me. It had been his idea to form a warband, his idea for me to be its leader. It had been the day after we had colluded to make Balomar king of the Marcomanni. We had been sitting in the shade of Balomar's hall, sharing a skin of good wine and simply enjoying the fact we had survived Balomar's scheme.

'What will you do now?' he had said to me.

'Me?' I had shrugged. To be honest I could have just stayed where I was, serving King Balomar and settling down with some woman or other. I might even have been happy. I'd had no plan, ever since the day I'd stormed off from Father's sorry little farm. I just wanted to earn enough coin so I would never have to go back.

'You should go out on your own. Start a warband and sell your sword for silver. People would pay good coin to have you on their side in a battle, Alaric.'

I remember rubbing my dark beard, which back then was by far less impressive than it is now. 'Why would they want me on their side?' I had asked.

'You are a leader, my friend. Not to mention the fact you seem to be as lucky as Loki in combat, and you are intelligent, generous but with a mean streak. You would make a fine leader of men. I will be your second in command,' he had said with a wink.

I thought back to that day so long ago as the first rays of sunlight crested the eastern horizon. 'Have I been the leader you always thought I would?' I asked Ruric.

'Huh?'

'That day, when we sat outside Balomar's hall and you first mentioned this crazy idea you had of me starting a warband. You said I would be a great leader, that men would want me on their side in a battle. Well, have I lived up to your expectations?'

Ruric did not answer at first. For a few heartbeats we rode in silence. I could see him weighing up the question. 'In the years since we helped Balomar steal the throne of the Marcomanni, what have you achieved?'

I said nothing. I had won more battles than even old One Eye himself could count, I had filled my chests with silver, brokered deals with chiefs and kings, gone back on many of those deals and slaughtered them in battle. I had attracted men to my banner quicker than a wounded deer attracts a wolfpack. 'I have done well for myself, I think.'

'Aye, you have, no denying that,' Ruric said. 'But have you done well by your men? That is the question. A lord can horde as much silver as he likes, he can carve himself a place in history with the edge of his blade. Kings can fear him; war chiefs cower under their furs at the very mention of his name. But what is the cost of this spear fame? It is no cost that can be weighed or shared, it is no treasure to be cherished or worshipped, like that torc around your neck.' Instinctively, my hand went to the golden torc, the one I had taken from Wulfric as payment for his treachery.

'The cost is in lives, Alaric. This last year has been the bloodiest in all the years I have served you, and let's face it, they have all been dominated by some war or other. But I say again, what is the cost in lives? How many men ride to those walls? Three hundred? How many men rode under your banner just a year ago?' I had tried to mutter some words in my defence, but he quickly cut me off. 'No, do not speak, Alaric. Two hundred souls have crossed into Hel's domain in this last year alone! By the Hanged, Alaric, this feud you have with Warin, this girl Ishild and Rome has gone too far. *You* have gone too far. I do not know what drives you to the edge of insanity, and to be truly honest I am not sure I want to. But you are my sworn lord and till this ends I am your man. But when this is done, when you have your victory and Warin's head is on a spike, I will leave. I will leave, Alaric, with your blessing or not. I am too old now for these games, for this life. I wish to grow fat and keep warm at the side of a small hearth; buy some land and find a fine plump woman to be my wife. This winter will be my fiftieth; fiftieth! Not many men live to see so many, especially men of the sword.'

I nodded, feeling slightly chastened by his words. Each one sent shards of truth charging up my spine, as if they had been fired from Donar's mighty hammer. I had not, I realised, become the great lord Ruric always thought I would be. I was too selfish, too self-centred. I spent my men's lives like coins of bronze, throwing them away whenever it suited my interests.

'So, to answer your question, yes, you have been a good lord for the most part. At times you have been rash, other times damn foolish. But no man is perfect in the eyes of the gods. You have won yourself a seat in the Allfather's hall, and a place in his shield wall at the end of days. Just heed this advice, my friend. Always, always, think of your men before you throw them into battle. Do not needlessly take away a loving son or father from this earth. Each life is precious. I know this after my long years treading the path of war. I see it so much clearer than I did when I was your age. I hope, one day, you will too.'

He reached out his arm and I clasped it. Tears streamed down my face. There was but one man alive who would speak to me the way Ruric just had, and once this battle was done I would lose him from my side forever. The mere thought of it made me sick with sorrow and worry.

'Thank you, Ruric,' I choked through my sobs. 'Thank you, for everything you have done for me and our men. My life will be poorer for not having you in it.'

He pushed my arm away, leant over and cuffed me round the back of the head. 'Don't be such a tart!' he said, though I could see the emotion on his face too. 'Now then, let us go and win one last victory together, shall we?'

39

Dawn broke across the eastern horizon. The light was blinding but the rush of warmth was glorious. A cacophony of excited shouts broke out amongst my men. Shielding my eyes, I squinted into the sunlight to see what had excited them so. Then I saw it and felt my spirits soar as high as a gliding eagle.

The gates were open.

All worries of assaulting the walls, of keeping my men organised and in unison throughout a brutal assault, dissipated to dust. The gates to Parienna were wide open, and I felt the touch of Loki in the sun's warming rays.

'What did I tell you?' Ruric said with a savage grin. He had a single-headed war axe loose in his right hand, and he swung his arm in a circle, the silver blade gleaming in the red and orange light of the dawn. 'One last day, Alaric. One more battle. Gods, I'm excited!' He grinned again then kicked his horse hard in the flanks, urging the beast towards the gate, which still hung seductively open.

I cannot remember ever being so elated at the prospect of bloodshed as I was right then, in the light of that glorious sunrise. I raced after Ruric, the Ravensworn all now at full gallop as we hurtled towards the open gate. What a fool Warin was, I thought as I bared my sword. And Dagr? Had he lost his wits? The man was an experienced chief, well-schooled in the art of war. How could he possibly allow his men to make such a blunder?

I passed Ketill, who was on foot with his men as always. 'Last one through the gate is a rotten egg!' I bellowed as I sped past him.

Over the thunder of Hilde's hooves and the tumult of the Ravensworn's excited screams and shouts, I faintly heard his reply: 'I don't mind missing the start, brother, as long as I'm still standing at the end!'

Baldo appeared at my right. He rode with just his knees with a longsword in one hand and a blacksmith's hammer in the other. I do not believe I have ever met a man who had a blood-lust like my loyal Baldo, and it appeared he would get his fill today. I heard Otto trying to restore some order to the men in his Hundred to no avail. As I watched, he threw his arms in the air in frustration and galloped after his disobedient men. I laughed, just for the pure joy of it. Otto, I knew, was still out to impress me, even though he was by then a well-respected captain among the men. He would have usually seen his men approach the gates in good order, keeping their lines and holding their discipline. I made a mental note to give him a good chiding once the battle was over.

Thirty paces from the gate and still we rode completely unmolested. Surely the thunder of our hooves had stirred the army inside? Surely even now they were raising the alarm, squeezing into their mail and brandishing their blades. And yet, no helmets appeared on the battlements; no banners were raised, no horns were sounded in panic and alarm.

And just like that, we were in.

I pounded through the open gate and let out a loud cry as I set my face to a snarl and raised my blade high. I had expected to find a multitude of men just rising from their cots, preparing to start the day. Cooking fires would be being lit; men would be leaving their huts or tents to go and take their morning ease, say hello to a neighbour or fetch water from the nearest supply. I had expected all of this and more; instead, we found nothing.

Nothing. Not a soul stirred in Parienna. Were they all deaf? Had they drunk themselves into such a stupor the night before that even the horrific noise of three hundred armed men riding to give a great slaughter had not woken them from their drunken sleep?

I rode on through a narrow street and I could make out the all too familiar footprints of Roman hobnailed sandals in the dust. A lot of footprints, far too many, especially for a half century. I looked around, fully twisting in the saddle. Parienna was a small and inconsequential town, little more than a collection of mud huts surrounded by low and flimsy wooden walls. There was a small hall in its centre, no bigger than fifteen-foot-long and six or seven wide. As I rode towards it I saw its thatched roof had caved in, some time ago it appeared. I frowned. Something suddenly felt wrong, very wrong.

'Ruric,' I barked, 'where is Birgir?'

'Not seen him, Lord,' he said with a shrug.

My frown deepened. All the savage joy I had felt on the wild gallop to the gate had vanished with the morning dew. I rode up to the hall, still scanning the huts and walls around me. The Ravensworn were all within those walls now, so too Ketill and his Harii. I looked behind me to the gates, which still sat open, one of my men standing guard on the small palisade on either side. That comforted me, and I made a mental note to thank the man who had ordered them there.

I dismounted Hilde, still scanning the walls. Between the rotting wooden beams on the eastern wall I thought I saw a flicker of movement, a flash of silver. It lasted no more than a heartbeat, and when I blinked and looked again it was gone. I studied that slit in the timber, waiting, waiting for the flash to appear again. It did not. Shaking my head clear, I turned and strode into the dilapidated hall; the floor was covered in weeds and rotting thatch, the benches were rain soaked despite the dry summer and most of the tables had been turned on their end. Something had clearly happened to the Arsietae, but it had not been done by Warin and the Suebi. This devastation had been caused long ago. I looked up towards the sky, where the roof should have been. Shards of wood dust and the odd straw of thatch danced in the flooding sunlight. It was an almost magical sight, and for a few heartbeats I just stood and watched what appeared to be flecks of gold falling from the gods. And then, just as I was in the midst of my entrancement, I saw a sight that turned my blood to ice.

* * *

Gerulf hung from the wooden beam that ran vertically from the east wall to the west. It was the beam that should have held up the highest part of the roof, but judging from its darkened and uneven state it appeared it could fall at any moment. And yet it supported the weight of a man.

Poor Gerulf's face was as blue as the ocean; his eyes bulged from his head and his tongue hung uselessly from his gaping mouth. He still wore his armour, arms held behind his back with thick rope. His body had not been defiled like the four men of his command we had found back west. For that, I felt oddly grateful. I stepped forwards until I stood directly underneath him. I reached up and touched the foot of one of my most loyal men and felt a burning shame mixed with anger. Gerulf was innocent of any crime Warin or Ishild perceived me of committing. He had wronged no one, done nothing but serve me well and set a perfect example to his men every day. He was the perfect soldier in many ways. Discreet, obedient, he had that knack for knowing when to stay silent or when to offer his lord some advice or his opinion. Tears streamed down my face, hot beads of rage. I swore right then, on all the gods in the Nine Worlds, I would not rest, I would not falter, in my pursuit of the men who had done this to Gerulf. I had not been much of a man for keeping oaths throughout my life, but with Wotan as my witness, this is one I would see through to the bitter end.

There was a disturbance behind me and Ruric stomped into the remains of the hall. 'Freya's tits, it's as dead as Hel in he—' He stopped mid flow, his eyes locking onto the swinging body above my head. 'Oh no. Oh gods, no,' he whispered. He staggered forwards, sinking to his knees and gasping, trying to catch his breath. He vomited then, sprayed it over the decaying floor. On all fours he panted again, wretched, then wailed. 'Why?' he bellowed at the top of his voice. 'Why do all the good men die?'

He had been close to Gerulf, I knew. Gerulf had been in Ruric's Hundred for his first few years under the Raven banner. There Ruric had passed on the knowledge gleaned in a lifetime of war. A young Gerulf had grown into a leader, until Ruric had virtually forced me to promote him to the role of captain.

I reached down and hauled him up by his broad shoulders. Bringing him in close, I engulfed him in a bear hug, his shuddering body thrashing violently in my arms. I needed to calm him, and quickly. Something was not right; I could almost smell the schemes of my enemies in the air, feel their blades pointed at my back. I was exposed, vulnerable, not a place I was used to being in. 'Ruric,' I said in a soothing tone. 'There will be a time to grieve, old friend, but this is not it.' I shook him gently; he raised his head and his teary eyes met mine. 'Think, brother. We were told the town was full of our enemies. Suebi and Roman, here to make a secret pact to bring about our downfall. So we ride here, quicker than a strong west wind, and what do we find?'

I left the question open, so it hung between us with Gerulf's body. I watched Ruric, saw the life spark back into his eyes, saw the great cog of his mind whirling. 'We were told the enemy had no rear guard, that they were completely unaware of our approach. And yet, my friend, when we rode through those gates we found nothing but ruin and Gerulf strung up on the beams of an old hall.' I was shaking now, shaking with rage and shame. I had led my men to this place; put my trust in someone I thought would always be my loyal man. It seemed I had been wrong.

'Ruric, where is Birgir?'

Ruric's mouth opened but he did not speak. He blubbered like a fish out of water. 'The enemy must have him,' he said eventually.

'No.' I shook my head. 'No, Ruric. We are betrayed. Get the men ready to ride, we leave at once.'

Ruric turned to walk away, out into the brightness of the dawn. He paused, turned back to me, a question on his lips. I have often wondered what it was Ruric had meant to ask me on that red tainted day. Would he have cursed Birgir for a traitor and a fool? Would he have perhaps offered some words in his defence? For surely he had not betrayed his brothers in the Ravensworn? I never did find out.

Just as he opened his mouth, a horn sounded in the open. A moment later there was a response from another. I suddenly felt very claustrophobic within the walls of that crumbling hall. I wanted to breathe fresh air, feel the warmth of the sun of my face and the breeze ripple through my beard. Another horn blared; this one came from the same direction as the first, I was sure. 'Ruric, rally the men, NOW!' I barked the last word, pushed past my oldest follower and sprinted into the sunlight.

I paused on the threshold of the hall. All around me men were in disarray, galloping this way and that, some bearing arms, others just seeking a way out. I scanned the faces, looking desperately for Ketill or Otto or Baldo. I could see none of them. I grabbed the nearest man, a greybeard on a black mare. He wore full mail atop a sleeveless tunic, his arms thick with silver rings. 'What is happening?' I asked.

'Romans, Lord. They're pouring in through the gate.'

I nodded. Looking towards the western gate, I saw a wave of red. Red shields, red cloaks, silver mail and a forest of spear tips. I squinted, not fully believing what I was seeing. They were two hundred paces off now, getting into lines as best they could with the sprawling mass of huts in their path. Painted clearly on the front of those red shields in brilliant white was a Capricorn, emblem of the Fourteenth legion.

40

'Orders, Lord?' Baldo screamed in my ear. All around me was chaos. My men were in full panic now, pushing past each other, desperate to be away from the dreaded enemy.

I said nothing. I just continued to watch as the Fourteenth moved ever closer. It was not a full legion, my brain managed to comprehend. A single cohort, five hundred men, no more. They marched in perfect cohesion. The uneven ground was no obstacle for them; they simply skirted round any building in their path. They were, I have to say, completely flawless.

'Is there another way out?' I asked Baldo in a quiet voice, not wanting the men to hear me thinking of retreat.

'Not without tearing the walls down, Lord. The only gate is to the west, where we entered.'

I nodded. I had thought as much. 'Baldo, Otto, Ruric, get your men together. Baldo and Ruric, your men are to dismount and form a shield wall here.' I pointed to the ground at my feet. 'Otto, keep your men mounted. You are to split them in two and harass the enemy flanks. Try and bunch them together, force them into the killing ground. We will do the rest.'

'And me?' Ketill was at my shoulder. Loyal Ketill, brave Ketill.

I grabbed him by the shoulder and pulled him back to the hall's entrance. 'Get your men out of here, brother. Go over the northern wall, get back to your lands and live your life well. I cannot ask you to fight this fight, I will not.'

He said nothing. He stared at me with such ferocity that I thought he would strike me. He did not, though; he just shook his head meekly, gripped my wrist in the warriors' embrace, and whispered in my ear: 'Wait for me in the Slain One's hall, brother.' And with that, he was gone.

* * *

Fifty paces off and the men of the Fourteenth were revealed in all their snarling glory. I stood in the centre of my shield wall, sword in one hand, my own red shield in the other, the black raven proudly depicted on the front. 'Ruric, the banner,' I said. Ruric gave a nod to a man at my back and he unfurled the beautiful banner. It was a glorious red, deep, rich and striking. The raven was blacker than the night, its head bigger than mine. Its one eye seemed to look straight at me as the standard billowed in the wind. What was it trying to say to me, that Raven? Was this to be my last day on this green earth? Only time would tell.

'Axemen to the front!' I bellowed, churning all the grit in my throat to that yell. My men responded in a heartbeat. A horde of battle-hardened veterans crouched low behind their shields, their axes held loosely in their right hands, ready to tear down the large rectangular *Scuta* of the enemy. I have often wondered just how a legionary manages to carry all that kit. Thirty miles a day they can trudge through whatever terrain or weather the gods throw at them. Their shields, or *Scuta,* are particularly ungainly. They stand almost as tall as the soldiers themselves, and when they plant the bronze rim in the earth and crouch behind them, all you can see is the iron rim of their helmets and the slits of their eyes. My men had smaller, round shields that were lighter and more comfortable to transport when strapped to your back via a leather strap.

At twenty paces I heard the call from the Roman line I had been dreading: 'Ready, *pila!*' I watched on, helpless, as the men of the Fourteenth moved their shields to their sides and thrust back their right arms, the deadly throwing spears gripped tightly in their sweaty palms. 'Shields up! Shields up!' I bellowed in my finest battleground voice. The response from my men was instinctive, thanks to the months of training my captains had put them through. Those of us in the front rank raised our shields to head height while the men in the second rank raised theirs above our heads so the shields overlapped, forming a solid wall of wood and metal. The men in the rear ranks raised theirs and locked them onto the shields in front of them. It was, in a way, our answer to the *testudo* formation the Romans used to such good effect. As I have said many times, I have no love for Rome or her cursed legionaries, but they do train the *finest* soldiers.

At an order from what appeared to be a tribune, the Roman spears launched into the sky and blotted out the sun. 'Steady!' I had time to call before death rained all around us. The *pila* used by the Fourteenth were long and heavy. Their leaf-shaped iron points snapped through our shields and suddenly the air was full of the cries of the wounded. Another order from the Roman lines; more spears in the air. Our shields were growing heavy now, tired arms quivered under their weight. 'Shields, shields!' I yelled, desperately urging my men to hold fast. Again, the snap of iron on metal, again the harrowing screams of the dying. The Valkyries would be busy today, I thought grimly. There would be many a warrior requiring passage to the Allfather's hall, there to feast and drink and fight to the end of days.

I lowered my shield after the second volley, seeing the Romans redressing their lines and preparing to advance. 'Wounded to the rear,' I said as I turned to Ruric. He was pale, was Ruric, paler than death. His eyes were red rimmed, and a trickle of blood ran from the corner of his mouth. 'Ruric?' I said as I lumbered to him, holding him by the waist to prevent him from falling.

'Never... forget... lad. One day... you must answer... for your sins.' He died in my arms. It was only as I held him that I realised my hands were slick with blood. High on the right side of his chest, a Roman spear had bitten deep, penetrating his mail and driving deep in.

I pulled him closer, bringing his face to mine. I prayed to every god I knew of to bring him back; how could I ever go on without faithful Ruric by my side? Arms grappled with me then. Baldo was screaming in my ear, but I paid him no heed. Nameless hands took Ruric's body and I watched him dragged through the ranks of *his* men, who waited with bated breath, ready to do their duty to *him*.

For the second time in almost as many days I was struck with a profound feeling of loneliness. Surrounded by men, my men, although for the first time I realised they were not really my own, never had been. We had segregated them into units of one hundred, years before when our numbers had swelled too much for us to function as a single unit. It was the captains who drilled them, the captains who paid them, ensured they were well fed and equipped. I had become nothing more than a figurehead. I was both feared and revered; a famous warrior who they would tell stories of round campfires when they were grey and old. 'I served under Alaric,' they would say, and brag about their heroics in this battle or that. But it was not really me they served, wasn't me who had their loyalty; it was the man they looked to to keep them alive. That man was not me.

I was only dimly aware of the boom of thunder and spark of lightning that was the men of the Fourteenth crashing into my front line. They held, they must have done, for I stood just yards behind them in my confused daze.

Baldo was screaming. I watched him as if from afar as he wrenched down a Roman shield and swiped his single-headed axe into the man's exposed neck. My spearmen were pushing past me now; they jabbed under our axemen's legs and over their shoulders. Groin or neck, groin or neck. They were lethal with those long spears, safely out of reach of the Roman short swords. 'That's it, boys, push 'em back!' Baldo screamed, and I realised we were indeed pushing the enemy back. Step by bloody step, we were gaining ground.

My senses came back to me, slowly but surely. What was it I had said to Ruric when he had seen Gerulf hanging from that beam just a short time before? *There is a time to grieve, but this is not it.*

I rasped my blade from its scabbard, relished in the feel the leathered hilt always gave me. My men on foot continued to push forwards; looking out to the flanks, I saw Otto and his Hundred were doing their job well, fifty men on each flank harrying the enemy, making darting gallops and engaging swiftly before retreating to safety.

I moved forwards with the men in the third rank. They were eager for combat, I saw; their blood was up and they howled at the retreating Romans, desperate for the call to rotate when they would be released into the fray. That call would be soon, I knew, for no man can fight for more than an hour without tiring. It was, yet again, another tip we had picked up from the legions.

Baldo would give the signal and the front two ranks would turn side on, allowing the third and fourth ranks through to take their turn.

No sooner had I thought it than the call was made and I moved forwards with the other men. I gripped my shield tight in my sweaty palm and sent my sword in a savage arc down on to the top of the helmet of the first Roman I saw. There was a mighty clang and the man dropped from behind his shield. His comrade behind him pushed him upright but it did him no good. As soon as I saw flesh above the rim of his shield, I jabbed forwards and my blade burst through his eye. I bellowed a wordless challenge and threw myself into the small gap I had made. Heedless of the danger, I slammed my shield forwards and followed up with a thrust to the groin. The Romans to my left and right were packed in too tightly and could not bring their blades to bare, neither could I turn to strike them – I just kept driving forwards.

The next man was tall and broad. He slammed his shield into mine with such force I hopped backwards three paces, desperately trying to keep my feet. I rebounded off a Roman shoulder just in time to block a low cut with my own blade then immediately replied with a high swing aimed at the legionary's neck. He stepped back and dodged it smartly, surprisingly quick on his feet for such a big man. He came at me again, feinting right, sending a backhand cut designed to strike my head clean off. I got my shield up in time and followed up with a direct lunge at his midriff, which rebounded off his segmented armour with a snap. The armour held, but the legionary lurched forwards in pain and I hammered my sword on to the top of his helmet, which fell uselessly to the ground.

When he rose again I saw he had to have seen fifty summers at least. He had short, shaggy hair the colour of rust, a clean-

shaven face with a livid white scar just above his chin. His eyes
were a pale green, but they were puffy and bloodshot. The hit to
the head had him in a bad way. I knew then he was dead. I came
in low, feinted right and flicked my blade over to his left. My eyes
never left his and I saw how he struggled to keep pace with my
blade. He stumbled and fell as he tried to make a desperate
block, and without giving him the time to rise, I drove my blade
deep into his groin.

Men seemed to be moving away from me. A small circle of
space surrounded me. I turned back to my own men and with a
feeling of utter despair saw they were a full fifteen paces behind
me. Their advance must have staggered against the overwhelming numbers we faced. We were just three hundred, and
one hundred of those were still mounted. My two hundred on
foot had been fighting hard against five hundred of the world's
finest soldiers for a good while now; I was just proud they were
still standing.

I turned to my front and watched as a giant burst through
the ring of red shields. He stood a full head taller than me, and
there were not many men I had encountered in my years who
did that. His face was a mask of blood and entrails, but under all
the gore I could make out a set of piercing blue eyes. His nose
was short and round like a button, and thin lips surrounded a
mouth that looked too large for his face. His shoulders and bare
arms were thick with hardened muscle; they were as taut as a
bowstring as he thundered towards me with his short sword
held high.

'Well, well, well,' the giant said as he stopped just five paces
from me. 'Alaric Hengistson, we meet again.'

I had not seen Silus this close for a very long time. In fact, I
had made it my business not to. He was the *primus pilus*, or first
spear centurion of the Fourteenth legion. The cohort my men

were facing were the First, made up of some of the hardest, nastiest soldiers in the empire. They were crack troops, and Silus, I knew, was a crack centurion.

Many times over the years we had crossed swords. I had given him a couple of nasty cuts on his sword arm once, but he had done far worse to me. Under my thick, dark hair there was a livid white scar that ran from the top of my head to the back of my neck, which he had given me nearly ten years before when I had been bareheaded in battle. I had another scar on my right thigh from a blow that had very nearly killed me whilst fighting Silus on the Danube border with Areogaesus and his Quadi. The last had been just three years before, when Silus had speared me through my mail and caught me high on my left side. If that spear had bitten an inch deeper I certainly would have breathed my last on that battlefield.

But I had survived every encounter with this monster, and I was determined I would survive this one. 'Centurion Silus, what a pleasant surprise,' I said in my guttural Latin with a small bow. 'How is that lovely wife of yours?'

'Shut it, dog!' he spat. 'Today you pay for your many crimes to the empire. Today you cease to be a threat to the peace between the tribes and Rome. Today, it ends.'

He lunged without warning, his blade thrusting as true as a flying arrow, and only my reactions saved me. I wrenched up my shield and the point of Silus' blade burrowed through the wood and missed my hand by a whisker. He pulled the sword back and tried an overhand cut at my head, but I met that with my own blade and stepped back to open some space between us.

My left arm and shoulder burned from the block with the shield. I was dimly aware that all around us was silence as the battle drew to a halt. If Silus won this fight his men would crush mine and the Ravensworn would die here, in this inconsequential town. If I won, well, then there would probably be a similar ending, but at least I would take this whoreson with me.

I rolled my left shoulder hoping to lessen the pain, but instead there was a loud crack as the bone jarred and I lost all feeling in the arm. My shield fell to the dirt with a clang and I slumped to my knees in a wave of agony.

I heard Silus laugh and there was a loud cheer from the Romans. My men were groaning in dismay. Baldo was shouting for me to get up over the rising tumult. 'Is that it, Alaric?' Silus asked. He leant into me and put a heavy hand on my left shoulder. 'Is that all you have? The mightiest warlord in all of Germania, finished with a single thrust that didn't even pierce his armour! What has become of you, old friend? When did you become so craven?'

I was about to get up. I was going to burst to my feet and cleave that piece of shit to death with my sword. My blood was boiling, and I used the pain to heat my anger. I would not die on my knees. I would not let *him* finish me. My life would end in battle, that I have always known. But it would not be *that* battle.

I was about to. But I didn't.

There was an eruption of noise and spraying blood to my right. The left flank of the Roman line was evaporating like morning dew. A hundred Romans died in three or four heartbeats as something savage and terrible ripped through them like a knife through butter. A wolf howled, and dark shadows darted past the bewildered red cloaks, killing at will with unbridled bloodlust. More howls, more blood, more shadows. But this was no wolfpack, I knew. Nor were those dark shadows *draugr,* come back to reap their revenge for past wrongs.

They were the Harii. Ketill had come back to save me.

41

For ten or fifteen heartbeats more I watched on in awe as Ketill and his savages carved a bloody path towards me. Ketill was a monster, a demon of war. He carried a sword in his right hand and a small single-bladed axe in his left, and when he whirled them together they were nothing more than a blur of silver in the sunlight.

Silus seemed momentarily dumbstruck. He stood over me still, his short sword pointed at my neck. 'First cohort, wheel left!' he bellowed at his men. To give them credit, they responded as one, even though they must have been devoured by fear. I have seen it before in men; one moment you are winning a battle, your blood is up and you think of nothing more than slaughtering your next opponent. A moment later, you are running for your life.

'Ravensworn, to me! Rally to me!' I roared, turning back to my own men, who suddenly did not seem as far away.

'Forward!' I heard Baldo cry, though I could not see him, and then all was mayhem.

This was no straight fight between two shield walls now, it

was a melee. The Romans defended their left and their front with the frustrating efficiency one would expect from the eagles of the empire. Their shields locked together and formed that impenetrable wall that had been the undoing of so many warriors all around the Mediterranean Sea. I stumbled to my feet, fresh waves of agony tearing through me. Every step was torture as I fought my way through three ranks of legionaries to finally regroup with Baldo. I say fought, I more bounced and slipped my way past them. It was only the will of the gods that kept their swords at bay.

Baldo was grinning like a madman, his blood-soaked teeth making him look even more disturbing. 'We lock shields and aim for Ketill,' I said to him, moving back through my men. I was hurting bad, my wounded shoulder getting worse with every step. I knew there was no way I could fight. Baldo led the Ravensworn, and led them well. My wall was solid as the men advanced at a steady pace, every step being called by Baldo. 'Step, push! Step, push!' Back and back the Romans retreated. I watched as their men began to look over their shoulders, eagerly seeking the eastern gate and freedom.

I looked to my right and saw Otto had grouped his remaining men together on the Roman left and was forcing his way through to Ketill. My heart sank to see how few horsemen remained, for it could not have been more than twenty. But still, they fought like wild beasts. Even as I watched Otto stabbed down with a long spear, taking a Roman through the eye then slashing across another's face, blinding the man and taking half his nose with a single blow.

Ketill was near the Roman centre now, still slashing wildly with both axe and sword. I screamed at my men then, urging them to increase the pace and reach my friend. We were just fifteen paces from him, so close, and yet we may as well have been on the other side of the Danube.

I watched Silus push through his men and deflect a blow from Ketill's axe with his shield. I saw him dodge a swipe from the sword, and then I saw him jab forwards, the blade biting deep in Ketill's throat. I could not hear if my old friend screamed or if he went to the Nailed One's hall in blissful silence; I just know his journey was a short one.

A short time later I stood over the body of Ketill. I knelt beside him, tears blurring my eyes. Still the battle raged around me, though I had long since ceased to care as to its outcome. First Gerulf, then Ruric, and now Ketill. I had lost too much that day. With relief I saw that my friend's hand still gripped his sword. I put my hand over his and tightened his hold on the hilt. I could make my own journey to the Hall of Heroes in peace knowing he would be there to greet me.

Howls of rage dominated the cacophony of battle now, as Ketill's Harii saw their lord struck down. Emmerich swept past me in fury. Screaming an incoherent war cry, he charged Silus and was rewarded with his own quick death, as Silus used his opponent's momentum and let him fall on his short sword. One by one the men of the Harii journeyed to join their chief. In their rage and grief, they sold their lives cheaply. And then it was just the remnants of the Ravensworn.

'Surrender to me, Alaric, surrender to me and your men can walk from the place, go back to their families.' It was Silus, of course, who spoke. The battle had ebbed again as both sides stopped to take breath. Slowly and painfully I got to my feet. My vision blurred and my mind swirled as I tried to stand upright. Hands on my shoulders and back steadied me. Baldo was at my shoulder, shouting in my ear, though what he said I could not make out.

I staggered away from him, my sword still held loosely in my right hand. 'I... surrender,' I slurred, though no one heard the words but me.

'Alaric! Surrender now! This is your final warning, your last chance to save your men's lives!'

'I surrender, I surrender,' I muttered as I collapsed once more to the dirt.

'Like fuck you do,' a voice said above me. Otto reached down and gently pulled me to my feet. He cupped my face with his hands and looked deeply into my eyes. 'No surrender, Chief, not to these curs.'

'You must go... Save yourselves... Enough men have died for me.' I coughed then vomited blood. My head swam; all I could see was a vision of my mother.

'Get up, you whoreson! We've all followed you this far, we ain't leaving you to die now!' Baldo's words were greeted with a cheer from the Ravensworn, which warmed my heart. Tears escaped from my unwilling eyes as cries of 'Alaric, Alaric,' went up from my men.

'How many men have we left?' I asked in a small voice.

'About a hundred, I reckon,' Baldo said, scratching his chin with his axe blade. 'Oh well, Chief, none of us live forever, do we?'

* * *

'SHIELD, WALL!' I bellowed one last time at my men.

'Alaric, do not be a fool! Save your men and lay down your sword!' Silus pleaded from behind his shield. He spoke in our tongue, I think wanting to make sure my men understood his offer.

I breathed deep and summoned the last shreds of my

strength. 'If you want my sword, Silus, then come and take it!' My men roared, a roar so loud it sounded as if we were a whole Roman legion, and not just a mere hundred men. 'My Ravensworn!' I said to them, my voice cracking with emotion. 'It has been my honour to lead you! Never has there been a finer band of cutthroats and mercenaries in all the land!' My men cheered and laughed. Baldo slapped Otto on the back and whispered in his ear. The two men embraced, and once more tears flowed freely down my face. 'When they speak of us in years to come, and brothers, they WILL speak of us, they will say we were the meanest fighting force Germania has ever seen! They will say we were savages, invincible and immortal!' Again the men cheered, but there was less heart in it. I think the word 'invincible' had them all thinking about their own mortality, and how they would be sent to their gods in the coming clash of iron.

'And immortal we are, brothers! As long as Germania is free, as long as our warriors continue to defy Rome, men will remember us! They will try to replicate our valour and fight on, just to equal our legend. They will fail; they must fail, for they are not *us*! There can be only one Ravensworn, only one immortal warband. We go to our gods, and we go with our heads held high! For surely each man here has earnt his place at the Allfather's table a thousand times over!'

I all but broke down then. I was ready for death; wanted it. 'We will feast with Ruric, with Gerulf, with Ketill and his fearsome Harii! Till the end of days the ale will never run dry, our plates shall never empty and a willing woman will always be at hand to warm our beds! Never again will we know hunger or thirst, never again will we feel the cold bite of winter. The end is now, brothers, but it is not an end, merely the beginning of our life at the Allfather's side. Are you with me?'

With a roar fuelled by passion, the Ravensworn charged for

the last time. I limped behind them, nothing more than adrenalin keeping me on my feet. Our men struck their shields with a mighty clash of metal on wood. There was no cohesion, no plan; it didn't matter now. We were dead men, and we knew it.

Otto fell early, a spear piercing his eye and sticking in his brain. I filled his space in the line and waved my sword blindly as I tried to keep focused on the man to my front. I could barely see and my ears rang so loudly I could not hear a thing. I was a spent man, long overdue a death on the field of battle.

Baldo fell from my right side, his throat slashed open. Red-cloaked legionaries streamed past me on every side as my men broke off and fought in ones or twos. I staggered, lurched left then right, waiting for the mercy of the death blow. I did not want to stand there and watch my men die; I wanted to be there on the other side. I wanted to hand them their first mug of ale by the warmth of the Allfather's hearth.

I swung my sword at a faceless legionary, but he merely swatted it away and scurried past me. I staggered forwards again, more uncertain on my feet than when I had first learnt to stand on them. Screams of the dying, my men, pierced through the incessant ringing in my ears; I just wanted to die.

A shadow fell across my back and I half turned to see Silus there, a wicked grin sitting between his thin lips. 'Nighty-night, Oathbreaker.' He crunched the flat of sword against the top of my helmet; the last thing I remember thinking is that I wished I hadn't abandoned my father, wished I had gone back to visit, if only to tell him how much I really loved him, how I never truly meant all the horrible things I said to him, before I had marched off that gloomy autumn day.

And then the darkness took me.

42

It was dark when I awoke. A cold chill ran through me as I laboured slowly to my knees. I wretched then, nothing more than bile mixed with crusty blood. My broken shoulder burned; the wound above my missing teeth had reopened and stung like a merciless bee each time I moved my mouth. I put a hand tentatively on the back of my head and felt the lump beneath my matted hair. I have gotten myself into some states over the years, but I do not think I have ever been as bad as that.

To my dismay I realised I was naked, my manhood shrivelled beneath a clutch of dark hair. There was an iron manacle around my left foot; when I followed the chain, it led to a thick round post that had been hammered into the ground. The smell of roasting flesh offended my nostrils. I vomited again when I saw it was my own men who had been unceremoniously piled into the burning pits.

Two legionaries guarded me, though they were too immersed in their game of dice to notice I had awoken. I cursed the gods then. How could the Allfather take my men into his hall and leave me here, on this godless middle earth? How could the great god of war Donar have watched on as the Ravensworn were cut to pieces? Did he not feel the urge to take up his mighty hammer and rush to our aid? Or was he so desperate to see such a fearsome host brought low? Most of all though, I wondered how Loki could have left me at my time of need. All my life I had considered myself a student of his teachings. I had betrayed good men, broken oaths and slaughtered good warriors all in his name. I was The Trickster reborn, or so I had thought. Where was my cunning now? How would I trick myself from this predicament?

Truth be told, I simply did not want to.

All my life I had known it was the spinners that determined the fate of men, that cackled in merciless glee as they destroyed men's dreams and tore them from this world just at the moment of their greatest glory. I had won great spear fame over the many battles and wars I had fought in. Men knew my name and shuddered at the thought of crossing my blade. All that work, all that bloodshed, all for nothing now.

'He is awake,' one of my guards said to the other. I studied them then as they approached me in the firelight.

'Calvus, let Vitulus know our guest is back with us,' the bigger of the two said with a smirk. The smaller man left without a word, leaving me alone with this giant. 'Your time is at an end, Alaric Hengistson. Soon, you will be with your gods.' He spat at me and his phlegm nestled into my beard.

'I will consider it a mercy,' I said in a small voice. I had no heart for a pointless argument with a nameless soldier.

'You will die without a blade in your hand. The Hall of Heroes will be denied to you.'

Tears welled in my eyes. All I wanted then was death, but death with my sword in hand. *Let the Valkyries take me to the warmth of the great hall. Let me taste the ale and hug Ruric, tell him how so very sorry I am.*

'That's enough, Bucco,' a short man said from the shadows. He approached and I saw he carried the long wooden staff that marked him out as an optio, the second in command of a Roman century, after the centurion. 'Go get yourself some food. I will stay with the prisoner. You too, Calvus.'

There was a silence between us as the two legionaries walked off into the night. 'You hungry?' the optio asked when they were gone. I just shook my head. 'Thirsty?' I nodded and gratefully accepted the skin of wine he passed me. 'For many years we have waited to bring you low, Alaric. Although I have to admit, I never thought it would end like this.' Vitulus made an empty gesture with his hands. I said nothing, just continued to empty the skin of wine.

'All men die,' was all I said when I had eventually quenched my thirst.

'Aye, but there are many ways to die. If I were you, I would have wanted the end to come on the field of battle, a blade in my hand and my enemies to my front. Not stabbed in the back by my own people, left alone to die naked in the dark.'

My head hurt like Hel as I tried to think. 'Birgir?' I asked.

'Aye.' Vitulus nodded. 'He had been Warin's man for some time. He led you into this trap, so you and your men could be killed like dogs.' He spat then, did Vitulus. It was clear he took no joy from the day's events.

'So Warin tells Birgir to lead me here, then has you and your men slaughter the Ravensworn. Bah! The whoreson even lacked the courage to wet his blade himself.' I shook my head at my enemy's shameful behaviour. 'That's about the long and short of it. And that woman, gods man, but she wants you dead.'

'Ishild?' I had almost forgotten about her.

'Aye, rare you see a woman of that beauty. By Jupiter she sure is one crazy bitch though. What did you do to piss her off?'

'Wish I knew,' I said with a shrug. I was a dead man. I had long since ceased to care what wrong I had done to her.

A huddle of cloaks moved forwards from the shadows. As they approached I saw Dagr led them, a wicked grin fixed upon his face. Warin was close behind, the others I could not make out.

'Good evening, Alaric,' Dagr said, holding his hands wide in greeting. 'A fine day for the crows.'

'Go to Hel,' was my only reply.

Dagr cackled: 'Ha! One day, old friend, I will leave this world and travel to the Allfather's bench and be reunited with my father at last. But you, you will not get to see the great hall, to drink the endless ale and feast till the end of days. You will die tonight, without a blade in your hand. You will suffer the same fate you gave my father.'

He wanted a reaction, did Dagr. He wanted to see my strain against my bonds as I raged in vein. He wanted me to shout and curse, to scream empty threats and behave like the barbarian the Romans thought I was. He would be disappointed. 'Fair enough,' I said quietly with a shrug. 'I tire of this life. Let us get it over with.'

'That's it, Alaric? No final words of defiance? You will not break free of your chains and slay us all where we stand? Shame, I expected more from you.' Warin stepped into the fire-light. His voice was high-pitched and childlike. If ever there was a man who deserved a bad death, it was him.

I sighed. 'That's it, Warin. It is over, you win. Now come, which one of you curs has the balls to finish me?'

Dagr and Warin both made to draw their swords. 'I will,' a voice said before either could take a step towards me.

Birgir lowered his hood and approached me. He knelt in front of me, wiped some dried blood from my cheek with an outstretched hand. 'Hello, Lord,' he said with a sad smile.

'Why?' I felt no rage at seeing the young man's face. I had no burning desire to throttle him there and then. I pitied him, I realised, and I was tired, so tired of life.

'Many years ago, Lord, you fought in the pit at Goridorgis.' I nodded. 'I first came to Goridorgis as part of the retinue of the Quadi king and his son, Areogaesus. Yes, Alaric, I am of the Quadi, not the Marcomanni, as you have always believed. I came as part of the retinue, because my father was part of the old king's guard.'

I studied him then, in a way I never had before. His blond hair, wispy beard, the frame of his face, the shape of his nose; it was all suddenly very *familiar* to me. 'Sisbert...' I managed to stutter out.

'Yes. The man you killed in the pit that day was my father.' A crushing wave of guilt smacked me straight in the face. Birgir had been four years old when I had slaughtered his father. Forced to watch, utterly helpless. I thought back to that distant day, me on my knees, stunned that I was still alive. Had I seen a small blond boy in the ranks of the Quadi? I thought then that I had, though it could just have been my mind playing tricks.

'You have been plotting your revenge ever since?' It was not really a question; only now was I able to slowly put together the pieces of the puzzle.

'Not exactly. I stayed in Goridorgis, as the Quadi had all but forgotten about me by the time they left. There was a new king of the Marcomanni, after all. I thought to kill you, and after a time I managed to steel a small knife from a blacksmith's forge. I took that knife and ran straight to your home, only to find you had left for good. After that I thought I would never see you again, and I tried to get on with my life. I worked in the kitchens at the king's hall, slept where I could, ate whatever scraps were thrown my way. And then, one day, this glorious warrior rides through the gates. He has a fine cloak of dark blue, solid-looking leather boots and a war host at his back. It was you.'

He paused then, and we both remembered our meeting at those very gates. Him begging me to take him with me, me refusing at first. But he was insistent. 'So why ride with me?'

'To kill you, of course. But all that time you were so well guarded. I could not do it in daylight, for one of your captains would surely see. Do you know how many nights I lay in the shadows outside your tent, just waiting for your guard to desert his post or fall asleep? They never did.'

'So you served me faithfully, all the while awaiting your chance. Gods, lad, I liked you, do you know that? Ruric suspected, at the end, but I could never allow myself to believe. You fought with me, at Ulpia Noviomagus, and many other nameless places, and fought well, if a little clumsily. I am sorry about your father, for what it's worth. He was a brave man.'

'Keep your worthless apologies, Oathbreaker. It is much too late for that.'

'I broke no oaths to you,' I said. And that, for what it is worth, is true.

'But you broke one to me, and Birgir is *my* man.' And there she was, in all her divine beauty. Ishild.

* * *

'You look like shit, which pleases me,' she said as she pulled a knife from within the folds of her cloak. Her pale skin glimmered in the moonlight, surrounding piercing blue eyes that seemed to lighten the darkness, and despite everything, still melted my heart.

'Sister,' I said. I was desperate to know what I had done to deserve this, but I was damned if I was going to let it show.

'Dear brother,' she said as she lowered herself to my side; with a flick of her head she dismissed Birgir, who moved reluctantly back into the shadows. 'You really have no idea of the trouble I have gone to to see you laid this low.'

'You look particularly beautiful tonight,' I said with a half-smile. Ishild struck me in the face, under my nose on the open wound with the hilt of her knife.

'Shut your mouth, you worthless piece of shit,' she hissed. 'You are not the great lord you would have men think, nor are you the invincible warrior. You are nothing but a traitor, an Oathbreaker.'

I kept my silence. Blood poured from the wound on my face; the gaps where there should have been teeth ached so much it was all I could do to keep the tears from my eyes. 'What have I done to you?' I said eventually.

'We are of the same blood, you and I, this you know already.' I nodded. 'My mother was your mother. But I was taken, given to another family to raise as their own. My parents were royalty, loyal to Agnarr and his tribe. Until one day my father decided he had had enough of Agnarr's tyranny and paid a man to have him killed. That man betrayed him.' My blood immediately turned to ice, my eyes fixed on the knife in her hand, tantalisingly close.

'My mother was called Frida, and she was the wife of King Gerhard of the Gythones.'

'Ahh,' I said with a slow nod. 'Agnarr really did clean up well after himself, didn't he.'

The Gythones had long now been part of the Suebi, but once they had been their own people. Many years ago, when I had just begun to form what would become the Ravensworn, Agnarr had paid me well to end the ongoing war between the Suebi and Gythones. *With a single stroke, you can end this struggle*, were the words he had used to me as we whispered over his hearth one winter's night. I had taken his silver, and with my faithful Ruric at my side, I had sneaked into their winter camp in the dead of night and slaughtered good King Gerhard and his queen Frida as they slept.

'Bah!' I suddenly blurted out. 'The Sly One really does know how to play with a man's life! That was you, you we took from that camp?'

Ishild nodded. Agnarr had been very specific when he had employed me. The king and queen were to die; their daughter, however, was to be brought back to him, and we were not to touch a hair on her head. I had paid no attention at all to the girl that had screamed and wailed throughout the two-day ride back to the lands of the Suebi. I had maybe fifty men under my command at the time. I had placed the girl under the command of two men, and left her at the back of our small column. 'I had no idea,' I said with a shrug. 'Doesn't make me an Oathbreaker though, does it?' I knew what I had done, of course, I knew full well. I had done what I had done a hundred times over in the following years; it was what I did best. I just wanted to see if *she* knew.

'I'll tell you what *does* then, shall I? I'll tell you about a young girl, peeping through the curtains of her father's tent, watching on as he made a deal with some stranger from the west. A chest of silver paid up front to kill the king of the Suebi as he slept. I looked on in awe and horror as these two men slit the skin on their hands before sealing the deal with blood. You broke a blood oath to my father, to my people!' She spat on me, then raised the knife.

'Stop!' Silus burst from the darkness. He tackled Ishild to the ground before she could bring the knife to my throat. 'He does not die, not tonight!'

'Like Hel he doesn't!' Warin roared, racing forwards and helping his wife to her feet.

'He is in the custody of Rome! You have no say in his fate. In fact, your presence here is no longer required. Our bargain is at an end; you may leave.'

'Is this how Rome treats her friends?' Dagr asked, his hand resting on his sword hilt.

'Friends? You are no friends of Rome! We had an agreement, to work together until the outlaw was captured. We have him, and now that agreement is at an end. Leave.'

And just like that, I watched Dagr, Warin, Ishild and Birgir as they were ushered from my presence. 'Kill me,' I said to Silus. 'Do not make me beg.'

'As much as I would love to, Alaric, and really, I would, I have my orders. Your life is to be spared. You are to be released back into Germania.'

'To what purpose? I would rather die than live to be Rome's puppet!' I meant every word.

'Ha! Always so full of yourself! Your army is destroyed, you have no men, no lands to call your own. Tell me how you could be of service to the empire?'

It was true, all of it. What possible need would Rome have of me? 'Then why? Why can I leave?'

'Fucked if I know, just following orders. I do, however, feel as if I should give you a little *present,* before you go on your way.' For the first time I noticed I was now surrounded by men in russet tunics, each showing me his teeth, their eyes void of pity. 'Hold him,' Silus ordered.

Hands grappled me. I was forced from my knees to my back,

where I lay writhing and kicking. Silus and his men had good cause to hate me, as did so many men in and out of the empire. Whatever the 'present' was, I knew it would be nothing good.

'Do you know how many men I have buried over the years, men forced to their graves by you and your ambition? Your schemes? Why, I have lost nearly two hundred just fighting you today! Their deaths will not go unavenged.' Silus rasped his short sword from its scabbard and thrust the blade into a small fire that burned to my right shoulder. I turned my head to look at that blade, and for the first time saw its beauty. It was short, as all Roman swords are, maybe half the length of my own. The pommel itself that sat on the end of the bone hilt was not the bland round orb that ordained so many Roman swords but was carved into the head of an eagle. The iron blade was patterned with gentle swirls which seemed to move in the light of the fire.

When Silus judged the blade to be sufficiently heated, he removed it from the fire. It glowed a deep orange; sweat poured down my face and I could feel my whole body shuddering in fear. 'So, Alaric, here is something for you to remember me by.'

Without further ado or ceremony, Silus thrust the tip of the simmering blade down into my left eye. I felt first an intense burning, followed by a wave unbelievable agony. 'And that's the last we'll ever hear of him,' I heard Silus say, before I passed into oblivion.

EPILOGUE
FIVE YEARS LATER

King Warin breathed deep the sweet summer air as he gazed out over the walls of Viritium. Life had been good to him, he considered as he watched the last desperate peasants rush for the gates before they were closed for the night. He was king of the Suebi now, and had hopes of taking over the Chauci too, if only he could rid the world of his father. The old man had become a nuisance in the years that had followed the death of the outlaw Alaric at the hands of Rome.

Too many times his father had tried to interfere with Warin's justice, his people. Always writing to offer his 'advice' on some matter or other, but Warin knew they were nothing more than barely concealed orders. He was his own man now, a king in his own right, free of the shackles of both his father and his enemies.

He was about to turn from the walls when a scuffle at the gates caught his attention. Two of his guards had stopped and were questioning a hooded man. Warin studied the newcomer, immediately feeling some small jolt of recognition, even though he could not see his face or hear his voice. But there was something about the way he carried himself, the way he moved his arms when he spoke. A longsword poked out from the back of his deep blue cloak, and Warin could see a knife hilt protruding from the top of his left boot.

He stayed a moment longer, deciding whether he should go down and get a closer look at this stranger. 'Lord King.' A voice interrupted his thoughts. 'The queen asks for you, Lord. She says to tell you that she feels "this is the night".'

Warin smiled. The one sour note on his reign so far had been his inability to put an heir in his wife's belly. The gods knew it wasn't from a lack of trying. Ishild remained the striking beauty she had been on the day they had married, the one advantage to her remaining barren being her body had stayed unburdened by the demands of childbirth. He felt the same heat in his loins then that he always felt when he thought of her naked. The swell of her breast as she held him to her chest, the thrusting of her hips as she straddled him... 'Tell the queen I will be there directly.' He set off for his bedchamber, all thoughts of the stranger vanquished from his mind.

* * *

Warin sighed as he spilled his seed, his body collapsing on top of Ishild. He lay there panting for a short time, breathing in deep the smell of their coupling mixed with the jasmine of her perfume.

Eventually he rose and filled two wooden cups with water from a jug on the table in the corner of the chamber. Turning to his wife, he stood silent and enjoyed the sight of her in the candlelight. 'If that doesn't put a pup in you, I don't know what will,' he said with a half-smile, passing her the cup of water.

'Tonight is the night; my woman has consulted the spinners.

You must regain your strength, my husband. I will not let you sleep yet.' Ishild put her arms round his shoulders and pulled him in close. Four wise women she had consulted now about her empty womb, and four wise women had gone to meet the gods with a knife in their back, having all told her the same thing: 'It is impossible. Some women just cannot bear children. I am sorry, truly.' It made her feel vulnerable, and ever suspicious of her husband.

Warin had, she knew, whelped bastards on two of the serving girls in their hall. Brazenly they had shown off their growing bellies as if they were his queen. She knew Warin felt no real desire for either and had only taken them to his bed to be sure it was not his seed that was to blame for their childless marriage. Night after night she allowed him to do more and more unthinkable things to her body beneath the sheets, whoring herself to him, keeping his eyes fixed only on her. She made sure to eat sparingly and exercised each morning, keeping her body firm and flexible. She had no wish to be cast aside for some fat milk cow who would give Warin a horde of children. He must stay infatuated with her; she would make sure he did.

Throwing aside her water cup, she turned the king onto his back and wrapped her thighs around him. Warin moaned in pleasure, as she knew he would. Sitting up, she let her hair fall so it nestled in curls just below her graceful neck, then she shook her body ever so gently so her breasts wobbled playfully, just inches from his face. 'You are a vision, and a tease,' he said, squeezing her buttocks.

'How much do you love me?' she whispered.

'Gods, more than life itself,' he groaned as he felt his manhood begin to ache. Warin lay back, groaning again. As much as he enjoyed the occasional romp with one of the serving girls, and the satisfaction the swell of their bellies in the months after gave him, there really was no other woman for him other than Ishild. No other woman who could meet his carnal desires.

A soft thud on the other side of the door to their chamber disturbed Warin from his pleasure, but only momentarily. 'I see Amalia remains as clumsy as ever,' Warin muttered, reaching to grab a handful of Ishild's hair.

'She grows worse the fatter she becomes, but you would know nothing of that, of course,' Ishild said innocently.

With a creak, the door to their chamber opened, a gust of wind rushing through the room and extinguishing the light. 'Damn you, Amalia!' Warin cursed, rising to his feet and searching for the means to relight the nearest candle. 'You know opening that door lets the wind in, and my wife does not like to sleep in shadow.'

Warin turned, ready to strike the serving girl, whether she carried his child or not. He had been so close to reaching a climax for the second time that night, and no woman could bring him there quite like his wife. 'It is not the shadows you should fear, dear Warin, but what hides within.'

A man stepped into the chamber. He wore a cloak of deep blue, and in his right hand he held a longsword with a pommel of black leather. He had long, dark hair, which he wore free-flowing past his shoulders. His right eye was as black as the night and as Warin looked into it he saw not a flicker of emotion. His left eye was covered with an off-white bandage. He had a great beard of the type Warin could only dream of growing, thick and curly. Beneath it sat a golden torc, depicting the Allfather sat atop his throne, winged by his Ravens Huginn and Muninn.

'No... no,' Warin stammered as he staggered back into the chamber, knocking the water jug off the small table.

'Yes,' the man said, an evil grin fixed on his face.

He raised his sword high, paused for one sweet moment, and then exacted his revenge.

* * *

MORE FROM ADAM LOFTHOUSE

Another book from Adam Lofthouse, *Outlaw* is available to order now here:

https://mybook.to/OutlawBackAd

HISTORICAL NOTE

This book is a work of fiction. There never was (to my knowledge) a Germanic warrior named Alaric, and he did not lead a notorious band of outlaws that called themselves the Ravensworn.

The Roman empire in the reign of Antoninus Pius – Titus Aelius Hadrianus Antoninus Augustus, to give him his full name – was largely at peace. There were wars in northern Britain, leading to the building of the Antonine Wall, which stretched Roman control of Britain a further ninety-nine miles north. Rome would not, however, be able to hold it for long. In the east there were the normal skirmishes between the Romans and the Parthians, and on the Danube and Rhine frontiers there were continual raids from and skirmishes with the unruly Germanic tribes.

Rome, for a number of reasons, never were able to stretch their dominance into Germania. Germania was some distance from the Mediterranean, her people very different to those in Hispania, or Greece, or Africa. They were not one people, for a start, but tribal and tended to hate each other as much – or maybe more – than they hated Rome. They lived in small villages or towns, and they had no roads, which made each tribe very much isolated from their neighbours. Rome made many attempts to conquer the eastern banks of the Rhine river, and for a time they managed to hold some sway of control as far east as the Elbe. But by the mid-second century, where this story takes place, those days were long gone.

When researching into the tribes of Germania, one must begin with Tacitus. Publius Cornelius Tacitus was a renowned orator and writer in his day. He was a keen historian, and the surviving portions of his two major works, the *Annals* and the *Histories*, examine the reigns of Tiberius, Claudius, Nero and the cacophony of the year of the four emperors. His other works were *Agricola*, which was an account of his father-in-law's triumphs in the conquest of Britain, and *Germania*. It is fair to say Tacitus did not think much of the native Germani people, or their land. On just the first page of *Germania* it reads: 'Who would leave Asia or Africa or Italy and seek out Germania, with its unlovely scenery and bitter climate, dreary to inhabit and even to behold, unless it were his home?' Sounds a bit like Britain, don't you think?

It is believed Tacitus wrote this some time at the end of the first century AD or early second century AD. Even though this novel is set just half a century later, the change in the tribes would have been dramatic. It was survival of the fittest in the wild lands: small tribes were being swallowed up by the large ones, villages were becoming towns, towns becoming capitals, capitals becoming fortresses. The Suebi, Marcomanni and the Quadi are known to have been three of the most powerful at the time, and Rome did never quite figure out what to do about them. Divide and conquer was the usual modus operandi for Rome, though with Germania, the 'conquer' part remained forever elusive. Through bribery and cunning they would continually pitch one tribe against another, their frumentarii agents scouring the land, whispering in the right chief's ear, dropping pouches of gold into the right hand. That was their only solution: keep them fighting against each other, help them to 'forget' that if they ever did unite they would pose a genuine threat to the 'Pax Romana'.

And that is where we find our Alaric. Outlawed from his tribe, he has a deep and unrivalled hatred of Rome and her meddling into Germanic affairs. This is, of course, not the first time I have met Alaric Hengistson. My debut novel, *The Centurion's Son,* is set on the Danube frontier roughly twenty years after this book concludes. Alaric was the antagonist in both that and the sequel, *War In the Wilderness.* If you have read them both then you will know his fate; if you haven't, then I shall not spoil it for you here. There has never been any doubt in my mind that Alaric is anything other than a scoundrel. He is, however, extremely enjoyable to write!

I finished writing *War in the Wilderness* in February 2018, and immediately threw myself into planning the third in the trilogy. But I found my mind wandering, my thoughts continuously going back to the same character. So, I thought, why not take a few months and write a short story, get the noise out of my head and then fully focus on the job in hand.

That short story ended up taking ten months to write, and became *Raven,* a full-length novel. I had absolutely no plan for the story, which was a first for me, and I found writing it to be my most challenging and enjoyable writing experience to date.

I have one or two sins to confess, and for any Roman historians reading this I better bare them now. Tacitus was, by the mid-second century, almost certainly long dead. There is no record of his death and we do not know when and where that happened. By the reign of Antoninus he was most probably entombed in one of the many mausoleums that filled the cemeteries around the city of Rome, and not running the frumentarii agents in Pannonia. It was a split-second decision to throw him into the story. I only decided I was going to do it as I found the clerk in Carnuntum speaking his name. My descriptions of Carnuntum, Ulpia Noviomagus and Colonia Ulpia Traiana are all of my own imagination. There is an excellent book called *Handbook to Roman Legionary Fortresses* by historian M.C. Bishop which gives us a basic understanding of the shape and layout of every known fortress in the Roman world, so I let my imagination build on those groundworks.

For further reading on Rome or the Roman army, I would highly recommend the following books, which I have found most useful in the last couple of years: *Roman Military Equipment* by M.C. Bishop and J.C.N. Coulston; *Marcus Aurelius* by Frank Mclynn; and *The Complete Roman Army* by Adrian Goldsworthy is an absolute must for those researching the legions. I could name another twenty, but I shall leave it at those for now. We are very fortunate to know as much as we do about Rome and her empire, but the amount of knowledge lost to time is staggering. For those of you looking for primary-source authors, check out the works of Suetonius, Tacitus, Plutarch, Virgil, Ammianus Marcellinus, to name but a few – the stories they tell shine a light on a long-lost world.

I will end by thanking you, the reader, for walking Alaric's path with me. I hope it has been as enjoyable to read as it was to create. If you haven't yet read *The Centurion's Son* and *War in the Wilderness,* please do hop onto Amazon and check them out.

Until the next time,

Adam Lofthouse

ABOUT THE AUTHOR

Adam Lofthouse has for many years held a passion for the ancient world. As a teenager he picked up Gates of Rome by Conn Iggulden, and has been obsessed with all things Rome ever since. After ten years of immersing himself in stories of the Roman world, he decided to have a go at writing one for himself. He lives in Kent, UK.

Sign up to Adam Lofthouse's mailing list for news, competitions and updates on future books.

Follow Adam on social media here:

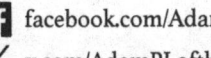 facebook.com/AdamPLofthouse
 x.com/AdamPLofthouse
instagram.com/adamplofthouse

ALSO BY ADAM LOFTHOUSE

Enemy of the Empire

Raven

Outlaw

WARRIOR
CHRONICLES

WELCOME TO THE CLAN ✕

THE HOME OF
BESTSELLING HISTORICAL
ADVENTURE FICTION!

WARNING:
MAY CONTAIN VIKINGS!

SIGN UP TO OUR
NEWSLETTER

BIT.LY/WARRIORCHRONICLES

Boldwood

Boldwood Books is an award-winning fiction publishing company seeking out the best stories from around the world.

Find out more at www.boldwoodbooks.com

Join our reader community for brilliant books, competitions and offers!

Follow us
@BoldwoodBooks
@TheBoldBookClub

Sign up to our weekly deals newsletter

https://bit.ly/BoldwoodBNewsletter